Hungry Generations

HUNGRY GENERATIONS

❀

a novel

Daniel C. Melnick

> For Frank Kermode,
> With my admiration and
> cordial best wishes,
> Dan Melnick

iUniverse, Inc.
New York Lincoln Shanghai

Hungry Generations
a novel

All Rights Reserved © 2004 by Daniel C. Melnick

No part of this book may be reproduced or transmitted in any form or by any means, graphic, electronic, or mechanical, including photocopying, recording, taping, or by any information storage retrieval system, without the written permission of the publisher.

iUniverse, Inc.

For information address:
iUniverse, Inc.
2021 Pine Lake Road, Suite 100
Lincoln, NE 68512
www.iuniverse.com

ISBN: 0-595-30803-1

Printed in the United States of America

In memory of my parents

Thou wast not born for death, immortal bird!
No hungry generations tread thee down.

—Keats, "Ode to a Nightingale"

If you have played a Beethoven sonata, then you know what the problems are of looking at a score and how it is to be turned into sound....Listening to a record, we neither feel the physical difficulty of realizing a musical text, nor can we witness, as in a concert hall, the exciting spectacle of the torments of the performer.

—Charles Rosen, "The Future of Music"

Was he an animal, that music had such an effect upon him? He felt as if the way were opening before him for the unknown nourishment he craved.

—Kafka, "The Metamorphosis"

Contents

❁

Part I   Allegro: Autumn 1972..........................1

Part II   Scherzo—Assai Vivace: December 1972........55

Part III   Adagio sostenuto—Appassionato e con molto sentimento: Winter 1973...............83

Part IV   Largo—Allegro risoluto: The Ides of March—Spring, Summer, and Fall 1973.....125

Author's Note:

Though historical figures appear in the following pages (Beethoven, Bartok, Schoenberg, Stravinsky, the Manns, the Werfels, Jack Warner, Jerry Fielding, etc.), they are imaginary—not historical—depictions and are not intended to render any actual events or to alter the fictional nature of this novel. On the contrary, as characters in the novel, they are mere figments of the author's imagination.

These imaginings emerge from many years of listening and reading, and the novel has benefited from the thoughtful responses of several people. Of course, the author is responsible for all the failures of perception herein, both intended and unintended, and the untoward distortions. For example, at one point, the reader will hear Beethoven speak unwittingly in the voice of Shakespeare's Dogberry: "Thou wilt be condemned into everlasting redemption for this."

We can only hope.

PART I

Allegro: Autumn 1972

1

Jack sat in the middle of the cavernous hall. All around him men in suits were seated beside women in gowns and furs. Occasionally there were young people, students who must have had passes or generous parents or enough desire to scrape up the cash to hear Alexander Petrov, the reclusive virtuoso pianist, at this October first concert. Jack had arrived in L.A. a few weeks ago, a graduate of the Cleveland Institute of Music in search of a studio job as well as time to compose. He remembered his parents' stories about the pianist, who was a distant relative of Jack's father. When he read about the concert, he wanted to hear the great musician, and he decided to go. Petrov was one of that select group of performers who had the power to stir even a resistant listener. On records and, it was said, especially live, the heavy old pianist seemed almost a godlike force—a Neptune bringing shape and order to the ocean of energy pouring through the music he played, as if all that wild risk and passionate surge were containable in a bowl of gold or a brimming goblet of glass. Petrov would be playing Beethoven's Hammerklavier after intermission; the pianist had made a classic recording of the sonata in the fifties. Now, twenty years later, he played in concert only once a year—in October at UCLA.

Janice occupied the seat next to Jack. Her long purplish hair circled her face so that she kept smoothing it from her cheek, and the strap of her black velvet dress kept falling from her brown shoulder. He had met her three weeks ago, on the day he looked for a Venice apartment, walking up and down the grid of pedestrian paths which sufficed for streets in the beach-front neighborhood between Rose and Venice. Several times, he had trekked past the Ellison Hotel when Janice leaned out the window of her first floor apartment and pointed across the Paloma walkway to the dilapidated stucco bungalow, a shack of a house on the corner.

"They're about to move out," she had said; her hair, dyed purple over brown, had hung below her shoulders, her black bikini loosely circling her. She was completely tanned, and her face had the weathered cast of a woman who had given months and years to the sun. She looked to be forty, about a decade older than Jack. She had asked his name, and she gave him the name of the landlord. When he moved in, Janice had been fascinated by the music pouring from his windows. She couldn't understand his obsession but she had wanted to attend when she heard he was going to this Sunday concert.

Now, as the hall lights dimmed, three people appeared at a doorway near the stage. A short, graying woman with a black fur folded over her arm must be Petrov's wife, Jack thought, and the blonde woman and the man were his children. The younger woman headed them toward three vacant aisle seats close to the stage. The man had unruly black hair; he would be Joseph, a pianist like his father, only just beginning his career. Suddenly there was a roar of applause, and Alexander Petrov emerged onto the stage. His neutral walk had the art the occasion demanded, with all the hungry souls clapping at him, many of them, it seemed, celebrating the fabric of their gowns and suits.

Petrov was big and stout, with a horseshoe of trim white hair rimming his shiny head. His face—familiar from record jackets—gazed blankly out at the only audience he allowed now in this yearly concert at UCLA. Suddenly he stepped forward to the verge of the stage and raised his hands to silence the crowd: "This concert," he said in an accented voice, "I want to dedicate it to the memory of my friend and great pianist who passed away this last month. Robert Casadesus."

He sat down and immediately struck his large and graceful hands on the piano keyboard: Bartok's Allegro Barbaro, designed to draw in without appeasing the audience. His clanging, plangent tone was astonishing, each note incredibly clear and full. The improvisatory liberties he took seemed always on the verge of exploding the work, yet every manic detail was balanced, in place. Then Stravinsky's Three Scenes from Petroushka: the heavy man became a circus master playing presto and with complete detachment the technically impossible work, as if it were a demonic joke, a throw of the dice. Finally, Schoenberg's Three Pieces opus 11. He played so quietly and with such clarity that Jack felt the auditorium recede, recede, and all the city leveled to its original silence; then Petrov would visit this silent world with moments of such dissonant shouts of tone immediately subdued that Jack smiled tensely to keep from crying out. Yet all the while he waited, his soul tightening. He kept recalling the sound of Petrov's historic recording and the score of the sonata which the pianist was to play after intermission.

The paneled foyer of Royce Hall was packed with people during the break. They stood by columns, under arches, crowding out into the evening air. Janice stood with him on the plaza under the clouded sky.

There was an odd static in the air, and the rim of nearby Bel Air hills seemed edged by a fluorescent charge. He remembered first seeing the Santa Monica mountains when he flew in from Cleveland three weeks ago; the plane descended over this squat ridge of mountains, floating and dipping over the etched and inhabited canyons and then skimming toward the great gray mass of Pacific water. On stereo earphones, he had listened to Beethoven's Eroica. "Welcome to Los...," the stewardess had cut in, and the music's homage to freedom vanished into silence. Inside LAX, Jack had bought the Los Angeles Times for September 6, 1972: Black September Attacks Israelis at Munich Olympics. Eleven Dead. It was not a summer of love. Another toll, an uncounted one, had begun with the bombing of North Vietnam, and just three months ago, twenty-five died in a bombing at Lod Airport in Tel Aviv. He had visited Israel as a boy, after his bar-mitzvah: the thin pine trees, the peeling eucalyptuses, the dark hallucinatory cypresses, the oleanders with waxen leaves and pink flowers, the billowing bougainvillea with veils of massed deep purple flowers and little trails of them amid the upreaching limbs of cactuses on apartment balconies in Tel Aviv. The arid beauty and expansiveness reminded him of L.A., yet this memory—like his sense of being Jewish—was dream-like, fragmentary, and remote.

"Hey," Janice said on the plaza now, "are you okay?"

"Sure. How'd you like the music?"

"Strange. Especially the last piece. Strange music," she said.

"You wanted to come."

"Why do you smile? You're laughing at me."

"What about the music I hear you playing?" He was wearing his jeans and blue sweater with a brown tweed coat, and he began to shuffle out a rhythm on the gravel, to dance. She tightened her psychedelic shawl around her black dress. Amid the blare of the crowd he began chanting a travesty of an Iggy Pop travesty—"It's nineteen seventy-two, okay"—and she laughed. She reached toward him and held him against her laughing body, her arms tight around his back to stop him. The Hall lights were blinking and the crowd returning now. At the open doors stood the young man with unruly dark hair, finishing a cigarette. He had Petrov's face and nose, yet there was an odd blankness to his eyes, not like his father's, not German Jewish or Russian. He looked at Jack, as if he recognized someone, and then calmly turned away.

The lights dimmed again, and the seventy year old pianist—his head shining—sat before the keys. Rapidly and at once, he relished Beethoven's opening leaps and the athletic intensity of the Hammerklavier. In the fugato development, chords slammed one after another over the keyboard, and dissonance held the air. Then the sonata's opening leaps returned at the unleashed pace Beethoven prescribed, and the Allegro raced to its end. Jack watched the sweating old man pause and begin to draw the stumbling Scherzo out, its assai vivace rhythm resistant and off beat.

Then the pianist hunched in the glare and silence before the Adagio. He raised his thick hands, and the slow music began to escape from the piano and spread out—appassionato e con molto sentimento—into the evening stillness where the audience sat poised. In the middle of the Adagio, Jack leaned back, his eyes shut, to hear Beethoven's variation, four notes for each pulse, twelve in each bar hovering, luminous and quiet. Finally the rhythm fragmented again and admitted to stretches of silence; the pathology of the sonata was carefully exposed, the long-breathed serenity of its yet living lungs, the still slowly pulsing heart. Then, the Adagio sostenuto ended.

Tentative tones arose: weak, curtailed breaths, an irregular pulse, and then the old man's hands acquired new sporadic life, improvisatory and unpredictable. Here notes disregarded the priorities of symmetry, free now to draw new breath. Here the sonata rose up, ghostly and vital by turns, and the spontaneous exhalations grew. Here, at the point of death, fierce spirits were stirred and unleashed, and suddenly the final fugue flew from its Largo introduction.

Now Petrov's temperament found free expression, a willingness to take the greatest risks. At moments, he played the Allegro risoluto with a ruthlessness, which seemed to stamp and hurdle with steeled cruelty. Dissonances and sforzandi, trills and leaps, were all absorbed into the shock and momentum of the unfolding fugue. Suddenly there was the boom and crackle of a disintegratingly violent climax, and Petrov grabbed the body of the piano. When his hands let go there was absolute silence, and in this silence he began the canon, barely audible, with a gentleness which was intolerable in its control of touch, and Jack had to keep himself from laughing aloud or crying out. Finally, the rigorous counterpoint returned, and wave after wave of music renewed itself in the face of the sonata's death.

At the final chord, there was a standing ovation. After the fourth, Petrov lifted his hands toward the audience like a surgeon wriggling his fingers at a patient, shaking them at the crowd and the Steinway behind him. He grinned and walked off, not to return.

Dazed, Jack made his way to the aisle with Janice. He felt compelled to go to Petrov's reception, and he walked with her against the flow of the exiting crowd. With a group of other fans or friends, they walked up onto the stage, past Petrov's black grand, and found their way to the room where the pianist held court, a lit cigar in hand. Sweat still poured from his face as he shook the hands of people who filed past him, received the embraces of furred ladies; warm and voluble, he passed some of these people on to his wife and daughter, who stood near him. Jack had been right. Mrs. Petrov was this small, gray woman who met those who came to her politely, with a detached, perceptive gaze.

The daughter stood next to her. She wore a suede suit, and her blonde hair was pulled tight around her head, though there were some untamed wisps at her slender neck. Her glance had a clarity and intensity suggesting a life apart from the social ritual in which she was engaged. Her eyes were dark brown, almost black, quite unlike those of the mother, pale and gray, or of the brother, who was nowhere to be seen. Petrov's daughter looked to be Jack's age.

He stood before Petrov and shook his hand. "Thank you for a wonderful concert," Jack said softly. "I'm Julius Weinstein's son."

"What?" the pianist boomed. "I remember Julius! The cellist. With the Cleveland Orchestra now. My second cousin. I'm delighted to see you! Meet my wife Helen. And your name?" He told them. Petrov asked to whom he should sign his autograph when Janice thrust her program toward the pianist, who carefully assessed her. "I like your shawl," he said. Mrs. Petrov told Jack he must call and visit. Their daughter Sarah stood before him.

"Good to meet you," she said. Jack was astonished by the beautiful resonance of her high voice as she spoke her greeting. She shook hands firmly with her thin hand.

❦　　　❦　　　❦

"You smile when you're listening at the concert, you know?" Janice said as they drove in his sixty-two VW through the night fog down Santa Monica to Main.

"I smile? Probably from pleasure," he said.

He felt outside the present. He glanced at her face, thin and weathered brown, the fine long nose, the high bones of her cheeks, the purplish hair. She began to tell him about herself—her mad Italian family, her past relationship to a folk singer in the sixties, and in the fifties the years she spent in San Francisco, the beat scene in North Beach, the protests against HUAC. Now she worked at a café on Rose, baking bread and pastries in the back kitchen. She survived, with afternoons off for the beach.

When she asked him in, Jack took automatic steps up the Ellison's front stairs and into her first-floor apartment. She handed him a glass of bourbon with ice and sat next to him on the couch. "Do you want something else—there's some hash around somewhere." He lifted his glass and drank—it was enough. The Hammerklavier still pulsed through him as they talked; in a while he would walk across the cement path of Paloma and work to compose some as yet unheard and unimagined music. She lowered the straps of her velvet dress; she smiled and said, "Welcome to Los Angeles." Later their bodies, joined and naked on the couch, moved together in an intricate, leaping rhythm.

❀   ❀   ❀

Beyond the beach a block away, the Pacific was clearly visible from Jack's bungalow on the corner of the Paloma path. The windows of the living room were open to the ocean shimmering in the October sun, and hot Santa Ana air pulsed through the room. He wore only cut-off jeans, sitting at his table by the open windows and looking through the swaying lace curtains. His back was sunburned, and his reddened legs were tender against the armless wooden chair. In the room there were second-hand chairs, a stuffed couch, a rented upright piano, and shelves with books, records, and a stereo. The volume was turned up, and Beethoven's music absorbed Jack. On the table were his journals—wire-bound, cardboard-backed volumes of music paper—in which he composed and occasionally wrote notes to himself.

The final fugue ended, and Beethoven's leaping cadence left him in silence. The phonograph stopped. He rose from his chair and walked barefoot to the kitchen to pour a cup of coffee from the pot he heated on the stove. He cut a slice of raisin-pumpernickel and began chewing the heavy peasant bread, savoring the seeded wheat, smelling its sweetness.

In the living room, he turned over the record, and pushed the lever to turn on the machine. The player's needle edged into the circumference of the vinyl, and again the Hammerklavier sonata leapt from the speakers—it was Petrov's great recording of the sonata. In the three days since hearing the pianist play,

Jack had been drawn back to his writing desk and to this recording, to the glimpsed idea of a new composition.

He reached to the pile of journals for an old one, which he placed over the current 1972 notebook before him on the table. The earlier volume contained musical sketches and diary entries from 1970, the year he received his Masters at the Cleveland Institute of Music. Jack turned to the last pages where he had begun work on a sonata for piano. He was ready now to return to these beginnings. He could imagine the entire promised structure, and he transposed from the old notebook to his latest one the initial ideas for the sonata's first movement.

As he closed the 1970 journal, he noticed the final diary entry: "Dec 31: I've written down my first musical ideas since getting my MA in May. Spurred by listening to the immense and wonderful Hammerklavier sonata (Petrov's great recording, the wizard). Not an homage to Beethoven: it will be a confrontation. Not with shadows, but presences, for I continually feel his presence." And then a postscript: "Molly and I have broken up. Shit, the long and winding road is permanently closing. She always claimed I didn't respect her going to law school. But I did respect *her* and the fucking intensity of our love, or was it the intensity of our lovely fucking? I don't know now, sitting here at midnight, staring out the window at snow falling, eddying in the light as if under water, like an ocean current."

His professor's office had overlooked a snow-clogged street, which bordered the squat, green, glassed-in building of the Music Institute in Cleveland. It was 1966 when Marcel Dick had first invited Jack into the stuffy office strewn with papers. Dick had a thick face, and a narrow upper lip knifed across it; glasses masked the refinement and intensity of his eyes. He had been the first violist at Vienna, Detroit, Cleveland, had studied with Schoenberg and helped found the Kolisch Quartet at Schoenberg's suggestion, and finally had headed theory and composition at the Institute. He addressed Jack, a new Masters student and son of his cellist friend from the Cleveland Orchestra, as Mr. Weinstein: "This much I can do for you," Marcel Dick said, "because you already have something yourself, Mr. Weinstein. You already know that the theme comes first. But then what do you do with it! In Vienna, Schoenberg looked at the first piece I showed him. 'Dick,' he said, 'you must pare this down. Prune and cultivate: you'll see what wonders that will do.' Why did he say that? Because a piece of music must be a unit, an organic whole. This was Arnold's view, and it is mine. Today the language we speak is dissonance. But that doesn't mean imagination and craftsmanship are no longer in cahoots!" So Jack had begun his four years at the Institute, from 1966 until two years ago. With Dick, Victor Babin, and Donald Erb. Earlier this year, when he decided to move to L.A., Erb had agreed to call an old friend, a studio composer, for Jack.

On the stereo now, Jack heard Beethoven's resounding leaps—Petrov's protean fists in flight above the piano keyboard—as they built toward the climax of the Allegro's development. He inked a corresponding leap over the bass clef at the opening of his new work. The Hammerklavier would speak out, an oblique resurrection, from Jack's sonata.

Three bald geniuses entered in a gust of laughter. Ashen and aflame in the September sun, Schoenberg, Bartok, and Stravinsky cast moving shadows over the living room. They sat on the overstuffed chairs and couch, and asked Jack for brandy to pour in three cups of coffee. They spoke all at once. He heard the Viennese Jew, solid and tanned, say, "I discovered the space between. The chasms in cliché." The pale, fragile Hungarian said: "Into all abysses, I bear the blessing of my saying yes." And the thin Russian shouted: "We belong nowhere now, so recently dead, possessing sixteen languages between us and we've not come this far to hear you grasp at nothing."

The opening notes of Jack's sonata lay before him in the early autumn sun, and he held the table's edge as Beethoven's final leaping cadence left the room in silence.

2

In the middle of October, he twice visited the deeply indented canyons in the low mountains above Hollywood and Beverly Hills. One visit was to the home of a composer who worked for United Artists. Jack had consulted a list of studio arranger/composers he had written in his notebook. Bachrach, Baker, Berry, Burns, Cameron, Cordell, Delerue, Fielding, Gold, Goldsmith, Hamlisch, Jones, Kandor, Kostal, Lai, Legrand, Mancini, Newman, Previn, Rosenthal, Scharf, Tiomkin, Williams—some with names of assistants and phone numbers. He had called one last week, the man his teacher knew, and he was invited to the house on a sloping hillside just north of Hollywood.

Brian walked with him around the yard, a ragged lawn with irrigated camellia and rose bushes. Both men held beers. "Maybe you can help *me*," he said in a British accent, punctuated by American idioms. "At least *you'll* get a job, working with Jerry and me, learning what the industry is about, the bullshit and general insanity of it. Peckinpah is going to start a brand new film, and he has Bob Dylan in it. He wants Bob to *score* it. What a half-assed idea. The son-of-a-bitch knows how to score like he knows how to conduct a fucking orchestra. But Sam wants it. And my job is to help out—i.e., keep him from fucking up. Maybe you can help me *communicate*." So, as October wore on, Jack began to make a daily trek to the music studio on Melrose where he learned the necessary skills of the trade from Brian.

Then, on Sunday afternoon at the end of his first week at the studio, Jack again drove into the low mountains intersecting L.A.. His green VW rattled up Benedict Canyon Drive, past a welter of close-packed mansions and ramshackle bungalows, their garages facing directly onto the circling street. Far up the Canyon, he discovered the Petrovs' address, the driveway indenting a mass of brush. It was wedged between two new luxurious walled-in homes. He walked up the hill, trampling on weeds, which covered the stone path, passing overgrown bushes and a yellowing garden gone to seed. At the top, a circle of trees—evergreen, a lacy pepper tree, a palm, and eucalyptus—towered over the old stucco house, its roof crowned with red-tiles, and the garage to one side on the edge of the hillcrest. That morning Sarah Petrov had answered the phone, and he heard the beautiful intensity of her soprano voice. She confirmed his meeting with her parents Sunday afternoon. He asked if she would be home—he would like to see her. She had said she wouldn't be there. It wasn't possible.

Now Petrov slowly paced over the oriental rugs and polished oak floor of his music room. He wore a pocketed linen shirt, pale plaid, and he gestured for Jack to take a seat on an armchair near the piano. Then he stopped before a cabinet of liquor and wines.

"I wish Helen could join us; she gives her regrets, of course," he said, a smile on his thick face.

"Is Mrs. Petrov ill?"

"Is Mrs. Petrov ill? She's a bit frail these days. Upstairs, not feeling well—maybe she'll join us later." He held up a blood-red bottle from the cabinet. "How would you like some Füking?" His jovial face stretched wider. "Good for the music. Or Scotch, wine, anything?"

Jack took what Petrov was having, Scotch, and asked for plenty of water. The pianist sat down on a stuffed couch. There were indentations in the plush where people had sat over the years. His back was to the sliding glass door and the gray sky beyond it.

"Now, why didn't you bring your ladyfriend, with the purple hair? What is her name?"

"Janice. A good person, but I…"

"I can see you're an extravagant young man. A genuine radical when it comes to women!" Petrov's laughter exploded in the room. "I received a letter last week from Julius Weinstein, my cousin. Rather, my second, or third cousin. We knew him and your mother Rosa when they lived here in the forties—before they moved to Cleveland. They were struggling, you know, and we tried to help. Also, I remember your grandmother in Berlin. She was a relative on my mother's side. A very pretty woman. When I was a little boy, she would lift me up in the air: 'Sashela, Sashela.' Very sweet. So now I know something about you from Julius."

Jack knew his father had written, at his mother's prodding. "Sasha should know what's become of you," Rosa had said on the phone, with her warmth and worry: her guards against all ill winds and ill will. "Maybe he can help you."

Suddenly Jack felt a sensation from childhood, as if he levitated up to the ceiling and looked down now at the music room. He remembered, when he was seven or eight, from just that height on the stairs, he used to watch his father play the cello. He would listen in pajamas, leaning his face against the banister bars, sitting there invisible to the adults below who played quartets—Haydn, Mozart, Beethoven, Schubert, Brahms. Always, his father seemed tentative, a satellite orbiting among the stars who visited Cleveland and sometimes filled the Weinstein living room with their force and brilliance—Menuhin, Stern, once even Heifetz. And Jack as a child felt like a satellite's satellite.

"I can imagine what he's written to you," Jack said to Petrov now, and lifted his glass in the air. "Don't believe a word of it."

"You're a man of many talents. A pianist, you studied with Babin. And you're a composer. I have composed too, did you know? Also I've known many composers. Their memories are dear to my heart. Gone now: my friends, almost all my friends are dead."

"You knew Stravinsky and Schoenberg."

"They would come here," he said, pointing at his own chair. "To this room."

"That's amazing." It was as if Petrov had casually identified Jack's innermost imagining as he composed, as he dreamed his deepest dreams.

"Oh yes. Every year we gave big parties. Once, I invited both Igor and Arnold! That was before my *first* concert at UCLA, in 1942. What a party we gave! And quite a little audience to play for: Schoenberg, the Stravinskys, the Manns, the Werfels—you know Alma, Mahler's widow—and Adorno...I remember even your parents were there, Rosa and Julius! My Helen cooked and baked for days. People loved the meses, the appetizers, the pastries. Not to mention the drinks that flowed, the Vodka and Scotch, the Claret and Sherry. I remember I went to the piano over there." Petrov pointed to the concert Steinway across the room from them, and Jack imagined him walking across the room, undaunted by the clink of their glasses and the gnaw of their eating. The pianist must have smiled before his guests for the full worth of his years (forty, then), height (at least six feet), and talent (immeasurable).

"I told them: 'Next Sunday is my first benefit concert at UCLA, at Royce Hall! You are so kind to listen: my undress rehearsal.'" He laughed as did Jack, as his guests must have then. "'Arnold, in your honor, I play the Suite opus 25, and Igor, in yours, the Sonata. After intermission, the Hammerklavier!'" Petrov looked away from Jack, his glance ranging across the room, beyond the glass door of the music room to the hill, the city, the ocean, the earth's ken.

"Do you know Schoenberg's Suite?" he asked in a detached voice now, and Jack nodded. Suddenly Petrov sprang from his seat. "I will play it for you!" he said. His old frame—heavy and lanky—swam across the room, as if time and space had become fluid and distorted, and then the pianist sat at his instrument like a general at his map. The uncanny momentum of Schoenberg's opus 25 gripped the sole, startled listener—its riveting ostinato repetitions, the angular leaps and askew couplings of high and low, the slammed chords and sinuous melodies giving way all of a sudden to silence.

The second movement began, its dancing rhythm sometimes leaping and eruptive, the Gavotte's row of twelve tones continually punctuated with moments of no sound like empty spaces inside the series of tones. In the middle of the movement, a macabre Musette waddled out, a parody of dance, lumbering and ironic like Petrov himself now, his big hands and arms busy building the brilliant structure. The Gavotte returned, beautiful and stricken, with its vanishing ghosts of feeling.

As Jack knew it would, then, the genuine ghost town of broken melody arose before him, its fragments of melody strewn across the keyboard. Here, in the Intermezzo, was an infinite scattering, where one breathed the air of another planet. Jack saw Petrov's face beginning strangely, palely to glow in the afternoon sun. At the drop of a hat, the pianist conjured this ashen landscape and summoned up evanescent voices, echoing across the crystalline infinity of the decrepit music room. Little, asphyxiated sighs intensified sometimes into hammered fortissimo chords, which rang out and then fell back, deteriorating toward the final silence.

Now Petrov's hands were all fire and air, energy and movement: this Menuette was no tragic travesty, but a mockery of dance, decorated by vicious filigrees of rapid notes. The pianist's finger work was fleet and dry, conscious of the barbarities it wrought. "Unbelievable," Jack kept repeating to himself, and his mantra did not cease as he heard the finale pour forth, the Gigue's ceaseless waves of power. Abrupt shifts from energy to stasis kept recurring, so that what was loud or soft, violent or tender, civilized or barbaric became indistinguishable from one another. Petrov tossed the final chords toward the younger man, and they clanged out to disappear into the frayed oriental carpet at his feet.

"Unbelievable," Jack said, clapping vigorously and alone.

Petrov was somber, and his eyes were practically shut. In his pocket he found a cigar and matches, and now he lit the stogie as he sat back on the couch opposite Jack. He reached another cigar toward his visitor.

"Thanks, but no."

"We were so young then!" Petrov said. "1942. Naturally, we were all struggling to survive."

"My god, I can understand. Of course, certain things haven't changed too much, Mr. Petrov. As far as survival in L.A. is concerned."

Petrov's glance absorbed Jack for a long moment, and the pianist said, "Please, call me Sasha."

"Sasha," Jack said gently, "I mean the struggle to earn a living. I've begun to compose here, but I have to survive. In Los Angeles, no less! Do you know the

Woody Guthrie song?" With an ironic grin, Jack sang the chorus of the "Do Re Me" song, and Petrov smiled at the roughly rendered folk lament.

"You understand," Jack continued. "California's no paradise if there's not enough…. Anyway, you may not believe it—I can't quite—but I've started to work in the Studios, god help me, at United Artists."

The pianist let out a loud laugh and sigh at once, a boom of delight and sorrow.

"You remind me of someone I knew thirty years ago," he said. "Yes! You remind me of Bruno Fried. A fine, sensitive man, like you. He would look around with his wide eyes, registering everything. He also worked at UA. Bruno used to sit just there, where you sit. Listening to my complaints. He knew what I was going through. Partly because he too was an exile. Uprooted just as I was, and hungry like me, but for what! I knew him slightly in Berlin, in the cafés, but it wasn't until I fled to this paradise, as you say, this paradise of no culture, that we became real friends. You even look like him. What a delight! You're taller, better looking. But your eyes, wide and sensitive—I must say, just like Bruno Fried's."

"Bruno Fried?" Jack repeated. He felt the force of the old man's words, almost his categorization, and also the warmth and need welling in the pianist's voice.

"Yes, a good friend," Petrov said. "In the early forties, he took a few composing lessons from Schoenberg. Because he had ambitions! Like Adorno—Teddy had studied with Berg. And when those two would meet at our parties, in 1942 and then…how they'd spark each other! Once when I proposed a toast: 'To all of you gathered here in my canyon home. Just like in Berlin. Who would have thought? Each of us a refugee, and here we are in sunny Los Angeles.'" Petrov raised his glass of Scotch now, as if it were still 1942 and he were still surrounded by emigrant musicians. "'Berlin or Los Angeles,' Bruno piped up, his brown eyes roaming around the room, his tongue always sticking out a bit from his mouth: 'Either way we're fucked. They're two coordinates in hell.' And Teddy said, 'True!' raising his glass of Claret: 'To the harrowing of hell!'"

Jack was moved by the pianist's outpouring, his overflowing words, and he felt a responsive warmth, a spontaneous empathy for the man forty years his senior.

"Mr. Petrov, I'd like to study with you." Jack had not wanted to say these words. He felt his face flush. Yet once spoken, they seemed inevitable.

"You must call me Sasha." Again Petrov's glance searched the young composer's face. "Let's get to know one another a little more, no?" Petrov sipped from his glass of neat Scotch. "Busoni was *my* teacher. What a demon he was as a pianist, what clarity as a teacher. An Italian. I am half Russian: the real thing," he grinned. "Though my father had nothing to do with my success. The ass opposed me at every step: I mean, even when I was five, he used to scoff at my mother as she taught me the piano. My dear mother. She was from a refined Jewish family in Berlin, your father's relatives. And she married this displaced Russian caviar merchant. For passion, I believe. For passion. When I began to have a career and everyone attended my concerts—everyone, Busoni himself, Alfred Einstein, Busch and Serkin, Schnabel, Eisler, Weill—my father began to boast: *he* was responsible for my success, my genius. He was a pathetic, ignorant son-of-a-bitch."

Jack was slightly drunk. As the voluble, intense old man gestured before him, blowing smoke from his cigar, he felt his own ego oddly evanescing, disappearing before Petrov's flow and glance. For a moment, the old man's intensity seemed to suspend, to erase Jack's identity and existence. Then the odd sensation passed, and words came to him. "My Dad said you met your wife in Berlin, but she's…"

"Helen is Greek. She used to open our house to people every Sunday. In the late twenties, the early thirties. What she fed them, baked for them! People loved her, and not only for her baklava. Everyone came. Or we met them at the Romanisches Café. And then again here, the same thing, after we arrived in 1939. We knew everyone. Even Brecht, sometimes we would see! Bristling, shrill, such a powerful temperament. L.A. is Hell! he would say. Bert arrived in New York in 1941 on the same boat with Chagall and Levi-Strauss, but he could never get over the feeling of illusion here, the emptiness. How disoriented he was, and bitter! Not that I was immune to that disease. You can't imagine what we went through. But I remember what it was like in Berlin a decade before—and earlier! How different it was, in 1928, when Brecht and Weill collaborated on Die Dreigroschenoper in Berlin…"

Jack began intoning the Ballad of Mack the Knife, and immediately Petrov joined in, broadly bellowing, lifting his bulk off the tattered sofa to refill the glasses of Scotch. Their German and English jarred and intermingled. The shark Macheath swam into the room, hiding his Messer, flashing his teeth.

Jack asked for a glass of water.

"You can't imagine," Petrov said, settling down once more on the couch, "Bert was a communist for sure, and Kurt was the son of a cantor, who just happened to have married a woman blazingly hot, incredible! And together, they made the music of our time and place: the wasteland! The triviality of it was so extraordinary. It said: you live in a trivial world, and the only thing of worth is the crazy intensity of your desperation. Only the torture you feel is valuable, all the rest is dross. So what's the answer? Embrace it! Go ahead: rub your nose in it, in the shit. The snide singers, the honking horns, the snarling strings, the shrill whistles!"

"That's not unlike the music of today. Klangfarbenfunk," Jack spoke the travesty of German tentatively.

"Weill started all that," Petrov said, a smirk on his face. "And Eisler: the music of political utility, he called it. I call it the music of the industrial wasteland." He paused. "I run on, don't I? My memories take me over!"

"Not at all," Jack said; then he asked: "When the Nazis came to power, tell me, did you have any sense of what they were going to do?"

"I refused to see for a long time," Petrov said softly. "But finally I did see. If the Nazis succeeded, we would all be killed. Every one of us! Impossible. Unspeakable. Beyond imagining. The grotesqueness of it, and the betrayals all around. Even people you admired, who you felt were friends, collapsed before your eyes. Of course, that could be rather melodramatic." His face widened back into a smile. "We had to get out. Those who could escape came here!" He gestured to the room and beyond to the window, the city, the nation.

Suddenly Petrov shot up from the couch. At the hall doorway Helen appeared. Her face was white, the sallow white which olive skin becomes. She was buttoned into a flowered housecoat, red and green. In her hand was a cup of steaming liquid.

"I'm so glad you visit with Sasha," she said, gliding up to Jack, who stood unsteadily. "I wish I could be a proper hostess and talk with you myself. I do remember you as a little boy, your curly hair."

"I understand, of course," Jack said.

"She's not well. Are you, Helen?"

"No, I'm not well," she said, her clear, brown eyes gazing at her husband and then to Jack. The aroma of her coffee mixed with the odor of bedclothes and perfume. "You must excuse me. Sasha is well taking care of you, I see, with his stories about our past. I know I'll see you again. Next time." She vanished, yet Jack felt her presence, as if she paced the hall just outside the studio door.

Petrov strode up to the piano, saying: "Let's have a go at some music. Did you bring any with you?" he laughed.

"Do you think there's any more of that coffee?" Jack asked. Petrov said, "I'll see," and left him in the studio.

He looked at the grass-cloth-covered walls, gashed here and there but intact, with plaques and diplomas, an array of vivid, framed photographs, and bookshelves of music. An Oriental rug, frayed at the edges, stretched under the coffee table in the center of the room. The purple and black geometry of its design rose in the circle of light from a lamp by the piano, and in the gray-white light from the glass door of the studio. At the glass, Jack glimpsed the vista beyond the hillcrest, the gray gap which was L.A. huddling below the clouds.

Jack swallowed now from the cup of black coffee, and Petrov sat at the piano.

"As an adolescent," he said, "I tried to screw the keys. Yes. I was twenty-one and filled with my success, the éclat. And I was filled with beer, so my ears buzzed. Also, I was filled with rage. At what, should I tell you?—at my ass of a father. So my ego bursting, my bladder bloated, and my heart breaking, I tried to screw the piano. Unfortunately I was too drunk to fuck. What do you want to play?"

He got up and took steady steps to the shelves of music, gesturing for Jack to come along. They agreed on late Beethoven.

"Let's begin with opus 111 and work backwards, my boy. Next year—in Jerusalem—the Hammerklavier!"

Petrov sat down by him on the piano bench, and Jack felt the force and bulk of the man next to him, a few inches and it seemed fifty pounds bigger than he.

"Go ahead, play!"

Jack combed his hands through his hair. Then he struck the opening dissonances of opus 111. Petrov began immediately to talk above the music, shouting when the Beethoven was loud, whispering when it was soft.

"Stop!" he soon said. "You play like a composer. Like Bartok did. You have all the notes. The form. Now add the will. Not this:" In the upper register of the piano, he played the opening octaves and chords of the Maestoso, but with a swinging pulse, as if he were Duke Ellington playing a C-minor blues, meandering off the beat. "But this:" The octave leaps had decisive force, high in the treble as they were. "Now you play. Yes. It must be massive. Primitive. Slow up. And more pedal. More shmutzig. Dig your hands in the primordial shit. Now fast. Always with precision. With open eyes. Each beautiful fragment ironic and precise. Each pause an end to sound. Slow here. Concentrate on the structure: the branches of one tree. Faster again. Fly through that dense network. Sing. Like a bird caught there."

Jack's blue t-shirt was soaking as he concluded the Allegro. Petrov left him at the bench now and drifted to the glass door.

"Go on," he said, and Jack began to work through the Arietta variations, the last twenty minutes of Beethoven's sonatas. "See. Is your neck in a noose? No!" He spit out his words at the glass. "Did you think your hands were hooves?" The music spoke a miraculous language beyond the compass of the two men, making their ordinary human speech sound like a bleat or gasp or yelp. Petrov, quiet and distant now, sat down on the couch facing the overgrown garden in the darkening Indian summer afternoon.

※ ※ ※

As twilight descended, Jack drove home from the Petrovs, down Benedict Canyon and right on Sunset Boulevard, toward the Pacific. After he had played Beethoven's Arietta, they had sat nursing their drinks, and Petrov regaled Jack with more tales of his first years in America. The writer Thomas Mann, he said, was a reckless driver, a speeder. Could this be true? As Jack drove west, he could not be sure what was fiction and what was truth in Petrov's words.

Suddenly a vivid queasiness took hold of him as he remembered reading Mann's *Doctor Faustus* and then Adorno's *Philosophy of Modern Music*. Adorno-like language began to stream through his alcohol-polluted synapses: Everything is being transformed into an object, a thing to consume, in the administered society: art, people, music. And in the packaging process all of us without exception are being mutilated. Schoenberg's dissonance is, like Beethoven's late music, an act of resistance against the complaisant acceptance of such deformation. The music of popular media, by contrast, reinforces self-satisfaction, inculcates acquiescence, and serves the status quo. Our responsibility is to adopt perspectives which displace and estrange the world, reveal it to be, with its rifts and crevices, as indigent and distorted as it will appear one day in the messianic light.

A Scotch-induced aura formed now around his fantasy of L.A. in the forties when Mann, Adorno, and the composers who shaped Jack's sense of what was possible in music had practiced their art, and their fellow émigrés had gathered about them to listen, to bask in the reflected radiance, to feel the force of their new music.

Driving toward Bel Air, he imagined Mann speeding past him on Sunset, heading thirty years back toward the Petrov home.

"Welcome to Los Angeles," his dour voice must have addressed his passengers, the novelist's black Chrysler flying down the narrow, eastbound lane. His wife, Katia, would have sat on the passenger's side, her head momentarily flicking to the left with an anxiety she always censored, never giving her patrician husband the corrective glance, not to mention the words his driving deserved.

Yes, in the back behind Mann would have sat Arnold Schoenberg. The car had swung out of the circular drive in front of the composer's stucco and red-tile mansion, a dwarf by Bel-Air standards, yet deserving in this carload's opinion a Riviera view. The whited building, however—two story with arching Romanesque windows—looked out to no sea or beach, no Sansury sur Mer, but onto a similar manse across the eucalyptus lined street.

It would have been the Indian summer of 1942, and hot noontime air poured through the open car windows onto the tan Viennese Jewish composer acclimated and now a US citizen after eight years in Los Angeles. The leg of the tense man felt the touch of a woman's hip situated next to him in back of the car. Vera Stravinsky sat by him, and on the other side of Vera sat his great antipode in music, Igor Stravinsky. Petrov had arranged it: a unique and never documented meeting. Carefully dressed, sweating, and bespectacled, Igor tilted his head into the wind from the open window and peered out over UCLA as it spread down the mountain by the careening car. Below were hills and meadows out of which rose the redbrick tower of Royce Hall. Stravinsky, the Russian and now Russian-American composer, had arrived with his wife by cab to breakfast at the Manns (smoked salmon, "Canadian" bacon—the rage at the time—and eggs, over-easy, scrambled, and sunny-side up). Then on the way to their destined appointment, they'd picked up Arnold Schoenberg, whose car was in the shop and whose wife looked after their son, Lawrence.

As they hurtled past the wild western academy to their right and Bel-Air's burgeoning little enclave on the left, the two composers and the writer yelled to one another above the engine noise and the hot Santa Ana air rushing in on them. Vera Stravinsky and Katia Mann interjected comments antiphonally. Impeccable Thomas Mann sped the car toward Beverly Hills. Their shouts drifted in and out of four languages. They spoke of the campus they passed, their fates in L.A., the world war's engulfing evil.

Now a forest, spotted with yellowing green oases, rolled down the hill on Stravinsky's side, into the valley below. Mann suddenly turned his head, his hands planted on the wheel of the speeding Chrysler.

"Here is the golf course for Protestants only," Mann said with some acidity, and he glanced at Stravinsky, whose mouth was about to form the words 'this fucking war;' "and to the south is one for Jews." Schoenberg sat in silence behind the German novelist.

The Russian's mouth narrowed. The little man leaned forward and spoke into Mann's ear, in a suddenly British lisp: "If you ask me, both Protestant and Jewish greens are mediocre. Too low for high praise, too brown for fair praise, too little for great praise!"

Mann smiled, and Katia Mann winced. Vera Stravinsky placed her hand on her husband's knee, and Schoenberg's left hand tightened on the hot, black skin of the car outside the window. Finally, they wheeled by the Beverly Hills Hotel, awash in a new coat of pink paint and rung round by a trim girdle of new-planted palms. The novelist swerved the car to the left, up Benedict Canyon Drive, past isolated compounds and the occasional, rambling shack. The car circled far up the canyon road toward the Petrov mansion. Rising above Los Angeles, the passengers stared at the city's rectangles of orange groves, its tracts of bungalows, its stretches of indistinguishable brush and farmland, the long perpendiculars of its boulevards and highways, the tiny dots of its new buildings, and the amazing finality of the Pacific far to the west.

Mann parked at the foot of a hill rising toward the Petrov's green lawn on the crest. As they emerged from the car, Igor turned to Arnold: "Too bad Bartok is not here, to complete our little triumvirate. This week poor Bela must tickle the ivories at some concert in Portland or Seattle."

Perhaps that was what it was like, fevered and off-beat, pervaded by the gratuitous energy of those who had hoodwinked certain death and arrived in L.A. almost too late, a bunch of brilliant escapees occupying assorted hillside homes and beachfront properties—certainly more regal, Jack thought, than his own Venice bungalow, which he now approached in his battered, green VW bug.

3

Erect and on the verge of climax, he kept slipping from Janice: the unwitting need of his body was to leap, as if he were diving beyond the woman beneath him into some abyss. The askew, offbeat syncopation interrupted the riveting ostinato of their coupling.

"Hold still," she said. She wrapped her thin arms around him, quieting his pulsing buttocks, and she rolled him over onto his back. He slipped into her again, and soon Janice rose on her knees, her arms stretching out like wings, her head tilting up and facing the ceiling of his bedroom. Together, they resembled a bird seeking flight, a dove or falcon, with Jack's hairy thighs and knees supporting her body, which thrust up toward the sky. She was calling out, as if her "Jack" or "fuck" confirmed the heightened state they attained.

Later, he wrapped his limbs around her and began to doze in the light of noon, filtering from the windows closed against the fog enveloping Venice in late October. As he fell to sleep, she slipped away from the bed. He was in flight, soaring beyond a precipice, and he heard a shattering music, as if he were an orchestra playing at highest pitch and volume, his bones the instruments, his flesh the staggering sound. Suddenly he was standing on the stage, hidden amid the shuddering basses and cellos, the violas and violins crying out in brief, aching shouts. All vanished. He sat there at a Steinway, composing this music, his sonata.

Guitars shrieked above a constant punching beat, and a male voice shouted the lyrics of a violent ride, up, up to the top, then down, down to the bottom, and then again up, up. Jack pulled on his jeans and walked through the hall to the living room. She was sitting on the rug in front of the shelves of records, books, and music along the side wall of the room. The records at the bottom were ranged on long, wooden boards supported by occasional, gray cement cinder blocks. She wore a blue workshirt of his. A cup of coffee was on the floor by her.

"I've never known anyone with so many records," she cried above the blare. He went to get a cup of coffee that smelled from the kitchen.

The climax of Helter Skelter approached, the shouted warning of crushing descent into breakdown, and then the ultimate judgment rendered: the lover might couple, but the lover made no music and could not dance. Then they let distortion loose. The empty white album—the Beatles, a present from an old girlfriend in Cleveland—was leaning against the bottom shelf.

"You know, that song was part of Manson's defense: it told him to do what he did, supposedly. It was subliminal," she said with disgust, as she turned over the record on the player. She coupled, yes, but could she dance?

"He was still convicted. The courts don't accept music as a defense," Jack said.

"I know, it was bullshit. They were all like that. Bobby Beausoleil used to come down to Venice, looking like a virgin hippie. Five years ago and it seems like yesterday. He fucked a number of people around here: and I mean fucked them up good." Down, down he swooped, crushing whoever was in the way of his descent.

Now the lyrics of Revolution Number One filled the room, a one and a two, a four count no account melody, sweet and shallow, mocking politics, activism, anything but what was sweet and shallow.

"Why don't you play Revolution Number Nine?" Jack said, wandering to the upright Knabe in the corner between the shelves and his large writing table under the windows. He held his coffee mug in his left hand, and with his right he began to play the tune they heard. Stressing the shoo of the shoobedo, he parodied the parody. She laughed, and when the song ended, she lifted the needle off the record.

He put his mug on the top of the piano and with both hands began playing a sound he vaguely recalled or imagined. Within him, he heard a confused music, generated by sounds or voices beyond the world, it seemed. He tried to reproduce the music on the piano. He played a set of shuddering trills, and they resembled the long, isolated trills which rang out an apocalyptic alarm in the sixth variation of Beethoven's opus 111, except Jack's trills encompassed the keyboard, both base and treble at highest volume: a quadruple alarm inferno. Then he alternated and shortened the trills. They became a version of the trills lashing out at the climax in the middle of the Hammerklavier's fugue.

"Jack, I'm going. It's Saturday, and there are things I have to take care of." She was dressed now and staring at him.

"I got distracted."

"That's all right. I have to go anyway," she said and kissed him on the neck. He reached to bring her thin face to his, to kiss her mouth, to confirm the sweetness of the connection between them. Then he returned to his four-alarm fire. But the sound he produced was not the sound he recalled or imagined, and he stopped. He walked to the long shelves, gazed at the sixteen feet of records, and pulled from one end a Vox album of Penderecki. He played the Stabat Mater at the start of side two.

Suddenly, helplessly, he imagined his mother sitting next to Helen Petrov in 1942, the two women on the music room couch and surrounded by émigré intellectuals at Petrov's Indian summer party. Noise filled the room, bouncing off the polished oak floor and rising up to reverberate off the high ceiling with its embedded redwood beams. The luminous blue and red oriental rugs below could not muffle or tame the room's overloaded acoustics. Petrov had just finished playing Schoenberg's Suite opus 25; lighting a cigar, he stood glowing and loquacious in front of the composer.

Rosa Weinstein—effervescent, pregnant, and due next March—whispered over the din to Helen, loudly enough for Adorno sitting on her other side to hear: "I love the cheese ball," and she pointed to the appetizer on the sideboard. Like Jack a lover of food, his mother-to-be asked, "How do you make it?" Helen Petrov spoke her recipe quietly, only the essentials, but enough for this American to understand. Then Rosa pointed at another dish and another. The recipes poured out in Helen's quiet accent, with traces of Greek from her Athens childhood, and German from her studies in Berlin with Edwin Fischer and then her marriage there to Alexander Petrov. The cheese ball: mash cheddar and blue (domestic now because of the War) with cream cheese; be sure to crush some garlic into it, and then once blended and formed, encrust the ball with walnut halves. The sweet eggplant: bake two eggplants—make sure to pierce them first, or they'll burst—and scoop them out into a pan of onion and parsley you've sautéed in olive oil and some salt; mix it altogether with a cup of mild, white Monterey Jack cheese (do you know Monterey, those beautiful beaches down the coast from San Francisco?), and then bake it until all melts together. The taramasalata..."Do you know," Adorno interrupted, lifting a cigarette to his mouth, "the beaches of Los Angeles?" Of course, Helen said with a sort of authoritative glee: Long Beach, Redondo Beach, Newport Beach, Santa Monica Beach, Sunset Beach, Malibu Beach, not to mention Venice. Et cetera!

Sudden, aching shouts and whispers of Christe, Christe—the agonized chorus of Penderecki's Stabat Mater—penetrated his consciousness, and at that moment the music of his dream came back to him. It was music he would now add to the sketches for his sonata, which were filling his notebook. First he took the record from the turntable, slipped the vinyl into its jacket, and replaced it in his collection.

The young man's collection was emblematic of his life. Confronted with the fullness of experience, he sought to affirm whatever signs of life he could find. The collection of records to which he listened was helplessly eclectic. As for the people to whom he listened, Jack was open to them in ways he did not fathom or control—like a latter-day version of Mann's Hans Castorp, exploring this new magic mountain by the Pacific. No accident then that the outer layer of his consciousness was especially permeable, admitting myriad forms of life which poured in on him: some he was familiar with, some he could not track, and some were creations thrust upon him from he knew not where—and these too he struggled to affirm, just as he strove to affirm signs of life in whatever touched or aroused him.

As for his record collection, six inches (or more) of records were devoted to each of the following composers (arranged, seminally, by birth year): Bach—1685 and twelve inches, Mozart—1756 and another foot, Beethoven—1770, eighteen inches and the cigar, Schubert—1797 and eight inches, Schumann and Chopin—1810 and a basic six each, Verdi and Wagner—1813 and eight inches of boxed sets each, Brahms—1833 and eight, Mahler—1860 and again eight of mostly boxed sets, and almost every recorded work (at least the basic six inches for each) of Schoenberg—1874, Bartok—1881, and Stravinsky—1882.

In addition, there were recordings of music by other composers: twenty composers before Vivaldi (1678—two inches) and Handel (1685—three inches); seventeen composers born in the eighteenth century (for example, Haydn—1732, with five inches of potent quality); seventy born in the nineteenth century (including Liszt—1811 and two inches, Debussy—1862 and over ditto inches, Webern and Varese—1883, Berg and Leverkühn—1885, Eisler, Dick, and Gershwin—1898, Weill and Copland—1900, etc.); and myriad composers born in the twentieth century (for example, Shostakovich—1906, Carter and Messiaen—1908, Zimmermann and Bernstein—1918, Xenakis and Hazelrig—1921, Rorem and Ligeti—1923, culminating with as many recordings as he could find of Penderecki—1933, as well as a host of other "voices" up to the most recent solace and cacophony).

Not to mention the jazz, the rock, the folk, and...

Jack was sitting at the large table where he worked at his notebook of music paper containing the sketches and journal of 1972. At the top of the page on which he was composing his sonata, he had jotted the following entry last night.

Oct. 20: A decade separates us, I told Janice. She said generations last three years now, maybe three months. Nothing you can do about it, honey, except lead your life the best you can. Amen to that. It's like a festival for me with her. Yes, she says, whatever happens to the two of us, that's the way to remember it, with no sense of violation or license. Except can't find enough time to work on sonata.

He began to draft a passage in the middle of the first movement. At one moment he looked up from the notes he wrote on the staves before him. *The pale Hungarian wandered into the living room. The old man sat down by him. He had sallow cheeks, small clear eyes, and blond-white wisps of hair trailing about his head. A numinous pallor illumined his skin, and a smile formed on his mouth. It was as if his eyes had witnessed all that Jack or anyone did, and yet the eyes and mouth smiled.*

"The rhythm is good, always shifting, searching, never predictable: everything from 2/4 to 15/16. And the terrible trills: they are good."

Jack laid his pen down and stared out toward the ocean. The fog was burning off; even now when it was nearly November, the sun had begun to draw bare bodies onto the cool sand.

"I first began seriously to compose when I was twenty-one. It was 1903, and my rite of passage was the first performance in Budapest of Also Sprach Zarathustra. Strauss came to conduct. What a gift he gave. To make available in music, just twenty-five years later, the essence of Nietzsche! New sound, new vision—ironic and bountiful at once."

The Hungarian's voice was thin and shy, yet it flowed out: "Zarathustra taught me to listen as a child listens. Keep the whole surface of your consciousness clear of all great imperatives, all great gestures or poses. To become what you are, you must not have the faintest notion of what you are."

He folded his slender, ravaged hands on the dark-brown wood of the table before him. "In you, all opposites must coalesce. But that is the problem: how does the spirit which bears the heaviest fate and the deepest task nevertheless become the lightest and most transcendent? To do so, you must live as you play or dance or compose, and do these as you live. Joy in the reality of life—even in the tragic, the ugly, the dissonant—grows from just such playing and composing and soaring beyond all ordinary hearing. Dionysian joy experienced even in pain is the source of your art and life. That is what your music must reveal. The playful construction and destruction of everything in your world is the overflow of delight."

"Excellent, Herr Nietzsche," the thin Russian said as he burst into the room and plopped onto Jack's couch. The Hungarian gave him a long, wry glance from his seat at the table. The third visitor sat on the stuffed easy chair by the couch. "As for our handsome young man: an excellent performance from you, Mr. Weinstein," the Russian continued, extending his arms like wings over the top of the couch, throwing his head back, and shouting: "Jack!"

The tanned Viennese Jew began to speak from his chair: "If you think Strauss conducting Zarathustra was a revelation, you should have heard Mahler in Krefeld, conducting his Third Symphony. I couldn't speak. I could hardly breathe."

He stopped dead still. Then his sensuous voice continued: "In the last movement, he took the adagio theme from Beethoven's last quartet and transfigured it, revealing the height reached only by one who soars beyond resignation to joy. He stood before the huge orchestra and, with almost no motion, made them play the massive chords with such clarity and loudness that I felt an engulfing terror. Then they played with such quiet—even unto silence—for seconds, for minutes, that here as in the face of the loudest weight of tone, sounds began to cry out helplessly in my chest."

Tears came from Jack's eyes as he stared before him. They welled from a hidden source. He too knew such sounds, and they would become the sounds of his sonata.

"Mahler was inventing the future where we now live," he swept his arm in the air of Jack's apartment and seemed to include them all. "Earlier, in the Misterioso, the contralto sang Zarathustra's song: What does the midnight say? How deep is life's sorrow! Yet deeper still is joy, and joy seeks eternity. That is the world our dissonant souls seek to inhabit; we yearn to be liberated into eternity. 'Cancel all hope, yet send me the light!'"

The Viennese Jew rose from his chair. He walked to the shelves of books and music, passing the Russian on the couch, who said: "Oh my god, another Nietzschean. Is this eternally recurrent as well? Give me chance over fate anytime."

"Pay no attention to him," said the Jew, who turned his back on them and began to note the contents of Jack's shelves.

"I was born to determinism," the Russian said, "to be eternally damned as the child of a collapsing land, but I have escaped my fate. Can you be liberated into eternity? I escaped! I survived by probability and sleight of hand." He fixed his round eyes on Jack. "I was born out of time, and now I tell time by no clock or watch. I would have been more suited by temperament to the early eighteenth century, to be a minor Bach living in anonymity, devoted to the service; I would have composed three times as much. Protect your talent, Jack. There will be momentary setbacks, and there will be genuine losses. For this is no time for music. What is its function here and now? Where is the money to feed your talent? Life is a game of chance, and to survive you must learn the rules and trust to determination and probability. Bonne chance."

Jack composed now at this desk, working further on his sonata. Its dense network—root and vine, blossom and leaf—grew across the lines of his music book. The themes he took from the Hammerklavier entwined the pages of his score. Beethoven's leaps echoed there in continual antiphony.

4

The next day, Jack made a second Sunday visit to Benedict Canyon. Petrov had agreed to monthly sessions with him, and their plan was to work crab-like, backwards through the late Beethoven sonatas. On the phone this morning, the old man had told him to bring along a copy of one of his own compositions. Just before two in the afternoon, Jack turned his VW left off Sunset and passed the palms circling the Beverly Hills Hotel, pink and green, and receding from the corner of Benedict Canyon Drive. The day was bright and smoggy. When he parked his Bug at the foot of the Petrovs' path, he left his sweater in the car and locked it. In a green tee-shirt and jeans, Jack walked again up the weedy path; in his hand was an envelope containing a copy of his Variations. By the garage, a gray jeep was parked, canvas-covered and a few years old.

As Jack approached the front stairs, he glanced at the yard gone to seed. He saw Mrs. Petrov hunched over at the end of the lawn. Her legs stuck out wide in front of her, and the long grass curled over her house coat. Her head of gray hair was bent forward, and Jack thought she was in trouble. He walked toward her and saw that she worked with a trowel in her hand. Leaning over the flowerbed, she seemed rooted in the yard.

"Jack!" she said, looking up and squinting in the sun. Her voice was labored and breathy. "Look at my chrysanthemums."

He hunkered down on the weedy lawn by her and admired the variety of blooms, rust and gold, purple, white and pink.

"This corner, at least, I keep up," she said. "Sasha doesn't like me to, but I can't help it. I love chrysanthemums. And the season lasts so long here in California."

"These are beautiful," Jack said, looking at the spider mums and the bunches of blossoms, double and triple normal size.

"He thinks I do this from defiance," she said. "Little does he know."

"Defiance?"

"He used to scream at our son when he played in the flowerbed. Even to beat him. I would run out here and throw myself between them."

She looked beyond the flowers to the rim of hills. She said slowly, "He's a big man. A powerful man. Imposing and enthralling. He likes you, Jack. My husband is impressed with you. But be careful. We all need protection in this life. My Sarah needs it. I certainly do. Even you need it. Now you go in. I think I'll take a rest. I don't feel very well."

"Can I help you?" he said, reaching out his hand to her arm, and she looked at him with her dark, exacting eyes.

"You are Julius's and Rosa's kind son. No, Jack, I'll manage. I'll stay just a few more minutes. You go on in."

Jack walked up to the front entry. When he pushed the ringer button, Sarah Petrov opened the door. She reached her hand out to shake his. Her wavy, dark-gold hair was tied back, and a rope of it trailed over the thin, embroidered fabric covering her shoulder.

"Father's not quite ready," she said in a high, clear voice. "My name is Sarah."

"I'm Jack. We met after your Dad's concert, at the beginning of the month."

"I remember," she said, smiling with quiet confidence. "My father speaks quite highly of you, you know."

Jack wondered what Mrs. Petrov had meant about Sarah, for she seemed in no need of protection, with her quiet alertness and the astonishing clarity of her voice. She walked with Jack through the dark hall, past the living and the dining rooms, to the music studio. They sat on couches opposite each other. The composer's back was to the sliding glass door with its green curtains pulled open. Sunlight brightened the room. A flower-pattern was woven around the collar and down the front of her white blouse, Greek or Mexican, it seemed. She wore a leather skirt which stopped above her knee, and her body filled the clothes fully. A quiet pride and singularity sounded in her voice as she responded to his questions.

"I live here. And my business is here. I manage performers and musicians, especially my father. And now my brother—the out-of-town arrangements, the concerts, Joey's new recording contract."

"Your brother's? Your Dad no longer performs much, does he?"

"Except once a year at UCLA." She hesitated. Then she seemed to decide to go on. "His heart attack was three years ago. But even before that, Father was sick of performing in public: 'The carnival,' he'd say. Now he calls it his extended sabbatical." She offered him something to drink. She was having a coke with ice, and he would too. She leaned over the liquor cabinet, pouring their colas, reaching into the bucket for ice, which stuck to her hands.

"I can't get over how fine this canyon is," he said. "It's like living in the mountains, except for the smog. All the trees, the brush, the high hills."

"Have you seen Laurel, two canyons over?"

"I've never driven through. It's a huge city. Impossible to…"

"Laurel is more developed. I lived there a few years ago." Again, she hesitated. Perhaps it was the imprimatur of her father's regard for Jack that made her continue. Her high voice never lost its assumption of intense separateness, yet now she spoke with warmth and a seductive openness; she seemed to take pleasure in her apparent trust of him. "Now, you know, Laurel *is* a carnival. The adults become adolescent, the young become goddamn infants."

He heard names of her friends and acquaintances, recognizing some of them, Sebastian and Nash and Taylor and Simon and Collins and Young. And the names of drugs.

"I lived in the apartment above a garage on Neil's grounds—a sort of converted mews. I used to photograph the band."

"Are these photographs on the wall yours?" Jack asked. "You took them?"

"Some of them," she said casually. "I lived with Rick, a guitarist who worked for Neil. What a scene! For two years among all those fucking flower children. Then three years ago, I moved home. I haven't smoked any shit since. I don't want any of that."

"I know what you went through, I think. What years those were." He leaned forward on the couch, one hand making a loose fist in front of him. He was absorbed by her Mediterranean eyes, and there was a kinship and call in her voice. The sound he heard seemed to connect with the sounds his music tried to bring into being. "I can understand how you feel," he told her.

"You can understand how I feel," she said, with a vague vulnerability, as if the two of them were caught for a moment inside a dream or movie, and then she seemed to wake herself, laughing.

"I still love Neil Young's music," she said, her voice suddenly teasing. "Have you heard his latest album?"

"I've heard Heart of Gold on the radio," Jack said, and he began to sing, ironic and too fast, that he wanted to live, he wanted to give.

He stopped, but she continued the song, her soprano voice forming an envelope of isolation around her as she sang now that she too was a miner for a heart of gold, for the true words and feelings she never could find; weary and yearning, though, she keep on searching. Again she began to laugh.

Petrov walked in, smoking a cigar.

"What have we here?" There was censure in his voice, and his face stiffened. He must have listened from the hall. "Romeo and Juliet?"

"Father," Sarah stood now, "I'm glad you're feeling better," she said with a smile.

"I'm fine, thank you," he said. He greeted Jack, shaking his hand. "Helen gives her regrets again. She's under the weather."

"Yes, I saw her in the garden. I'm sorry she's not feeling well," Jack said to his host, who turned away to the liquor cabinet.

"I'll see you again, I'm sure," Sarah was leaving, and he shook the slender hand she held out formally to him.

"What can I get you to drink?" Petrov asked from the cabinet, pouring himself a Scotch.

"I'll finish what I have, thanks."

Petrov sat down where his daughter had sat. The man's vigor and bulk filled the indented couch.

"Don't believe everything Sarah tells you, Jack; she's a bit subjective, I should say. Her 'scene' was not very romantic. Squalor, she lived in. And I know whose fault it was: a so-called musician. He hypnotized her, the son-of-a-bitch. But that is all in the past. He's no longer a consideration. So, Jack, how are you doing?"

"I've started to earn my keep," he answered cautiously. "You know, at the UA studios on Melrose? I'm doing some arranging for…"

"Son of a bitch! Bruno Fried—he worked at UA too! I told you about Bruno, didn't I?"

"Yes, you mentioned him…"

"He was a composer/arranger, as they say. Starting in 1940. He worked for Max Steiner and hated every minute: Studio work, he would way, fuck it, fuck it! Steiner had studied with Mahler in Vienna; of course that didn't prevent him from composing crap. But he respected my friend, and with good reason. Bruno was such a fine, gifted man. He understood the hell we inhabited during the war. I remember his voice filling this room: 'I can't even play my violin,' he'd say. 'Moving my fingers on the strings—just pure habit—is impossible. We are frozen men, Sasha. No home, no life, only death everywhere.' He knew, Jack, he understood. It was not only the death, the war, not only the kitsch everywhere, then as now, not only the hell of what your wife or child puts you through. It is the isolation, the being alone of your spirit. What do they say: face the music? When we face ourselves, we are totally alone. What do you think, Jack, really? You think it's easy?"

"No, Sasha. It isn't easy, for anyone. My god, not at all," Jack said. "What happened to Bruno Fried?"

"Bruno was so poor, you have no idea. Especially when he first arrived. Once at the Beverly Hills Hotel, Wallis paid him ten dollars to jump in the pool with his clothes on. Bruno was a friend and fellow-traveler of Hanns Eisler, Oscar Fisch, and Teddy Adorno—you know their work?" Petrov asked, lifting his glass to drink.

"I studied some of Eisler's music. And I've read some Adorno," Jack said. "Vaguely I remember, did Oscar Fisch work with Kenneth Anger, on a film?"

"Well then, you know about them," Petrov almost shouted. "Bruno, Oscar, Hans, and Teddy were all Marxists! May I tell you a story?" Petrov asked with a smile.

"Yes, of course," Jack said.

"Now, I was not personally a Marxist, but I liked Marxists. Especially the snobs among them. That was Bruno!" Petrov glanced intensely at Jack and then, with animation and a certain urgency, he began his story.

"Remember I was telling you about my grand party in 1942. It was just before my first benefit concert at UCLA. That afternoon, Bruno and Teddy, the Marxists, had an argument with Igor Stravinsky. Yes! I was about to play Igor's Sonata—for *him*. But first I said: 'Before the war, before fascism descended, Igor wrote this Sonata. I play it now in memoriam for our earlier lives, there in Europe.'

"Suddenly Igor started up, and I froze at the keys. 'In 1924,' he said, 'I composed it in Paris. In an extraordinary state of readiness: I always love that feeling of awakening—to life. Not that feelings have anything to do with it.'

"'Feelings have nothing to do with it?' Teddy piped up.

"'I prefer feelings,' Igor said, 'if they must be called so, that are concealed in form, that obey the rules of the game. Your feelings and my feelings are much less interesting than form itself.'

"Teddy answered, first puffing on his cigarette: 'But I always hear a definite pathos in your music, the pathos for the past. And for the vanishing present too. Your Russian tunes or your Pergolesi tunes or your Tchaikovsky tunes. Always the nostalgia for what is and was. But I never hear the pathos of becoming, of discovery. I mean of what may yet be.' Now everyone was smoking away, Teddy at his cigarette, also Mann and Werfel; Igor had lit one of my cigars, and me too! It was as if we all were exchanging smoke signals. I gave up waiting at the piano and sat down on an easy chair to listen.

"'The pathos of what may yet be?' Igor said. 'I am not an anarchist. Feeling that demonstrates itself as some blind stab at the future—as a "spontaneous" eruption—is false, grotesque, even absurd. Games require rules!'

"'Pardon me,' Teddy said, 'you don't understand. In music other than yours, I hear another relationship between feeling and…'

"'You mean Beethoven!' Igor practically shouted. 'Pardon me, but *you* don't understand: I wrote the Adagio of my Sonata after I made a study of Beethoven, especially the Adagio of his opus 31 number 3. Before that, I couldn't bear how emotive his rhetoric is. His "pathos!" False! But then I understood. In the first place, Beethoven isn't conveying his "emotions" at all, but his musical ideas. And in the slow movements, how prodigal those ideas are! Even more radical than in his sonata expositions. How inevitable every line, every ornament, every…'

"Suddenly Bruno interrupted Igor, and everyone turned to my friend, whose eyes glanced about the room and whose tongue roved about in his cheek: 'For sure, you are only at the beginning of understanding Beethoven. "Prodigal! Radical! Inevitable!" Or maybe you're at the very end of understanding him. In our day, to listen and respond has become mere habit, formula, cliché—for you, for me, for the whole fucking world. When this happens, when something vital becomes a thing, memory dies and bodies turn to ashes. A permanent forgetting is about to occur, Igor, and that will truly be hell. Don't eulogize Beethoven, or he'll become just one more monument. The next step is Nazi shit.'

"Then Teddy's patrician voice rose up. The words poured from him, blending Marx and Nietzsche according to his own special recipe. My Helen was sitting next to him on the couch, and as he spoke she got up and swam through the cloud of smoke from the cigars and cigarettes and went to open the glass door.

"'Igor,' Teddy said, 'in what you say and what you compose, I hear a latent message: an identification with the authoritarian. Yes, Beethoven plays the game brilliantly—all that disciplined force and invention. But there is another mode of his creating, and of listening to him: for Beethoven is breaking new ground of feeling. Always, he strives to explode the game rules so that he can join discipline with *freedom*, objectivity and subjectivity, game-playing with the risk of discovery. But for you…for you form is only objective, only the game, as you say. You acquiesce to the authoritarian trend of our age. Music is a language game for you, and that's your guarantee of authenticity. Your melodies and rhythms and harmonies advertise themselves as the positivist absolute, all that can be. Accept them! Embrace them! Nothing else is. After all, it's all according to Hoyle: "I am not an anarchist!"' You could hear a pin drop after Adorno's mockery, it resounded so in the room.

"Then Igor said elegantly, his eyebrows raised: 'I'm always unprepared for the explosions my music is attended by, whether the revulsion or the fawning.'"

"Teddy said nothing. And what could he say, anyway, in this beautiful room surrounded by my oriental rugs and the oak floors and that magnificent piano, waiting for me to play it! Could he say, your brilliant music is false and has the logic of the shit hole, or it should be so lucky? No! Though I must say, such a scream of soul would have been interesting to hear. Excessive, of course. And incorrect about Igor! Anyway Teddy remembered the possibility of another appointment, or maybe he needed to go home to Gretel. He stood before Helen and gave his apologies. 'I must leave,' he kept saying. He shook my hand warmly, then each of the others', including Stravinsky's!

"'You're sure you must go, Teddy?' Bruno said, when Adorno approached. I remember so vividly, as they shook hands Bruno reached to hold Teddy's arm. I liked them both so much, you know. Especially Bruno. He united the best of the Jew and the German, especially Germans like Stefan George, you know his work? Usually the Germanic is so insufferable when it speaks on its own, but it became brilliant and ironic in Bruno. What seemed like deference was really sarcasm. 'The next step is Nazi shit!' He could be acid. But you know, finally, he killed himself. And not because he worked at United Artists. He lost his family at Auschwitz."

"My god," Jack sighed. The room was suddenly silent. Then Jack said, "It was Adorno who said to write poetry after Auschwitz is barbaric."

"Really? And have you brought any of your own work with you?" Petrov smiled and pointed to the large, brown envelope on the coffee table between them. His own brand of poetry, Jack thought.

"Yes," he said and unclasped the envelope; "I'll have some of that Scotch now, if it's okay." He walked to the Steinway, not sitting on the bench, only placing the score on the music holder. Petrov handed him a glass of watered Scotch and sat down before the music.

"Variations for Piano. Don't give anything away." Petrov looked at each of the eighteen pages, several of them with fleeting sweeps of notes over only a few prestissimo bars, others with many bars in adagio. When he got to the bottom of the last page, he went back to the top of the first, stopped and turned to Jack, who stood by him. "While not constant," he said in his fluid, accented voice, "your direction is firmly fixed. You're an incorrigible revolutionary. You know I did some composing in my day. Sometime I'll show you. May I play this?"

"Of course," Jack said. "I'd be grateful. You'll play it now?" He sat on the worn plush red armchair near the piano and heard Petrov mumble and then begin striking the keys. Sight-reading the score, he maneuvered among the theme's rhythms with phenomenal precision. Jack took a swig of the Scotch, which teetered in his hand. With immediate mastery, at sight, Petrov played almost twice as fast as Jack had conceived his piece. Always before he had played it emotively, with an apocalyptic cast. This pianist was exposing the music's true character. He was playing it as if he were a being from an alien time and space, fallen to Earth to reconnoiter. Experimental sonorities became transparent; brutal rhythms became fresh and springing, and they alternated with passages of inhuman delicacy.

Petrov laughed aloud as he moved from variation to variation. "Chopin!" he shouted, his hands sweeping up and down the keyboard, quoting the double octave runs of a late etude, but transmogrified now into an avalanche of dissonance, a pure and tragi-comic motion without consonance or center, plummeting into the silence of the break. Each of Jack's travesties and quotations—of Chopin or Liszt, Schumann or Schubert, Beethoven, Bach or Brahms—sounded now like the visitation of an angel or a god descending into chaos, bestriding a time each had not dreamed could exist. Petrov began the last variation warily, as if finally this were a new earth and heaven, yet soon he was oriented to its assumption of freedom, the oddity of its sense of space and motion, the strange and brave sonorities, the keys scattering sparks of tone, scintillant and aflame, a phoenix taking flight. This ascending god of new sound was a Dionysus, not merely of the fucking root but of garlands and aureoles of flowers he gentled into being.

"Christ," Petrov boomed with laughter, which echoed in the studio as he finished. "Did you have to make it this difficult!"

"Unbelievable," Jack kept saying, his green tee-shirt wet with sweat as if he had played the Variations. "Your playing! Unbelievable. Unbelievable." He rose as the old man stood and headed for the liquor cabinet. The younger man—with his brown hair sweaty and looking electrocuted—walked up to him, took his hand, and shook it. "Thanks," he said. "I'm amazed."

"So am I," Petrov said and with his free hand raised his glass in the air. "I drink to your work. You're quite a composer." He swallowed. "And, I must say, quite a thief."

Jack burst out laughing, and the two men sat down on the couches opposite each other. "You know the lesson of the masters: anything, in or out of the canon, is fair game. It's not learning and using what you learn that cripples. It's gentility, not giving one's all to art. But, my god, you plunder the corpus of the canon like the devil!" The studio, like a demonic den, resounded with laughter, knowing and unknowing.

"You know the sonata I was telling you about, Igor's?"

"Of course. Now in that work, Stravinsky didn't hesitate to 'borrow,'" Jack said. "From Bach, from Beethoven, as you said."

"I feel like playing it! You mind?" Petrov gave Jack a warm, almost fevered smile, and he went to sit again at the Steinway. In a sweeping movement his big, long-fingered hands began the first movement, Commodo. Jack realized his touch had drastically changed: now it was motoric, a detached legato—a sound capable of constructing or destroying at whim, transforming whatever it contacted, and always with elegant insouciance. The grand piano sounded like a beautiful machine, humming out the mock-baroque figure Stravinsky "borrowed," and it unfolded, in turn cynical and seductive, indifferent and incandescent. When a sinuous melody rose up in the treble, its graced gestures became knowing exposures. The terrain of such melody was beyond the terrain of irony; there was not a crevice or rift in this wall of sheer play where the spirit might hook a fingernail.

After the first movement, Petrov said: "When I played this for Igor, I overheard him whisper to Mann, 'Listen to this extraordinary Jew, how he gives himself to my piece—heart, mind, and soul to boot. I must use him to perform other things!'" Petrov turned then and flashed a smile at Jack, a strange, almost maniacal smile, filled with unspoken pride and rage and knowledge.

He began the Adagietto, summoning up the ghost of Beethoven. In slow time, the left hand sounded a motoric four beats per measure with self-conscious regularity and an occasional pirouette which numbed any purpose Beethoven might have imagined for such an accompanying figure. In the treble, an elegant, heavily painted, salon-version of a Beethovenian tune was dragged out, sullen in its dress of travesty, its over-wrought trills, decorative runs, and drunken arpeggios. Drugged and decorated, the melody grew more and more grotesque, yet it was beyond all sense of horror or loss or ugliness. This was not a dance of death, it was purely a dance, an elegant game.

Immediately, then, Jack heard the Finale soar out, another gigue, a beautiful and machine-like travesty of baroque momentum. There were occasional pointed, Mephistophelean assertions with octave drops and percussive decoration, and then a neo-classical anthem of salon elegance. Louder and louder, any tension the gigue generated was transmuted into pure motion and resolved finally by the sweetly consonant chords.

Petrov got up and walked up to his single clapping listener.

"Igor rose when I went up to him afterward. On his little face, there was a delighted grin, and he said: 'I'm so pleased, Sasha!'"

"He must have been amazed," Jack said, "how brilliant his work sounds when you play it, and how true you are to its essence!" He reached toward his new friend's hand and arm. With an unstable blend of warmth and formality, they shook hands, and Jack imagined the Russian composer, thirty years before, pumping the Jew's big, heavy, magical hand.

❦   ❦   ❦

Through late October and the start of November, Jack searched for the hours at night and on weekends to compose his sonata. Amid the draft unfolding on the musical staves in his 1972 Notebook, he made several journal entries during these autumn weeks. Among them were the following:

Oct. 29: Two weeks since my last Sunday afternoon with the Petrovs, and it still amazes me: what a revelation, how he unveiled the Variations. Am deeply moved too by his memories, his wonderful stories! Even if he's polishing and burnishing them, it's astounding how he captures the essence of those amazing people who created the music I love. Just like his ability in playing to capture the essence of the music—case in point: the Stravinsky sonata, and my Variations! Also saw Sarah, now for the second time. She reminds me of Molly, without the limitations, i.e., the law-school careerism. (Of course, I am not the Jack I was when I was insulated inside the circle of academic life.) Her high voice has a beautiful intensity and tenderness, both. She is somehow hurt, isolated, but ambitious too, somehow, in spirit. A sort of muse: in her presence I feel I can bring something to life, in myself, in her; I find myself wanting to surround her vulnerability, to protect her. But from what?

Oct. 31: Halloween Tuesday. Only a few kids braved the salt air for candy, my dumdums and gum. Tomorrow will bring the day of the dead, but not here, elsewhere.

Every workday, Jack drove to a cluster of two story buildings on the edge of Hollywood, fifteen miles from the ocean. There he worked with Brian and with Jerry, the music director for The Getaway. Jack was brought in "basically to listen and learn," Brian explained, avuncular and his British accent dense with Americanisms. He looked about forty, with a thick, reddish-blonde mustache and thinning, blonde hair brushed back behind his ears. He was Jerry Fielding's fireman, he said, his jack-of-all-trades, his workhorse.

"Listen to me," Brian had said on the first day. He was a union man and had made sure Jack was a Federation musician. "Show up and do your fucking work, drudgery or not. That's the *minimum*, and some of our 'colleagues' hardly do that! Once you show up and do competent work, they *owe* you. You know you'll get benefits. Fuck yes. We worked damned hard for them. You'll understand when you have a family." He sucked on the Cavendish in his pipe, and a crowd of monkeys sauntered by the window of the glassed-in office. Their heads and bodies were spray-painted gray-brown and covered with hair.

Through early November, they worked together on the movie score Jerry wrote, helping articulate the music to the pace of shots, adding tracks, adjusting details. Over and over they watched scene after scene at the video monitor by Brian's messy office desk. The score always played against the scene, tense when it was calm, conspicuously relaxed when violence was unleashed. "Jerry didn't get his Oscar nominations for nothing," Brian said.

Jack felt bored by the process and the music. "This is pretty commercial shit," he once told Brian.

"You don't like getting paid to write music?" Brian said.

Jack learned what was possible and what impermissible in his new job, and he began to feel the pleasure of working hard with others, making imperfect things less imperfect. Mostly, though, he felt frustration, which turned into bitterness at the trendy effects, predictable harmonies, empty rhythms, and trite tunes. Yet in three weeks, Jack had earned enough extra to pay three months' rent. Late one night in early November, he made the following entry next to the unfolding sketch of his sonata's first movement:

Nov. 7: Stayed up listening to the bitter end—Nixon wiped out McGovern. The corruption of it, with some mad scandal going on, yet the papers hardly report it. Sarah called for her parents: The Petrovs invited me for Thanksgiving. I want to ask her out, but should I? Need to talk with Janice first. At work, something odder than usual has happened, but Brian and Jerry are not saying what's going on, what disaster is occurring. In ten days, the fucking film gets an invitational showing. The Getaway, indeed. The drudgery at the studio from day to day is insane: the need to work with bits and pieces of crap, to go to the factory each day and be allowed no vision let alone freedom or control in what gets produced, not to mention the need to salve rampant egos. In the administered world, I am a low-level industrial worker, servant of the status-quo, an accomplice who transforms music—which I love as much as life—into an object of consumption, a drug to create complaisancy and consent. Brian says I have to do my time. A narrow man, he knows whereof he speaks.

❦ ❦ ❦

The lights came on in the theater, and the screen turned white with a sheen of silver flecks. The clapping welled and then subsided. Eyes blinked against the light, as they had against the dark. Dust and rubble had billowed toward them as a blast blew open the house. Cars careened, thundering into trucks. Bullets whizzed and riddled, bursting into bodies, blood and guts splattering the earth. And at the start, gentle deer had grazed behind the barbed wire of a prison yard.

Someone nudged him to get up and make way. He stood and followed Brian into the aisle. Jostled by the crowd, he obeyed its flow into the lobby and reception hall. He was pushed into a thin, blond man with tanned skin stretched tightly over the fragile bones of his cheeks and forehead.

"Excuse me. Sorry," Jack said.

"No problem," he said. Jack realized it was the film's star. The taut skin and thin bones were transformed on the screen into a graced, translucent face. The co-star held his arm. Her dark eyebrows framed extraordinary, almost sunken eyes, so thin was the woman. The screen had transformed the two emaciated and handsome freaks into McQueen and McGraw.

Brian tapped Jack on the arm and handed him a glass of champagne.

"Time to zelebrate," he said in a slur of British English. "Our fucking score will never be heard. Did you hear the shit replacing it?" He sucked intently on his pipe as they sauntered through the reception hall, invisible to the crowd of guests, money men, actors, agents, production staff. Brian and Jack were handed refills of champagne by a waiter in a white tux jacket, with the Roman profile of an aspiring actor. Jack was suddenly conscious of the jeans he wore and the rumpled crew neck sweater, his concession to the L.A. autumn.

"Brian, Jack," Jerry stood at the bar and called to his assistants. A short man, clutching a beer, was standing next to him. Jerry looked hypertensive and furious; he gestured irritably for them to join him. "Sam, you know Brian. Meet Jack Weinstein. He's working with us now."

The man with a beer was Peckinpah, the director. He wore scuffed boots and a pressed safari shirt with deep, unused pockets. "Shit, I hate previews," he said.

"I can believe it," Jack said. The short director looked assessingly at him, as if he were a prospect paraded before a fight promoter.

"You're a pleasant son-of-a-bitch," Sam said in a loose, leering California drawl. "Have you ever been in a movie?"

"Jesus, no," Jack said.

"He's an arranger. Excuse me, a 'composer.' From Cleveland," Jerry said.

"Well, Jerry knows who you are, dozen' he?" He slurred his words in a parody of drunkenness. "I'll want to get in touch with this man," he said and walked into the crowd.

"He's under a lot of pressure," the studio composer said to Jack, and then he turned to Brian. "Do I need Sam to fuck around about him? Do I need this shit tonight, of all nights? For what? For some bright-eyed, bushy tailed kid, straight out of grad school no less?"

"He's doing great work, Jerry. You won't regret it."

"Yeah, yeah, yeah," Jerry said, swinging around to stare for a moment at Jack and then turning to talk with a plain woman dressed in a shower of gold, diamonds at her ears.

"Jerry likes you. It's just not a great day for him," Brian said, puffing on his pipe.

"'Yeah, yeah, yeah.' Do I need this shit?" Jack said.

"I'm not kidding. Sam likes you, too."

"Who gives a fuck," Jack said.

"Who gives a fuck, indeed. He likes you. He never says more than two words to me. Look," Brian pointed across the room to a man in a fashionable, oddly cut suit. He emanated energy, and people eddied around him. "That's the mother who replaced Jerry's score with his own, with every cliché in the book."

Jack wanted to be driving west on Wilshire down to the Pacific.

"Which you can do if you're the producer. Money talks, the rest of us walk," Brian sneered in his British lisp.

"I have to go, Brian."

"Where to?"

Outside, on Wilshire Boulevard, the sun's glare off the facade of the silver building blinded Jack. He smelled the newly hosed concrete sidewalk of the Beverly Hills address and the exhaust from passing cars. He felt the wind rustling the dusty date palms, which swished and swayed above him toward the five stories of glass and steel. In the movie, the grazing buck and clear-eyed does had pricked their ears at a distant sound and then had lowered their heads to the wide green field. The Wilshire traffic pounded and drummed by Jack. Then the prison fence had sliced across the field of deer. Men with hopelessly alert faces were imprisoned inside the fence. Then they lowered their heads to look at nothing in particular, you pleasant son-of-a-bitch.

5

With a sharp, silver-handled blade, Petrov sliced through the skin into the white flesh of the turkey he stood above.

"Do you want white meat or dark, Jack?"

The young guest sat on one side of the dining table by Sarah and near Mrs. Petrov at the end. Petrov forked the steaming white meat onto the plate Jack passed him. Joseph sat on the other side, opposite his sister and Jack. The table was laden with the paraphernalia of Thanksgiving: bowls of olives (California) and cranberry sauce, candied yams, stuffing (with oysters), and pasticcio (made meatless—a Greek dish which Sarah had made, following her mother's directions: egg noodles, jack cheese, parsley, nutmeg, etc., all baked together; Sarah had made the entire meal following the ritual Helen had set for over thirty years in America but was now unable to perform).

"Why have you put oysters in the stuffing?" the small woman glanced with dark eyes at her daughter.

"I love oysters," her husband said as finally he served himself slices of breast and thigh.

There were bottles of wine on the wide table, Riesling and Oxblood. Joseph put his hands on their necks.

"Which will it be, Jack?" He tried the Oxblood.

"Pour, please. The Oxblüt," Petrov said, his fork piercing an oyster and bringing it to his mouth.

Joseph did not reply, only poured the dark red wine into his father's goblet. He had said nothing more than yes or no to him all evening, and no glance or word came from Joseph now as he filled the glass almost to the brim.

Sarah drank ice water, Joseph and his mother the Riesling. There was a small, crystal dish of pale caviar spread from which Jack took a spoonful. He had praised the taramasalata when they had had their drinks before dinner. Sarah brought the bowl with them to the dining table, discreetly placing it near him.

Earlier, in the music room, Joseph had sat with a glass of vodka in hand, asking how Jack liked L.A. and where he lived. Joseph's own apartment was in Hollywood, on Franklin near Highland, "a jog from Hollywood Bowl," he had laughed, a muted laughter which distanced him from his words, from the Bowl and Hollywood, from the room and canyon in which they talked. What struck Jack most was how ascetic the man on the couch next to him seemed, how intense his brown eyes—like his sister's and mother's only darker—how haunted he seemed despite the fine suede shirt he wore and his legs stretched out in black pants, lanky and relaxed, and the thick shock of black hair. As he chatted, there was warmth in his voice: an underground telegraph seemed to make its way through the Petrov family, that Jack was to be accepted on sight.

"Look at the credenza in back of my mother," Joseph said during dinner, pointing off-handedly at a dark, carved sideboard with doors and drawers. "It was made by her father in Greece and shipped from Athens when he died."

"My mother told me, take everything you want," Helen Petrov said, gazing in Jack's direction. "After the funeral. 'I want nothing for myself,' she said. Of course we took only a few things. But they are fine. I've often wondered why she…"

"Your father was a peasant, a mild man and a peasant, and your mother…" Petrov said, as if by rote; his words briefly interrupted the rhythm of his eating.

Helen stiffened and continued, "They are fine things, nicely carved. He was a cabinet maker." On the wood of the doors on each side of the credenza, a god's face had been carved: his forehead, cheeks, and chin were framed by leaves as if the powerful face stretched from the dark burl of the wood itself and generated a dense and gentle vegetation which flowed from him, brown and thick, toward the borders of the door.

"The crystal bowl is from our grandparents too, Mother," Joseph said, slowly pointing at the bowl near Jack.

"I suppose so," she said. She ate with one hand held in her lap.

"Joey keeps track," Sarah said and smiled at Jack.

Toward of the end of dinner, Jack asked the young pianist, "Do you travel much, to perform?"

"In January," Sarah answered for her brother, "he goes to the northwest, Portland, Eugene, Seattle. In March, he's going east."

Petrov was sitting, silent, deliberately cutting the remaining piece of turkey on his plate.

"In December, you have a concert here, no?" Jack said. "What are you playing?"

Joseph held a small fork-full of pasticcio in the air, ate, and then said, "I'm starting with the Berg Sonata and the Webern Variations."

"I remember them; they were Schoenberg's pupils," Helen Petrov said, gazing pleasantly at her son and placing her knife and fork carefully on her emptied plate. Her tone was insistent, even as it coolly assumed Joseph knew what she spoke of: "They each visited us in Berlin. And of course Arnold Schoenberg visited us here in Benedict Canyon. You were a babe in arms; Sarah was three. I should say that Arnold was full of himself, but really all those people were. Except Teddy Adorno: him I liked. Didn't he recently die, Sasha?" Petrov bridled in his seat and oddly did not reply, as if speech were suddenly dangerous for him. Helen resumed, focusing again on Joseph: "The others were pleasant enough, but ego-maniacs all. Alma Mahler and Franz Werfel, for instance. To see Alma Mahler Werfel sit here in a taffeta gown, sipping from a glass of Füking—it was quite something. And to hear her interrupt the conversation to recite Rilke…'Hore, mein Herz: we must all listen to this music like the saints listen!' Yes, the ego-maniac said 'Saints'!"

The room was silent. It seemed as if Helen were speaking in code, and no one was willing to intercede, to try to break the code. Jack came to the rescue, zeroing in on Joseph.

"What a powerful contrast, Berg and Webern. You know about Webern's death?" he asked.

"A terrible logic to it. That an American soldier would shoot him in Salzburg, while he was going out for a walk to smoke his pipe, in 1945."

"And Webern had always tried to oppose the totalitarianism dominating the century. To overcome the dead-end of his culture."

"'To live is to defend a form,'" Joseph said with a flourish, his elbows on the table. "That was one of Webern's favorite quotes."

"Hölderin," Petrov suddenly spoke up, putting down his knife and fork. "That's Hölderin." Joseph cringed and then held himself still, looking straight ahead between Sarah and Jack, at nothing.

"You should read *The Autocrat of the Breakfast Table*, Joseph," the father said, smiling and irritable at once. "You surprise me. You never speak to me so eloquently. You never speak to me at all. I can't decide: are you a chip off the old block—the same force in you as in me? Or some oddity, no son of mine? Though you are a pianist, aren't you?" Silence again fell over the group.

"The Schoenberg you played," Jack ventured, turning now to speak to Petrov, "two months ago, that's related to the Berg, especially the…"

"Two months ago?" Petrov said. "Impossible. It's more like two weeks."

"That was October first. Today is November twenty third. It was a great concert."

"Two months."

"How do you think he did?" Jack asked Helen Petrov, who smiled mechanically as he turned to her.

"She doesn't know," Petrov said.

"She knows," Jack said.

"I don't judge," she said.

"The newspapers said I played fine," Petrov said off-handedly, putting an end to the matter.

"Do you want me to say he played badly?" the small woman began rapidly to speak from her end of the table. "Or do you want me to proceed with the adulations? I remember Franz Werfel was very good at that: 'When a great artist touches the piano, there is something absolutely unique about it! You always know who it is! What a privilege to hear Sasha play. He is a visionary genius!' Would you like me to rave like that?"

"It looks like you've all had fine appetites," Sarah interrupted, standing and beginning to gather the plates. "You're no less than stuffed men." Then she said to Joseph and Jack, "Will you give me a hand with the dishes?" She forked the remains from each plate into a bowl, the flakes of meat and noodle, the clumps of yam and stuffing. Joseph and Jack helped her clear the table as the old couple watched.

"Relax. After, we'll have dessert," Sarah told them.

In the kitchen, she stood at the sink, her hands in suds. Joseph held a dish cloth and wiped the crystal and silver pieces. Jack was told to take a seat at the breakfast table. He watched brother and sister, one almost thirty and the other just turned thirty three, performing the ritual they had practiced on and off since youth. Their movements syncopated perfectly, Sarah handing him a bowl and Joseph leaning his lanky frame to take it, rub it dry, and place it in a row on the old formica. Her dark gold head tilted to one side as she spoke to him or to Jack, who sat across the kitchen from them.

"We're told to be neat and clean," she said as she washed.

"We're told to be good and straight," Joseph laughed, as he dried.

"And we do it."

"Goddamnit, we do it," he burst out, gently lowering a silver platter to the counter.

"But do you think they did? Did they do anything they didn't want to do?" Sarah asked, her hands in the suds and under the faucet. "Mother is one of the most spoiled, bitter, tight-assed women I've ever known, and we allow her to get away with it. As for father..."

"Please, Sarah." Joseph stopped wiping. "Jack doesn't want to hear this." He crumpled the cloth in his hands.

"Don't worry about me. I have parents too," Jack said.

"Of course, she's old now, and I do feel sorry for her. But there was a time," she turned to Joseph and wiped her hands on his dish towel.

They brought the desserts to the dining table. There were cookies—butter-almond, dusted with powdered sugar, the one thing Helen had made that morning—and two pies, pumpkin and apple. The Petrovs were asleep in their arm chairs at each end of the table.

"Oh," Helen said with a start, "I was just telling Sasha to get me a cup of coffee."

As Sarah poured coffee and served slices of pie, Petrov started telling a story. It was as if he were continuing a conversation conducted in a dream while he slept, or perhaps he was answering—half an hour later—Helen's criticisms of Schoenberg.

"I told you, Jack, that once we brought together Schoenberg and Stravinsky, here. I don't know if Joseph and Sarah are aware of this. At one point, I remember, Igor talked about illness and creativity. 'One half of all artists are manic-depressives,' he said. 'And maybe alcoholics to boot. The other half are just more subtle about what makes them sick!'

"Your parents were there that evening, and Julius spoke up then: 'Sometimes it's not so subtle: the stress is tremendous, with the war.' I remember how your father leaned forward as he spoke in his chair, next to your mother. With his dark hair close cropped, very earnest, he said: 'Not that my pain is anything compared to all the death and disaster. But there is so much anxiety everywhere, and it comes out in small odd ways, in all of us. Migraines, ulcers, heart murmurs, lumbago. It's true. Just to play your instrument can be a challenge now.'

"Then, Thomas Mann spoke from his couch, by Katia and my friend Bruno. A cigarette was lit in Thomas's hand, and his other hand was wedged in his suit pocket—like this—his neck stiff and erect: 'The war takes an incalculable toll. But even before the war, my generation grew ill. And I know at least one cause. We were especially prone to the fevers and aches of romanticism, in its death throes. Even now, we keep trying to purge and cure it. We who came of age at the fin-de-siecle, who—secretly or not—loved Wagner, we were all sickly art-worshippers and symbolists in our youth!'

"'I certainly lapped up Wagner when I was young,' Igor said, 'those unpleasant sounds to which all our music is indebted. When I was fifteen, in the dark of Petersburg winter days, I would sit at the piano for hours, numb from playing through Tristan and the Ring. Even Webern—Arnold, you tell them—even Webern was a Wagnerian as late as 1905. We're all rebelling against him, still!—pulling ourselves from the grip of his autocratic rule, his iron-fisted clichés, his colonization of the chromatic scale, his imperialistic rule of music's new terrain. Nietzsche said his greatest experience was to recover from Wagner, who was merely one of his sicknesses.'

"'Yet,' Thomas said, 'music can also be the art most removed from our illness, most remote from life. Even Wagner's music. Potentially it transcends what makes us sick.'

"Then, finally, Arnold spoke up. He had been listening from the other couch, sitting next to Alma and Franz. 'You're deceiving yourself,' he said, his lips pursed and bitter. 'Look at you, look at all of us now. We have no home here. A culture? There is no culture here. I'd just as well see America disappear than accept its compromises. My world no longer exists. Music, form itself, has vanished. My very language, my words, my tones disappear: O Wört, du Wört, das mir fehlt.'"

Petrov stopped talking then.

Neither his children nor his wife said a word. Only Jack once again interceded, with helpless wonder, pleasure, and sadness.

After dessert, Sasha and Helen went upstairs to nap, and Sarah told the two men to relax—she would join them after taking care of the dessert plates and cups.

In the music studio, Joseph lit a cigarette and opened the sliding glass door to the dark. They walked out into the cool air. The yard was palely illuminated by a half moon. It was eight o'clock Thanksgiving evening, and Los Angeles's lights constantly blinked far below the hillside. The endless charge and flash, the lit intersecting lines of Wilshire and Santa Monica, and the occasional pools of blackness all seemed dwarfed by the flanks of hills and the dark trees, a palm, an evergreen by the house, and a leafless pepper tree arching above the yard. The limbs hung beneath the starry sky, and fallen leaves matted the ragged lawn. The air smelled of the dusty canyon brush, the damp grass, and the acrid fragrance of the leaves.

"I wish I had some weed," Joseph said by Jack, on the edge of the hillside. "I think there's an old stash in the garage. Come. There's something I want to show you anyway." Jack followed him across the yard and the paved drive.

The previous Saturday, Jack had asked Sarah out—to see *The Godfather* at a Westwood Village theater. They had exited into the night; his arm held her waist, and he felt the warmth and fullness of her body. Cars filled the intersecting streets in front of the movie house, cruising Comets and Valiants, MGs, Malibus and Mercedes, the occasional limousine inching its way through the crowd. If he had walked now past the chimeras he had just seen, he wondered whether these actors—Brando, Pacino, Keaton—would look as freakish as those Friday afternoon—McQueen and McGraw. The cross-cutting of the movie's climax, baptism and murder, water and blood, still gripped him even as he ordered cokes and falafels at a stand on the corner. He brought the tray to Sarah, who sat at one of the picnic tables inside the tent-like café. Through dirty plastic windows they saw a crush of movie-goers, teen-agers, UCLA students. She talked about Joseph. He was living in Hollywood near Laurel and the Hills, and he was doing drugs. "Just before you picked me up, I got a call from one of Joey's friends. Someone we know just ODed. Jesus, Danny was twenty-nine, Joey's age." She reached to hold Jack's hands in hers. There had been an implicit plea in her voice, as if it were possible for Jack to help her help him help himself.

Joseph opened the creaky door to the garage and flipped on the light. Sarah's Jeep was parked next to a big, white Chrysler sedan from the early sixties. Joseph disappeared into the rows of storage filling the back space.

"It's dry as dust," he said emerging from a row he had not entered, "but it'll do." The light bulb burned above them. There were rows of bruised trunks. Their leather, cracked and torn, bore the stamps of other countries, some with German lettering, some with Greek.

"Your parents keep all this," Jack said. The odor of marijuana joined the smells of dust, old leather, automobiles, and leaking oil.

"Yes, it's been this way ever since I can remember," he said. "My parents fled from Nazi Europe and plunked their shit down here in Los Angeles, the home of Aryan cults, white supremacist religions, and the John Birch Society. Brilliant planning." He held the roach toward Jack.

"No thanks," he said. Joseph took another drag, holding the smoke in his chest. He looked around, as if expecting the sight of other visitors, of strangers. Leaning against the piled trunks, he was a little taller than Jack, with long limbs and big, pianist's hands. His hair was unkempt, some of it covering his ears and falling toward his eyes.

"Look over here," he said and walked to the back. A rod jutted a few feet across a corner of the garage, and over it fabric was thickly folded, a gold Byzantine brocade beneath a clear plastic cover. He turned back the plastic and lifted a fold toward Jack, who felt its dusty pile and flashing metallic threads. Joseph leaned his head and smothered his face in it.

"In here at least, you smell what shit there is to smell."

They walked out onto the driveway, past Joseph's sports car, a low black Triumph, looking ten years old. Clouds had begun to clot the sky above the overhanging limbs. As they crossed the yard, Joseph talked about Jack's Variations.

Daniel C. Melnick   49

"I found it on Father's piano. I asked him about it," Joseph said. "He sat down right then and there to play a couple of variations, muttering all the while. He's impossible."

"Why impossible? Difficult, I can see, but there's so much amazing life and vitality in him."

"He's just impossible." An affectless mask covered Joseph's face. Then he turned to Jack at the glass entrance to the music room, and a smile appeared now on his lips. "Your Variations, they're an extraordinary work. I'd love to perform them."

❦   ❦   ❦

The Friday after Thanksgiving, Janice knocked on Jack's door as she stood in the rain, which had begun that day sheeting in off the Pacific. She hurried in, wearing shorts and a loose, purple sweater.

"You are never home, honey. Hell, what's happened to you?"

He repeated what he had told her on the phone, going over details of how demanding his work was at UA, with Jerry and Brian. He held back any mention of the Petrovs. She stood dripping on his living room floor, and he went to get her a towel from the bathroom. When he returned, his front door was open, and rain blew into the empty room from the paved patio which was his yard.

❦   ❦   ❦

It rained for a week after Thanksgiving, and now tiny winged insects and small spiders in flight crawled up the screen of Petrov's music studio. The rain had driven them out of the yard and brush, and they sought the light and comparative dry of the door. The quarter-inch of glass dulled the pattering and the thud of distant thunder. Jack glanced out into the drenched dark at the evergreen jutting up next to the eaves of the house. Sarah stood near the piano, in the corner where Petrov kept his phonograph. She put on one of the records from a pile she had brought from her room; next to her records was a small camera in its case.

She sang along—about his wanting respect and her getting it—laughing and swinging her hair in back of her. She danced toward him, and the two beat movements of her hips gave a hint of bump and grind. Aretha sang from Petrov's big speaker against the wall by the Steinway. He abjured stereo. He and

Mrs. Petrov were out for the evening; the brilliant violinist Michael Kramer had driven them to the home of their mutual friends the Weisbergs, to play chamber music. In the late afternoon, Sarah had called Jack and invited him over.

She grabbed his hand, and he danced with her, mimicking her motions, a smile on his face. Another song came on, and Sarah turned to peer out the glass.

"I've watched that fir tree grow for thirty years," she said, her high voice filling the room. "When I was just three, they let me help plant the sapling. And when I was thirteen, I carved my initials in the trunk. The tree was just a little younger than I, but already it rose to the roof. I remember I found Joey's pocket knife to carve with—my own SP on that thick trunk. Father saw it, and he took me out by the hand. He was so angry, and all I was trying to do was put some sign, some little sign of myself on this fucking property. I remember, he held me by the wrists in his big hands. God, he held me tightly. 'You must never, never deface our property, Sarah. Never. Promise me. Never.'"

She stared out at the fir in the rain. The limbs, black against the clouds, stretched from the tile roof out into the yard.

"When I promised, Father gave me a hug and held me almost as tightly as before. 'My good Sarah,' he kept saying. Mother came outside and made him let me go."

Jack reached for her hand, which he loosely held. "This place must have meant so much to him; it was a refuge," he said.

"Mother and father were in flight from the Nazis when they came here. In 1939. Father bought the house with money he had inherited—his mother's family kept it in a Swiss bank. The house is a classic, no? Before it was ours, it was a small-time producer's. Strang must have used this room to watch movies in. Then he moved on to a bigger monstrosity."

At the phonograph, she changed the record and put on the song she had sung here a month ago. She picked her camera up, walked across the music room, and sat down on the couch which faced toward the sliding door.

"So here we are," she said. "Shit, I'm thirty three and living again with my parents. When Father got sick, they needed me. And I needed help. You can't imagine what it was like, though maybe you can. Living with musicians. I had friends in the Weathermen too. So much anger and chaos, and there were the drugs. We were always high on rage or on shit. I was a mess. I didn't know how to get out. In his own way, Father came to the rescue. He had a heart attack.

Now that's depressing. And nothing much has changed in three years. Mother, son, and daughter depressed out of their minds, and Father into himself."

"Your mother seems ill. Has she been to a doctor lately?"

"Sure. The same doctor for over a decade. A brilliant internist with a practice filled with decrepit European émigrés. He couldn't care less."

"Why not take her to someone else?"

"Father is taken by him. You should never see the respect the doctor lavishes, the fawning. Anyway, she's a hypochondriac of the old school."

"There are small strokes she could be having. Your father too for that matter. People have them at that age. They're not dramatic, but they happen."

"You're right," she said. "I have to get it checked out."

On the player sounded a son's song to a father, a plaintive wail, a call for recognition that his old man look, that he see they both were sufferers and yearners for love.

Jack walked to the wall of plaques and photographs in back of Sarah on one of the old couches. She sat still, fiddling with her camera, not turning toward him, and he looked at the framed black and white photographs hung on the frayed grass cloth.

"These are yours," he said, and she hummed her assent in her clear soprano. Each shot had a heightened brightness and clarity, as if snapped in a highly polished mirror. One photo showed Joseph standing next to the Pacific, which swelled in the background. His face was masked by the gleam off his sunglasses. One arm was folded across his rigid body, and in the other raised hand he held a cigarette, the smoke trailing toward the camera, away from the luminous ocean.

Another frame held a photograph of Petrov and his wife, bright and precisely focused. The big man had tufts of white hair circling his head, and he stared out irritably. He wore a suit of dated, European cut, his hand held a cigar, and he stood a pace away from his gray-haired wife, short and elegant in a formal dress. Her stare moved beyond the ornate frame to envelop the room and measure what she saw.

"Don't look at those photos," Sarah said, getting up from the couch. She walked to replace the Neil Young on the phonograph.

"They're fantastic," Jack said. "It's wonderful they're here."

"Father insists." She eased the needle onto a record and stood on the oak floor in front of the single speaker by the piano. She pointed her camera in Jack's direction. Guitar distortion climbed up the scale, and Jim Morrison's voice strutted from the box.

"Here's a photograph of you. A self-portrait?"

"Yeah," she mumbled, "from college." In the photo, a girl of about twenty-two was wearing a tight, black sweater: Sarah stood behind a leather couch, her hand resting on it, her back to a white wall. Looking up, her lips parted, she leaned slightly over the couch; its hide was in careful focus.

"They're fantastic," he repeated. "They…they suggest so much." He turned to see Sarah was shooting his picture. "Oh jesus. Now there's a record of my being here." He walked over and sat down cross-legged by her on the oak floor.

"Let's not talk about them," she said, putting down her camera by the records. She sat next to him and in an objective voice began complaining about Nixon's victory over McGovern and the *Times*' suppression of stories about Watergate. "You didn't vote for Nixon, did you?"

He laughed, shaking his head no. He said, "Do you remember when he first appeared on television, when we were kids? Somehow, I remember him at the piano: Ike's vice-president on TV, tickling the ivories. Like a regular guy, the son-of-a-bitch." Sarah laughed, and he leaned gently toward her, kissing her golden brown eyebrows, her shutting eyelids, her smiling mouth.

The room's acoustics were remarkable. Its resonant surfaces could reveal the unique timbre of any instrument played there, a violin or cello, the guitar and bass blaring by them, or the black grand which loomed above them as their hands reached to soothe and touch on the polished floor.

The speakers bellowed out a harsh and swinging lyric about the city of lights, city of los angeles, the angels, who were like titans consuming their young under the cover of night.

"Come with me," she said in her quiet, full soprano voice. She got up and turned off the phonograph, gathering her records and camera in one arm. She switched the music studio's lights off as he followed her out.

Drawn to her, he had a vague sense that this woman merged with an elusive dream he could not yet fathom, but yearned to inhabit. He did not know what form the dream would take, and he wondered whether it were possible to realize it here, now. Whatever his destiny, he knew that the dream compelled him now to reach out to this woman, who was capable of such beauty of voice yet of such neutral silences. And he knew also that both voice and silence drew him. A bond had begun to grow, a kinship larger than he understood.

They walked to the end of the hall and up the carpeted stairs. At the top, a single fixture was on. The darkened rooms they passed were open. Sarah's one hand clutched the stack of records, and in the other she held Jack's hand, leading him down the unlit hall. An Orpheus, only led by Eurydice, he gazed into each room they floated past: Joseph's room apparently kept intact, Sasha's and Helen's room with a large, silken canopy looming over the big bed, a separate bedroom sparsely furnished, yet with its bed sheet turned down for someone to nap or sleep. At the end of the hall, Sarah led him into her room, turned on the light, and shut the door behind them.

She laid the records and camera down on a long desk built into the wall, with a typewriter, calculator, and a stereo at one end, files and drawers below, shelves above. He went up to her and began kissing her forehead and eyes; he smoothed her hair from her face and brushed his lips and tongue against her slender neck. She turned off the light, and they stood together by the bed and undid their clothes. Jack heard the incessant pinging song of the rain which poured down on the front drive, the dark, unweeded yard and path outside her window. As their bodies touched and joined, he was conscious of the surrounding trees and hills, the cited plain, the ocean. Then, an inner time obliterated the real time of rain and night. An intensity filled them, strangely silent, nearly motionless at first, and finally their bodies began to rock together in a restless surge of motion.

PART II

Scherzo—Assai Vivace: December 1972

1

The mounting melody approached the climax of the development, quadruple forte. Joseph's left hand punched the massive downbeats, his right exaggerated the skipping sixteenth notes, and the Berg sonata—OOOM pah OOM—became the parody of a scherzo by Brahms or Chopin. He held his hands always flat over the keys, and when the loudest octaves danced out, skipping and macabre, his flattened fingers betrayed no curve of effort. Little furious groups of six notes would erupt with scrupulous smoothness and control. When the opening lament of Berg's melody returned, Joseph restrained his shimmering tone so that it was shallow and unbeautiful.

Jack listened—from an aisle seat—to the refusal of beauty, the mockery of depth, and he glanced at Sarah by him, the Petrovs by her, and the riveted audience—many of them young—packing the Wilshire Ebell Theater. Joseph kept tossing back his black hair as he glanced at the corner of the theater's ceiling, and a smile kept forming on his lips. Isolated on the stage, he seemed on the verge of breakdown or violence, about to disclose some secret form, beyond all allure of surfaces. Yet he would tease and step back from the abyss of discovery. Sometimes he exaggerated the obvious, the four-square underpinnings of structure; sometimes he mocked the sonata's inward utterances. It was not the forward-looking Berg of Lulu or Wozzeck, nor was it any kin to the Schoenberg of 1908. Joseph revealed a Berg looking backward. Such maniacal Chopin, Jack thought, like some newly discovered fifth Scherzo written at the age of ninety-eight.

The shallow stage seemed to thrust piano and pianist forward as Joseph rose, bowing to the applause, and it magnified him in his black suit and silver-gray turtleneck. His eyes questioned the clapping crowd before him. Immediately, he sat down to continue.

Joseph played the notes Webern wrote in 1936 as if he were cognizant of an enveloping absence of sound, decades long. With care, he noted each note and the nothingness which surrounded it. One leg was stretched akimbo from beneath the piano stool, as his flat hands concentrated on phrases of two and three notes at a time, balanced against each other, like tilted mirrors, asymmetrical and always punctuated by silence.

Then, a scherzo raced out, a panicky joke or travestied waltz, the skipping, skittering notes divided between his hands in a flurry of motion. Suddenly it ceased.

The final movement began: single notes pinged high in the treble, answered by single bass notes, dryly hit. Note mirrored and answered note in ever more complex combinations, in violent descents, in gentle emptinesses, in vicious silences, as if Webern sought to anatomize sound and silence both, to see which was less redolent of death, which more resonant with life. Jack had heard Piatigorsky and Babin perform a similar autopsy at CIM two years ago, but here Joseph was revealing the profounder refusal in Webern's music, the refusal of performance itself. His eyes searching the far wall of the theater, he exposed the music's need to stop, to oppose (and by opposing, end): to stop time, to stop all complaisant, mechanical motion, to stop the century's brutal invalidation of music's language, to stop the noisy chaos of world culture's collapse, its totalizing usurpation of the popular, of any common language: to oppose through acts of non-communication, through a pristine and defensive stasis, which finally would end the motion of performance itself. To live is to defend a form.

Yells of bravo erupted. The roaring, youthful crowd yearned to witness just this last performance, the last waltz, to be present at the last gasp of a culture Webern gambled—through silence and stoppage—to preserve. The twenty-nine year old pianist bowed to the applause and fled the stage. "I hope he's all right," she whispered to him. On her other side, the elder Petrovs sat serenely still, waiting without emotion, it seemed, for their son's return.

After a minute of staticky silence, Joseph strode to the concert grand, sat without acknowledging the audience's clapping, and bent his frame forward to play: a single note, the C repeated and repeated again, higher, then lower, in exploratory rhythms, finally in wayward improvisatory double octaves. The single C again returned: the note repeating, then ceasing.

Joseph made his way now through Ligeti's Musica Ricercata. The pianist seemed released by what he played, his eyes elevated beatifically toward the high wall, a child-like smile playing now on his lips. Where before he held himself stock still at the ground zero of Webern's scorched world, he sat now delighted, playing Ligeti's second section, with tonic and the newly added dominant, C and G, as if they were mud pies or tinker toys.

Each section added another note of the circle of fifths, another building block: in 1952, Ligeti had tried to rebuild music from scratch. At nine notes, an apogee of his searching Ricercata was a stricken Adagio in memory of Bartok, the composer to whom Ligeti had most deeply listened. At ten notes, Joseph let rip his manic technique—capriccioso—his legs stretching, finding footholds as his hands played the dissonant din. He seemed to thumb out glissandi which were actually racing chromatic scales; he slapped notes onto the keyboard in great gobs and clumps, with a drunken, teasing dancing and slamming.

There was suddenly silence. The last movement, using the full chromatic scale, emerged, a penitential Andante. Joseph—visibly sweating and still smiling—played the homage to Frescobaldi with a reactionary simplicity, which denied the chromatic flux any kinship to twentieth century dissonance. As he rose from the piano and the audience rang out its approval, the child-like smile stayed frozen in place on him. He bowed awkwardly, in a sort of continuing refusal.

After the applause subsided, the house lights came on for intermission.

"I have to go see him," Sarah muttered to Jack. "Keep my parents company, would you? And keep them away from him." She vanished down the aisle toward the stage.

He felt her urgency and pressure, and he moved over a seat to where Sarah had been, next to Helen; Petrov sat on the other side of his wife. A heavy yet refined man in an ill-fitting suit edged into the now empty aisle seat and leaned over Jack and Helen to greet the old pianist. "Michael," Sasha boomed out, and the two men shook hands.

"Would you like to go out to the lobby?" Jack asked when they were alone. "To stretch or anything?" Still he saw Joseph before him, playing Ligeti's music, and Jack could not keep from smiling. He put his hand to his mouth. The Petrovs sat quietly in their seats. Jack felt restless. The Adagio—to Bartok's memory—kept resounding in him: Ligeti understood there how to listen and compose with Bartok's own deep openness and baring.

"Child's play," Petrov smiled, mind-reading from his seat. Mrs. Petrov's wrinkled face showed no sign.

"The Ligeti?" Jack said.

"Ligeti," Petrov said. "I'm impressed. The conception is so clear."

An elderly couple headed for their row. They leaned over Jack to greet Helen and Sasha. Jack heard the names Morris and Sandra, which Helen said, and then the words brilliant and son, which the woman said to Helen.

The couple seemed vaguely familiar to Jack, and he got up. "Please, sit while you visit," he said, and they thanked him and sat in Sarah's and his places. He walked to the high, shallow stage with the Steinway looming on it, and he made his way backstage to the dressing-room door. He knocked, then tried it, and the door swung open. Jack looked in and shut it behind him.

In the toilet, Sarah was leaning forward, her hand on Joseph's back. He was bent over the toilet bowl, gasping.

"Shit," he said between dry, wrenched heaves. "Shit."

As he vomited out the emptiness in his gut, his sister became aware of their visitor. She gestured for him to sit on one of the chairs. When they emerged, Joseph looked up at Jack. His skin was paper white, and the front of his gray shirt was spattered with wet flecks which Sarah rubbed off with a dampened towel.

"Why, Jack?" he said, "Why is it happening?"

"This doesn't happen to him," Sarah said.

"Fuck no, this doesn't happen," he said. He lay down on the cot in back of the small room. Sarah went to sit by him.

"You shouldn't have to see this, Jack," she said.

"Your parents were visiting with some people," Jack said, "Morris and Sandra, I think. So it seemed all right to leave them."

"Dr. and Mrs. Weisberg…they're friends. He's an amateur violinist," Sarah said.

"That's who they were. I think my parents know them too, old L.A. friends. More and more it looks like I'm becoming part of your family. Which means we're all in trouble."

Sarah looked at her brother by her and put her hand on his arm. "I told you he was one of us, just not as screwed up."

"Yeah," Joseph said and smiled. After some seconds, he laughed. "You know I was here early, and when I walked through the foyer, there were these two bitches in furs and diamonds. They asked me when was Joseph Petrov going to perform."

Sarah and then Jack began to laugh.

"Don't waste your money, I told them, just to hear some asshole get it off banging the piano. I guess I deserve this, for that." Laughing, he sat up now.

"Hell no," Jack said.

"Don't tell Petrov," he said.

"This is what you get for practicing six hours a day, fucking with shit at night, and not eating," Sarah said.

"It doesn't usually happen," Joseph said, lying back.

"I know," she said, her hand smoothing the silver-gray shirt over his stomach.

There was a knock at the door. It was time. Sarah helped Joseph into the black jacket of his suit, and she kissed him on the cheek. Before a mirror, he combed his black hair and then took deep breaths like an athlete before a meet. She gathered her suede jacket and purse, took some mints from it, and handed them to her brother.

They arrived at their seats by the Petrovs just as the crowd's roar met Joseph, pale and striding to the piano. He nodded at the audience as he sat. Immediately, his hands reached to play Mozart's melancholy A-minor rondo. The six bass beats per bar were dry and detached, as if the nine-foot grand had been transformed into a fortepiano. The touching melody endured in the treble, but barely breathing amid the almost airless purity of Joseph's playing. He withheld any of the rhetoric Mozart, late in life, was forecasting. When the bass octaves sounded out and the sixteenth notes sang out in the treble, they were reined in, made to serve a precise and finally complacent classicism. It was a neo-classical travesty, Jack thought.

The pianist gazed at the top of the high wall. He turned to the triplet figures of the middle section and played them with dry irony which never disappeared through the rest of the rondo. It was as if he would prefer not—would prefer the music not to search, not to open outward, not to forecast Beethoven or Schubert, but instead to turn back on itself, to mirror its own past, its own conventions, to admire only itself. And yet, when Joseph finished, there was a convulsive clapping. This was Mozart as the audience believed Mozart understood himself.

He stood for a single bow and then sat back down to begin the final work. Slow surging octaves and chords leapt out, Drammatico, and Scriabin's Third Sonata poured forth, a molten Chopin. Just as in the Berg, Joseph's playing abjured the abyss over which the music teetered. It was a drama of impulsiveness and deprivation, shadowed always by the power he withheld and the erratic violences he allowed as now he punched out the stamping march of the Allegretto scherzo, his arms tense with violent energy.

Suddenly Jack imagined how Joseph must make love, how he must arch himself with a violent thrusting, how he might be capable of tenderness but, bereft, must finally hold it back, left with merely fucking. Jack could not trace the origin of his imagining. With Sarah two weeks before, but now also with the images of her hands touching her brother, his imagination began only barely to glimpse the cavern of desire into which he was descending, to perish or revive.

The Andante sang out. Unlike in the Berg, Joseph gave himself now to the beauty of the music, and the effect was of floating, of hebetation, of a sentimentality he was helpless to purge. Then the violences returned in the convulsive transition to Presto con fuoco. Waves mounted on waves of agitation, and here Joseph finally allowed a tragic, Russian torment to speak through each wave of sound. Amid this tragic grandeur, Joseph's hands wrought the sonata's climax with the demonic power of a pianist in the great tradition, a last emissary, descended from Beethoven, through Czerny to Liszt, Busoni, and now Petrov père et fils.

Yet Joseph's Scriabin, Jack thought, still looked backwards: it was again belated Chopin, and Joseph refused to draw this ghostly Chopin forward to witness the future, to visit the desperate end of the last century, when Scriabin actually composed. The pianist had trapped this ersatz Chopin in the prison-house of nostalgia, of the pianist's own refusal and resentment. The torrent of applause descended yet again, flooding the stage, pouring over Joseph who stood wryly smiling and drenched, by the black piano.

Afterwards, after the ovations, after the reception line, the elder Petrovs sat on the cot in the backstage dressing-room, and Joseph sat on a chair. Sarah and Jack stood by the table with an open bottle of Stolichnaya given to Joseph by the sloppily dressed yet refined-looking man who had greeted Sasha at intermission. The five of them now lifted paper cups of the faintly anise-scented vodka; even Sarah had a sip. Together they cheered the son and brother. Joseph lit a cigarette after the toasts, and Petrov began: "Excellent though, of course, the last work…"

"Full of Slavic excess as Scriabin can be," the son spoke in the father's tone of voice and pulled his face away, exhaling smoke sharply to one side.

"Such a work," the father began again.

"It disappoints," Joseph's voice had disintegrated to a whisper.

"Now the Mozart before it!" The brilliant old man's eyes were laughing. He lit a cigar and held it in his down-curved mouth.

Sarah squeezed Jack's hand, leaving his side and exiting through the door. "We'll be right back," he said to the other three. Joseph sat smoking, unspeaking, as Jack was leaving and Petrov continued: "Such fine humor. Like Stravinsky you played it. His irony, teasing his own conventions. His sharp laughter. Like wise obsceni…"

Jack emerged into the back of the stage with its curtained obscurity, its ropes hanging from the rafters, and the back of the stage's thick acoustic wall at the front. A ladder was tilted against it. Sarah was nowhere to be seen. Why were father and son so opposed and cut off from one another? Jack did not understand, yet he felt caught between them: like Sarah. She walked steadily toward him through the near darkness, composed and leading him back now to the dressing room.

It was Beethoven's birthday, Jack realized, though Joseph had played no Beethoven. It was eleven thirty on Saturday night, December 16, 1972, his two hundred and second.

2

He strode down Paloma, across the cement pathway of Ocean Front, and onto the beach. Through the morning he had worked at his sonata, and now at noon he felt driven out of doors. The wind blew off the ocean, and the sun beat down from the cloudless sky. Flecks of sparkle glinted silver, like static charges, in the carpet of gray-white sand, and grains sprayed off the undulating sand hills nearest the shore. Wave after wave broke and spread a white foaming film up the sand toward where Jack walked. It was Monday, Christmas day, and he saw few people on the beach. The wind drove the temperature down near forty, and he kept his hands in the pockets of his windbreaker, zipped over his blue sweater.

The ceiling of blue above the ocean drew him to the foaming shore. Though its force and primal threat sometimes seized him, he walked steadily along the edge south into Venice. In the wind's hiss and the splattering roar of the breaking waves he heard the music he sought. How could he compose this hiss and roar so that the performer and listener understood that power—and their own? Their capacity to swim, to dive, to hold themselves afloat in the rising water, to reach out with purposeful strokes in the alien surge. He walked over the yielding sand, his face turned inland as he headed now back toward Paloma.

A half-block away, a man stood on the cement, near the sand's edge. He was stripped down to red shorts, and his oiled body shone in the cold sun. In his hands, he held a bar of weights above his head. The huge circles of iron bore down on his wrists, his trembling forearms and biceps, his barrel chest and legs. A skinny man in a parka crouched to spot the weight-lifter. The admiring little spotter was riveted in the self-regarding gaze of the bloated, lifting muscle man. There was no audience except Jack, who stopped a hundred feet away to watch this carnival Hercules, stretching and puffing and flexing in the mirror of the spotter's eyes.

Jack walked to Paloma across Speedway and into his paved yard with its hibachi, its bushy banana plants and low palms lining the edge of the brick fence. There were wind-beaten chrome and plastic chairs and a recliner for sun-bathing. Once inside, he went to the toilet to piss, washed and walked to the kitchen, to fix a sandwich: sliced turkey, avocado, sprouts, and mayo on wheat. He took it on a plate with a coke to the dining table he used for work in the front room. In the sunlight from the shut windows before him, his notebook was open to the second movement of his sonata. Wiping his hands between bites, he wrote in new tempo marks, two and three alternative tempi for each episode he had so far composed of the Scherzo. This would be a resolution of the problem which drove him—an hour before—to walk out to the waves: to tap the performer's power to create, to draw his listener too into the Dionysian motion and risk of choice. Performer and listener would have the freedom to read and hear his work as violent or tender, entrammeled or releasing, morbid or joyous—each according to his need, temperament, and imagination.

Pushing the empty plate away, he hunched over the paper. Through the score, he had threaded allusions to the second movement of the Hammerklavier, its Scherzo rhythm stumbling resistant and off-beat through Jack's second movement. His music now contained both choices of tempo and choices of themes to emphasize, intermingle, or suppress. Composing with a driven restlessness, he drew more and more to the surface the tense hesitancy of Beethoven's assai vivace, growing from stumbling to hammered, presto violence.

He let go of his pen and went to lie down on the couch. He imagined the alternative performances of the movement. Allegro, it would sound like a harmed panther, loping yet hobbled, snarling yet turned in on its pain. Presto, it would become a fluttering bird rising up toward the consuming sun. Andante, it would sound like a fey rock band, the bass and guitar distortion turned up so that the brute anger and sentimental clichés were wiped out in a wash of hobbling, dissonant sound. Awake yet dazed, he napped on the couch. No bald geniuses were present to witness or provoke.

He felt the emptiness of the day. His parents had never celebrated it, only Chanukah, and that without fanfare. A new album leaned against the bottom shelf of records, Neil Young's Harvest; he had listened to his Christmas present earlier, to the self-conscious hymn and wail of Neil Young's primitive band. Sarah had given it to him two days ago, on Saturday, and he gave her a sheer, silk scarf, with subtle, swirling, dark-blue paisleys edged in white, like breaking waves at night.

They had sat together in his Volkswagen, parked next to the Beverly Hills Hotel at the base of Benedict Canyon Drive. After they exchanged presents, Sarah had handed him a paper bag, and he took from it a matted eight by ten black and white photograph of himself. Jack stared, startled by the image of himself: human imperfection had somehow disappeared into the intense presence of the image, which stared quizzically back at him. The skin had no blotch or flaw, the mouth no twist or gap, the torso and legs no bend or slump. He looked at himself, at the aura of shaggy hair, the wide questioning eyes, the Roman nose, the warm speaking lips, the chest filling a dark t-shirt, the young man's body framed against the wall of photographs in the Petrovs' music room, and then he looked up at Sarah.

"Not bad, eh?" she said, smiling with pleasure and pride.

"Is that really me?" he asked, laughing and reaching to hold and kiss her face.

"Of course, it's you," she said; her high voice was proprietary and assured.

His embarrassment and pleasure—that this was the being she saw in him—erased the brief flicker of awareness that her photo had somehow pinned and fixed him against the Petrovs' wall. "Come over to my place," he said. "It's Saturday night. You can spend it with me."

"It's not possible," she said with a sort of tragic urgency. "Christmas doesn't just happen at our house. And we celebrate Joey's birthday Monday too. I can't stay out long. Father and Mother aren't feeling well either."

"Let's not just park here then," he said. He gunned his VW, and they lit out down Sunset, speeding left on Laurel Canyon.

"Let's not go up the canyon, okay?"

"Why not?"

She was silent. Then she said, "I used to live there. I just don't want to go by it."

Jack slowed the car. At a widening in the road, he waited for the traffic to thin and then wheeled in a circle, screeching within a few feet of a dirt embankment and heading back south down Laurel to Sunset.

"What's bothering you, really?"

"Nothing," she said in her quiet, intense soprano.

"Nothing? Tell me what it is."

"I was so messed up when I lived there," she said, her voice welling up, dramatic and breaking now. They drove west and south into Beverly Hills. "I told you I lived with Rick. It was as if I was caught in a nightmare and couldn't wake myself. Rick thought he knew what the fuck is up, but all he knew was what the fuck. Everything had to be easy, according to him, just a matter of his supposed charm and talent, and meanwhile I was picking up his shit and everything. He just wanted a slave. And what he really wanted was to be a record producer! 'I'm considering being a millionaire,' he'd say. He was a good guitarist, but that was nothing to him. Because it was too real, because what he truly wanted was fantasy, including as much shit as he could pop, snort, or smoke."

"It must have been terrible for you," Jack said, and he marveled at what she offered him this evening: that brilliant photograph, this pained confession told in her high voice—the spirit of each joining passionate clarity with decadence and disarming glibness.

"Tell me," he said, "how did you get away from it?"

"I kept trying. Every time, he'd say he couldn't live without me. I was the light of his life, et cetera. Finally, Father was paying one of his rare visits there. He looked around the apartment, the clothes on the floor, the dishes in the sink. He lifted a pot lid and gasped at a moldy chicken inside. Otherwise he was silent, and the only sound was me crying, helpless. Suddenly Rick came out of the bedroom door, only his shorts on. I couldn't believe what happened. Father lunged at him. He just came at him like a truck, to mow him down, saying: 'How dare you treat my daughter like this!' Then he stopped dead in his tracks, his hands in the air, and he collapsed on the dirty floor. His face turned blue. I screamed for Rick to call an ambulance, and I held Father until they came."

She was crying now. Jack had parked the car on Olympic by Roxbury Park. He held her and then led her out of the car. His arm around her waist, they walked past the swings and sand. They huddled silently on a park bench in the dark of the winter evening.

"That's all in the past now, Sarah," he said, gently stroking her hair and face. "We're together. We're together, and you'll be okay." They began to hold each other closely. Then, in the VW's cramped seats, they reached through clothes to touch and stroke, breathlessly kissing, struggling toward orgasm, bound and wrapped and striving in hobbled hugs, limbs cramped and clothed.

Later that night, when he returned home, he had opened his notebook and made the following entry.

Dec. 23: I want a fucking union of soul and body, for which this is not the place or the time, and there are no words. So fuck you, Jack. All the hope that a visionary like Lawrence felt even for the word itself, fuck, all that yearning has been perverted and reduced by the spoiled stupefied soulless bullshit of this time and place. We're so fucking desperate and petulant—case in point. It's the same struggle I feel in music: there are no words, no fit language, and the language we have is cynical and dead with torpor, when it should arise floating and luminous, refreshed and transcendent—in fucking as in music.

He stretched out now on the living room couch. The phone rang on the side table. He reached to answer it.

"Jack," a distant, half-audible rasp sounded.

"Hello."

"Jack, I need help," it was Joseph, his voice shrunk down to this gasp. "Can't talk on the phone. I need help."

"Where is Sarah? Aren't you spending Christmas with her and your parents?"

"Sarah can't help. I'm here, at my place. Can you come? Please come."

Jack asked for his address on Franklin. He put on his jacket and walked out again into the windy day. In his VW, he drove to Hollywood and passed record stores, jazz and comedy clubs, porno palaces. He glimpsed the high spires of a Christian Science cathedral and Grauman's Chinese Theater. He sped north on Highland (passing a three story bookstore shuttered closed and movie houses forever open). He turned right on Franklin where he ground to a halt.

Jack walked through the arched, open-air entry of a two-story apartment building, ornate with chipped cement patterning and plaster gargoyles, and he crossed the vacant inner courtyard. There was a child's scream and silence. He found Joseph's ground-floor apartment door. He tried it as he had been told, and walked into a white-washed hall.

"Joseph," Jack called out. The room in front was sparsely furnished, with piles of music and books strewn about. A Steinway was at the left end, six feet of black against the white walls. Boxes with torn wrappings were open on the tattered couch—a brown cashmere sweater, an old volume of music with the title, Satie, in large art-nouveau letters, and a thick book with an oriental carpet red and purple on the cover. The air in the living room was dry and overheated. To the right was an open door. Jack looked into an almost empty room with a single dresser and a mattress.

Joseph lay there naked, the blanket bunched behind him against the wall. He was curled in a foetal posture, his hands cupped together under his blankly staring head. His body was blanched white with sparse tufts of hair on the skin stretched across his chest. There were curling tufts above his penis, tucked pale below the black.

"Joseph, what happened? Have you taken drugs?" he asked. The man on the mattress did not move or speak. "I'll drive you to the hospital." It was intolerably hot in the apartment, but Jack still wore his windbreaker over his sweater. He grabbed the pants and shirt strewn on the floor and kneeled before the man stiffened into an infant's posture.

"I can't stand it," Joseph whispered. There was a red canker on the pale skin near his mouth. His voice was raspy and deadened.

"I'm taking you to the emergency room."

"I've not taken any shit," he said hoarsely. "You here, now, you're medicine enough."

"What can I do?"

"He'll never let me be. I'm sick, sick to death of him."

Jack put down the clothes he held, stood up, and took off his jacket.

"This morning," Joseph said, slowly sitting up on the mattress, cross-legged, "they gave me presents. I was born tomorrow. They always celebrate today. Petrov started in about the music he'd given me, about what a willful shit I am, in so many words. I told him. Don't try to alter me. I won't be made over in his image. I won't hide what I am from him. I am what I am," he suddenly shouted, his hands rooted on the bed, the bones of his chest tautly stretching.

"My god, Joseph," Jack said, feeling the force of grief and rage in the man's words. This was Isaac, but without the staying of Abraham's hand, so consumed must he have been by the altar flames of his childhood. Jack sat down on the floor beneath a window he opened, and he listened patiently to the naked man.

"Did I really will my fucking life before I was conceived, like Schopenhauer says? This shit-prison of myself. This stupid sorrow. How, Jack? How could I have imagined the hell of being born to him? From his seed." He fell back with his arms outspread on the sheeted mattress.

Facing the poor, forked creature before him, Jack wondered at what he saw and heard. Joseph's white, affectless face with a red sore near his mouth yielded a raging stream of speech from deep inside his agonized self-absorption.

"The witnesses who don't close their eyes to such horror, they're my true blood-relations, but one way or another they always destroy themselves. Bernd Zimmermann committed suicide, like Kleist, shooting himself on the Wannsee in Berlin. His music reminds me of yours. Always conscious of life's horror."

Joseph's voice was nearly inaudible now. He began to dress in the clothes Jack had gathered and left by him. "It's my only comfort, that others before me experienced this too. Maybe Zimmermann found the right answer." A bitter grin clutched his face. "The final solution."

He stood up, and Jack stood now next to him. "Can you take me out of here? I can't drive, and I can't stand it here."

Jack drove his battered, green VW down Highland, south past Hollywood, Sunset, and Santa Monica. In silence, they passed raw-faced teenagers, prostitutes, winos, their coats and jackets billowing like wings in the brisk wind. The glare from the Christmas sun slanted in on the passenger's side. Smoking from a pack of Camels, Joseph hunched in a black leather jacket.

"Do you want to eat?" Jack had asked when they got in the car, and Joseph had said no. At Santa Monica, Jack said haltingly: "I think I understand. The emptiness you feel, at least some of it. I wish I could help. At your concert you had so much force. Even after being sick. How you confronted the audience. How you educated and moved it."

Joseph was listening now, smoking with his right hand, and with his left he held a finger tightly against his face. Jack saw the concentration and intimacy of his listening, his finger planted at a spot below his eye which must in infancy have been a source of primal pleasure and security.

At Beverly, Jack said, "You don't know your own force. Like in your apartment just now, when you sat there and talked about dying. I understand. I feel like dying when I think I've stopped—when I'm composing and I begin to repeat myself—just fucking, without love, without letting the music grow and flower—when I can't go further. But you have so much power in reserve, Joseph. It's always new for you. Like when you performed the Ligeti."

Joseph smiled briefly, mildly, silently. At Wilshire, he said, "Turn here," pointing to the right with his cigarette.

"It took real courage," Jack said. "That's what I'd like my compositions to be, that miracle. I want it always to be the first time. With all the desperate discovery that goes with it." Jack knew that he was negotiating a fool's path between being sincere and being authentic, between compassion and truth. As masked and layered as he believed everyone and himself to be, he felt that contradictory path was the right one for him, though still he was oblivious to its potential dangers and destinations. It led him to say what more he said to Joseph.

"Your playing is so fucking powerful, you're so perceptive and aware, my god, but why do you still withhold yourself? There's more than this turning in on yourself. You know that, but you still withhold yourself. You're so sad, I feel I'm watching you die before my eyes."

"How do you know I'm not already dead?" Joseph said, cold and distant. They drove in silence past block after block of closed businesses. At Hancock Park, he said, "Stop here."

Jack turned and parked in the nearly empty lot. They sat in the stopped car. Jack said, "You know we die so many deaths…I only know that there's no pianist who says more to me. You're so sad, but I prefer your sadness to…"

He put his hand on Joseph's shoulder and smiled. "You're the last, great hope. And I'm the one after that." He laughed. "I'm not clear-headed or perceptive enough, so I use stupid terms for what I feel."

"No, Jack," Joseph said and reached to his own shoulder, holding Jack's wrist there. "I love what you say. It gives me hope." Joseph held his hand on him. Both of them were quiet as they sat, looking at each other.

"What is Hancock Park?" Jack said.

They got out of the old VW and walked across the parking lot, then up to the top of a slope. The glaring sun lowered toward the horizon. There was a stench of tar and gas in the air. Below them, bordering Wilshire Boulevard was a small lake, dirty with oil slick and a bracken of fallen leaves and blown dirt. At the furthest end, frozen two stories high was a hairy, tusked, gray-brown mammoth, its mouth trumpeting a permanent, silent alarm. They walked down the hill and up stairs to a platform, with the lake point-blank below them. The wind had picked up, hitting their faces, blowing at Jack and tossing Joseph's black hair about his head. Instructional plaques were built into the restraining fence along the edge of the platform.

The Lakepit: This lake fills a quarry where asphalt was mixed in the nineteenth century. The oily slick on the lake surface, composed of less volatile chemicals from crude oil, escapes with the bubbles of natural gas (methane) from fissures below the lake.

"Gas, water, and fissures in the earth," Jack said. "Only in L.A.."

There was another mammoth knee-deep in the foul, bubbling water. Its head rose twisting to their eye level, fifteen feet in the air, its mouth open in a frozen, gaping scream. Two small mammoths, six and eight feet high, stood helpless and appalled in the sharp shadow the trapped animal cast toward the shore.

Joseph began to read a plaque, somber and mocking, shouting the words into the empty park:

"'Life-size fiberglass models of an Imperial mammoth family stand at the end of the lake. The mother has become trapped; her offspring watch helplessly. For thousands of years, here at La Brea, thick oil has seeped to the earth's surface from sticky pools of tar. These pools became unique death traps for countless Ice Age animals and birds, making La Brea the richest deposit of Ice Age fossils in the World. Over 100 tons of fossil bones have been recovered.'"

Joseph's laughter grew manic. It became indistinguishable from a broken cry. Jack stepped up to him and put his arm around the shoulders of the crying man. Joseph broke down, crying spasmodically, without bound in the shelter of Jack's arms.

3

"Yo' Mama," Joseph sang along with the radio, turning up the volume and bellowing out the pop indictment of old folks' inability to dance. He was driving across West L.A. on the Santa Monica Freeway.

"Please, Joey," Sarah said, reaching to his hand planted on the steering-wheel, but suddenly her intense soprano joined his tenor to mock moralistic, undancing Mom and Dad. "Yo' Daddy" rang out in a mocking, scherzando trio for brother, sister, and radio.

He sped the black Triumph from lane to lane, weaving through the New Year's Eve traffic. Jack, sitting cramped behind the brother and sister, held tightly onto the back of Sarah's seat. Her hair and skin shone in the flashes from headlights and the freeway lighting overhead. She wore a flowered dress, the gauzy purples and greens of the sheer fabric falling to her knee, wrapping over her soft shoulders next to his hand holding the seat back.

"Finally, we get to see your secret hideaway," Joseph had said at the door to Jack's Paloma bungalow when they picked him up. "It's wonderful," Sarah had said. When he showed her around, she gazed, thoughtful and assessive, at the shelves of books, scores, and records, at the Knabe and the couch, at the wide table with a stack of notebooks and a view past Speedway to the beach. He had walked them onto the sand the hundred yards to the ocean. There was a chill wind and light fog streaming through the darkness from the water. They heard the menacing surf and could make out the glow from a freakish herd of tiny, radiant plankton shimmering in the swelling waves. Jack had sheltered her in his arms against the breeze.

"I'm going to have to get back just after midnight," she said now from the passenger's seat.

"Oh shit," the two men said almost simultaneously and laughed. In the flashes of light, Joseph's skin—pale olive and healthy now—contrasted starkly with his shock of black hair. A song about pills and thrills and fame blared from the radio; Joseph turned it up and began to sing again, with abandon.

"They're not feeling well," she said apologetically. He turned the radio down.

"They're getting old and dependent, and they can't face it," he said. "Or at least, Father won't."

"He counts on my being available to help. So does she."

"Sure he does. He's possessive. And possessed."

"So who isn't?" she said, turning her head to look at her friend, who was going to agree that he—Jack—was as possessed as the next fellow, when Joseph answered.

"Reality doesn't exist for Petrov: a father is a reality-concealing machine. At least he is. Tell Jack about the lessons he used to give me." Brother and sister burst out laughing, and Sarah turned her body in the bruised leather seat so that one leg was bent beneath her. She looked warmly at Jack, who smiled, leaning back as relaxed as he could in the few cubic feet allotted to the back seat.

Joseph squealed the Triumph onto the freeway down ramp and swerved north to Robertson.

"Joey was the perfect little five-year-old. Father would sit him down at the piano in that studio where you meet with him, and he did everything he was told to do. Christ, and more. First, little pieces, then scales, Mozart, Bach, you can imagine. The only problem was whenever Father left the studio—to talk on the phone, go to the bathroom, anything—Joey disappeared. Father would storm around the house, yelling his name. 'He must be more serious!' he'd shout at me, as if I were a Siamese twin. Finally, he'd find him—playing in the garage, or up in his room with his toys, or most likely digging in the flowerbed, model streets and drives in the dirt. He'd roar at him. You should never see how he washed him up and toweled him down. But it never stopped Joey. Father was his teacher until he was twelve. Then neither of them could cope with the other. He went to study with Pennario."

Again Joseph turned the radio up; it and he began to sing a song about suicidal young men—with gusto and teasing pleasure.

"So then he went to Juilliard, and the rest is…"

Joseph's voice, manic and mocking, was calling out to an unspecified, presumably unhearing youth.

❦   ❦   ❦

Petrov had drawn the thick, green curtain over the glass door yesterday, when Jack met him for another of their monthly sessions.

"I can't stand the light," he had said, frail and edgy, pointing at the overcast afternoon beyond the curtain. They were studying opus 110, and when Jack began the last movement, the arioso passages introducing and interrupting the sonata's final fugue, Petrov gestured for Jack to get up from the piano bench.

"This is a gift Beethoven has given the piano," he said. "Succinctly, pianistically, he has given us the sorrowing beklemmt of the Cavatina in opus 130. Only written years earlier! Such sadness, such a gift."

The old man began to play with incredible gentleness and nuance, with agonized silences between notes, between phrases, and Jack felt rising in his chest the rare, untraceable, answering sounds which were his music.

At the end, Petrov suddenly turned to the younger man and said: "So, I see you're spending time with my children. You like my Sarah, don't you? And she likes you."

The old pianist lifted himself from the piano bench, and waved for Jack to take his place.

"Sex and love, oh god, Bruno, they're such a pain in the ass."

"Jack. You said Bruno."

"Yes, yes. Jack, Bruno. I seem to have had this conversation before." Petrov kept standing next to Jack, and he talked with a strange, tense glee, as if his words had to be spoken and needed to be heard. "Bruno used to joke...once he asked Mann if he'd met Oskar Fisch, the cabaret singer, who then became an avant-garde director: 'He moves in your circle, no? Not part of the upper upper, naturally. Nonetheless, like you, he is a profound pessimist. Have you ever attended one of his poker parties? You would recall. Not exactly strip poker, but not exactly kosher either. I'm writing music for one of his films. He's originally from Vienna.'

"Alma Mahler Werfel was listening to them; she ate a Napoleon from her plate, and she said: 'Ah, Vienna, the city of my greatest joy and my greatest disasters! No, Franzi?' Arnold spoke up then—yes, your friend Schoenberg."

Petrov gave Jack a tight smile and continued: "'Vienna,' he said, 'is a city of fools given over to sex and drink and gourmet food. Yet it has produced an artist like Mahler—a man whose passion for ethical and intellectual order can be compared only to the ruthlessness of a Conquistador. In his music, the earth becomes a place worth living for, and more...he was the future, and we follow.'

"Alma licked her fingers and replied: 'He was pure oxygen. One got burned when one came close to him. He told me, "Alma, give up your 'personality' and dedicate yourself, your freedom, your being to me." I loved his mad aura, and I filled myself with it. Everyone else I've known have been mites compared to Gustav.'

"Franz winced; no one spoke. Later, Bruno and I amused ourselves by making up lists of men Alma fucked: Adorno, Brecht, Caruso, Debussy, Eisler, Fisch, Gieseking, Hitler, Ippolitov-Ivanov, James Joyce, Kokoshka, D. H.

Lawrence, Mephistopheles, Orpheus, Proust, Don Quixote, Franklin D. Roosevelt, Max Steiner, Tchaikovsky, Ulysses, Viertel, Wagner, St. Francis Xavier, Yankee Doodle, Father Zosima, et cetera."

Petrov let out a laugh, but Jack remained silent, waiting.

"I want to tell you," Petrov said, "fucking seems rather simple, but it can be very complicated. I can't tell you how much, but I must try. Sarah's mother, for example. At a certain point, she began to dislike it, Jack. After we left Berlin, 1938, 1939. The dear woman! Is it my fault? But why then, in 1939? Helen withheld herself, she begrudged me. On occasion, yes, but then only with disgust—and with a purpose. Usually she wasn't interested: no sex, no, none! So, sex and love can be very complicated, Jack. Beyond controlling. Beyond understanding."

Petrov paced back and forth in front of the younger man at the piano. Riveted, Jack saw that he had not finished, that his need was still deeper—to speak, to contact him, was it to absorb him into the family, or to help him, to steel him against fate?

"Now, let me tell you, Jack, Sarah has been hurt. The last man she loved was Rick. He tortured her. I don't mean physically, but mentally. She would come to me crying, Rick this and Rick that. He led her on with dreams, but actually he was a drunk. A sot, for days on end. Sometimes he wouldn't even come home. Finally, I visited her. Do you know she's a photographer? Album covers, even. Her Bachelors from UCLA. When I saw her photos in frames on the walls of that squalid place, I couldn't bear it. Her sensitive, brilliant pieces in that shit hole! It was repulsive. Unbelievable. I took steps, Jack, but it cost me. The stress, it nearly killed me. So now that son of a bitch doesn't bother her anymore. She lives here." Then Petrov had stopped. He had walked up to Jack, speaking into his face, threatening and imploring. "Love is never easy. You must respect its power. Know what you want and need, and treat it with respect, Jack. Don't be a genuine anarchist with Sarah. Not with my daughter!"

❀ ❀ ❀

Sarah turned down the car radio now, and she said, "Joey, show him your invitation."

"Oh yes! Randy's." Driving with one hand on the steering wheel, he reached into a pocket of his leather jacket and handed the folded sheet back to Jack without looking. It was the heavy cotton bond of a legal document. Along the left hand edge was printed the name of a legal firm: Wantu, Phrolic & Kavort, P.C. Attorneys and Counselors. Jack laughed. "Who is this, anyway?" he asked.

"Randy is a gangster," Joseph said. "A very rich hood who owns a large chunk of Tri-Star. Rich and mad enough to rent the Polo Lounge for his New Year's party. He's also a lawyer, and a collector—manuscripts, antiques, artists, musicians, writers, directors, stars, gossips. He has one of the finest collections in L.A.. Ask to see his manuscript of the Schubert B flat posthumous sonata. He's very good with all forms of the posthumous. He won't be interested in your work until you're dead."

In the broad, central California drawl of the director on whose project he had worked, Jack read as follows:

"State of Goodtimes in the Supreme Court of Intoxication. The People of the State of Goodtimes. Plaintiff: Randolph Schott. Party Action. File No Xcuses. B. R. Guest, Defendant. SUBPOENA to: Joseph Petrov. You are hereby commanded, that laying aside all and singular, your business and excuses, you be and present your person—and that of any significant other—to this Supreme Court on the 31st day of December, 1972, at 8:30 o'clock in the P.M. for the purpose of gaining your testimony at a New Year's Eve Party. Court will sit in session at the Polo Lounge of the Beverly Hills Hotel. If major illness or death prevents your attending, call 1-800-BULLSHIT, otherwise failure to attend will be deemed a Contempt of said court, and you will be responsible to the aggrieved party for the loss, hindrance, hurt or damaged feelings sustained thereby. RSVP et cetera."

The car jerked to a stop, and a valet opened the Triumph's door. They walked into the pink adobe-colored hotel, and they checked Sarah's suede coat, Joseph's black leather jacket, and Jack's blue windbreaker. It was just nine, and there was an obbligato of conversation coming through the arched, pink and forest green entry they approached—Sarah in her floating, flowered dress, Joseph wearing a dark red turtleneck and black pants, Jack in an earthen purple-brown sweater and jeans. Joseph showed his subpoena and ushered his sister and their friend into the throng.

At one table in a crowded corner were seated several gaudily tailored, older men. Burly body-guards stood nearby in plaid suits. There were extra seats, yet when a new gentleman arrived, one of those seated always bolted from his chair, zeroed in on his body-guard, and they shot over to the bar in back. Joseph told them it was the gangster Jimmy Valenti and then Herman Kahn making a bee-line for the bar.

At the other end of the room, under windows, Joseph introduced Sarah and Jack to a clutch of writers who frequented the hotel. Two of them seemed to belong to each other, and the man and woman had an odd code of silences between them, as if such deep violations were possible in talk that either they scrupulously noted trivia or quietly told grotesqueries; the ordinary struggle to live was not mentioned. Each wore sunglasses against the dark. Their friend—who spoke with an Eastern European accent—knew Joseph and asked Jack who he was. He had no immediate answer, and the man questioned him relentlessly. Joseph pulled Jack away to find their table on the enclosed patio. He tapped a handsome young waiter on the back, said something pleasantly into his ear, and the young man led them forward.

Servers in green uniforms handed them drinks. Jack was beginning to feel the effects of a second Polo Lounge Manhattan, when he stumbled into Brian, whom he had not seen for two weeks, in a break between films. After introductions, Brian sneered in his peculiar Anglo-American, "Old sport, your buddy is in the corner with his motley crew." Jack saw Sam Peckinpah sitting by the fence, thick with the leaves of tropical plants. He was surrounded by men, some with mustaches and beards, and by women in lace and buckskin. A slight, Jewish-looking man in a sequined, western shirt sat next to Sam.

"*That's* our next project," Brian said. "Bob Dylan and company. Can you *communicate* with that?"

The waiter took them to a table at the other end of the patio, and they were served caviar and Chateau Paradis, stuffed quail and frites, endive salad, then Queen of Sheba cake and Chateau de Nerval. As they ate, Joseph was an acid guide to the passing party-goers, a host of luminaries. Searching for reflective surfaces, some of them stopped to talk:

Andre Previn, who knew the Petrovs, and evanescently thin Mia Farrow, who did not; John Kandor and Liza Minelli, who knew Joseph and burlesqued a bit of a cabaret song in front of him; Kenneth Anger, who said hello and strode on with Anais Nin, her face a perfect mask, floating in his wake. Etc.

Toward midnight, a short, heavy man came up to the table; he looked like Truman Capote (also present). "I hope you're enjoying yourselves," he said in a deep baritone with a raw Chicago accent.

"Randy, I want to introduce you to my sister, Sarah. This is Randolph Schott. And our friend, John Weinstein." They all stood, thanking the host. Randolph seemed to examine the composer as they shook hands—Jack's jeans, his earth-colored crew-neck, his shaggy hair, his green eyes.

It was almost midnight, and Jack needed to use the facilities. He walked unsteadily to the bar. The Mexican bartender told him where to go but, then, continued talking to him. Where was he from? Was he on vacation? The bar man would get a vacation, long over-due, next month. He was going to Mexico City. As Jack began to leave, the man said, "Lo esencial es invisible a los ojos." He exited the Lounge and saw a dark bearded man enter. "Jodorowsky," he heard the Eastern European-sounding novelist shout out, but the man strode past to the patio, up to Peckinpah whom he punched in the stomach and then kissed on both cheeks.

Jack wandered out of the building into the maze of paths in back. It had begun to drizzle slightly. He passed darkened bungalows and bushes (into one of which he pissed helplessly). He walked over to the swimming pool. It was softly lapping and lightly dotted with droplets from above. There was the sound of honking, of screamed cheers and singing within. He sensed the ragged army of people who had passed this spot, the stars and starlets, the hangers-on and gofers, the desperate and blasé. A whole stream of talented men and women had dived fully clothed into this pool.

"Happy New Year, Jack," nearby Sarah's high voice called to him. There was her face glowing in the pink light from fixtures in the bushes. He stepped to her and held her in silence. He smelled her hair, soft and moist against his face, the light perfume, and the rain. They clung to each other, dislocated in drunken isolation.

Joseph swung his Triumph out of the half-circle in front of the hotel. The wipers were on. Bearing right on Benedict Canyon Drive, he lit a cigarette and drove, smoking. The three of them were quiet. Only an occasional laugh or comment punctuated the silence. At the Petrov's driveway on the hillcrest above Benedict, Sarah got out of the car. Jack scrambled out of the back, almost falling against her, and holding on, he kissed her mouth with blind sensuousness.

"Take him home safely, Joey," she said as Jack sat in the passenger's seat. "He needs a good sleep."

"I will," Joseph said and drove down the asphalt driveway. "Brother, are you hot tonight," he laughed as he turned right, climbing up the Canyon Drive toward Mulholland, and he reached his right hand lightly to punch his friend's chin. Jack felt a reciprocal warmth for Joseph, and his feeling arose from one more obscure chamber in the structure which housed his bond to Sarah and her family. His head was humming and lax now at the end of the evening. Joseph took a metal flask from an inner pocket of his leather jacket, which creaked as he had a swig, and handed it to Jack. "Stoly. I know you don't like weed or coke." The son, it seemed, had a capacity as great as the father's.

"Just a little," Jack said, took a small sip, and handed the flask back. Joseph put it down between them and wheeled the car suddenly at the crest of Benedict, left on Mulholland, the high road which topped the wedge of mountains cutting L.A. in two.

"This is my favorite road in the city," Joseph said. "I wanted you to see what it's like, even in the rain."

A single, blinding light roared toward them. Joseph swerved the Triumph onto the dirt verge, with Los Angeles's clouded bulk spread out on both sides of them. The maniacal face and streaming hair of a Hell's Angel shot by on a motorcycle.

"Jesus," Jack shouted. "We could have been killed!" The wipers slapped back and forth across the windshield.

"Fuck. That was close," Joseph said. He started the car and drove in silence, cutting left down Beverly Glen to Sunset. He smoked from his pack of Camels, and occasionally they took swigs and sips of the vodka. Driving up the San Diego Freeway entrance, he said, "Now you know what Petrov's lessons were like for me." His smile was a bitter grimace.

"What was Juilliard like?" Jack said.

"Oh shit," Joseph said. "When I'd turned twenty, I was a junior and my teacher Rosina Lhevinne told me I must help a graduate that year, Vladimir Kline. He had to have a trainer, twenty-four hours a day. She told me to move in with him. He would pay." Joseph laughed, weaving around the slower cars out now on the freeway in the first hours of 1973. "He was up for the Leventritt, so for a month that summer I lived with the son-of-a-bitch in his Manhattan apartment. He had incredible technique. But little sense of music. And none of meaning!" Joseph had been entrammeled again, Jack thought, in the mesh of another man's needs, now Kline the flashy technician. The car swerved off the exit ramp at Pico and sped west.

"I taught him every bar, every note of the competition pieces. He was one of the most ignorant pianists I've met. His father's blind creation: a music-loving psychiatrist named his son Vladimir after Horowitz and wished this monster on me. I was holed up in his apartment for a month. Training him, cooking for him, sleeping on the couch. At first." They were driving down Main toward Paloma; the wipers on delay erasing the film of drizzle every few seconds. "I fucked the son-of-a-bitch for weeks. And he won."

Joseph parked the Triumph. The two men were silent. Jack sat in the passenger seat, and he stared in dismay at the windshield in front of him, the patter of drizzle on it. His sense of location was obscured. Opening the door, he took drunken steps out into the lightly misting rain. Joseph walked next to him. They headed down Paloma toward the beach, away from Jack's flat.

"I'm gay. At least partly? Subliminally? Entirely?" He put his hands up, arrested, and smiled a bitter, long-suffering smile Jack had seen before. "There were others I…"

Names flashed through Jack's mind. Who were these others? Alcibiades, Byron, Cavafy, Diaghilev, Encolpius, Forster, Ganymede, Hockney, Isherwood, Jonathan, Kinsey, Latini, Michelangelo, Naphta, Orton, Proust, Peter Quince, Rimbaud, Socrates, Tchaikovsky, Urizen, Visconti, Wilde, Xantippe, Yahoo, Zeus?

At the edge of the beach, there was the blur of a lean-to.

"It's drizzling. Stand over here, under the roof of this penthouse," Joseph said, mocking and driven. "Like a true drunkard, I'll tell all to you. Do you know what a deformed thief this fashion of fucking is? How it consumes so many hot bloods between fourteen and thirty-five? How giddily it fashions some into those Herculean soldiers in dirty, worm-eaten magazines where their dicks are as big as bats?"

Jack shouted, "You're fucking giddy with…" Wordless and drunk, he lighted out into the foggy drizzle toward the breaking waves. Enveloped in the driven mist, he felt the pull of the sand on his calves. He looked slant-wise toward Joseph following behind, and he swerved to the ocean's edge. He heard the sound of sea-wrack and squishing foam under foot. He welcomed the endless, cracking clap of the surf. It no longer frightened. The real danger was nothing more than the risk of being. The ocean lived and spoke, roaring in his ears. He fell flat on his face in its rolling foam, and he discovered that the ocean's edge was only one more boundary he plunged through, the water seeping through his pants and shirt and against his cheek. In the surf, he curled into a posture of sleep.

Joseph lifted him by his arm, holding him up as they stumbled across the sand, back to Paloma and the flat. At the door, Joseph helped him get his keys uncaught from his wet jeans. Inside, he walked him to his bedroom, supporting Jack, whose teeth were chattering. Joseph undid the man's soaking pants and shorts, pulled them down to his ankles, sat him on the bed, and pulled off shoes, socks, pants and shorts. He took Jack's windbreaker off of him, his crew-neck sweater, blackened with ocean brine, and his blue tee-shirt. He took a towel from the bathroom and silently began to rub him down.

His legs and torso and arms warmed beneath the motion, motoric and detached, of Joseph's hands. Jack's teeth stopped chattering. The sheet and blanket were pulled warmly over him. The light went off, and the shadowy ceiling continually revolved above him. A body pressed against him, invading the blurred circle of warmth beneath his covers. Jack's consciousness halted its drift toward dreams. For a moment, alcohol-fueled fantasy took hold of him, and in his stupor he imagined hands arousing him, a disembodied mouth exploring him. Then he realized the sensations were real, not imagined. He let out a brusque grunt, and girded, blurred, he plummeted into blackness.

O bald geniuses, where were you now—to allay Jack's fears, to transfigure each sound, to hallow each wave of water, grain of sand, drop of liquor, shadow of night, particle of light? Where had you fled?

PART III

Adagio sostenuto—Appassionato e con molto sentimento:
Winter 1973

1

He opened his eyes and saw the blank ceiling overhead. There was the patter of rain outside, and a raw, gray light came through the window. The clock read noon. His limbs ached as he pushed the sheet and blanket off his body and stood on shaky legs.

A wave of nausea engulfed him. He sat back down on the bed and looked down at his body, his legs, groin, and stomach; blurred sensations from the night before returned to him, fragments of memory. It was as if a curtain had been pulled over the experience, and a terror of lost memory, of imagined violation, gripped him at the base of his being.

A new wave of nauseated anger hit him now, and he forced himself to stand, to walk. The bone and lining of his skull ached as he made his way to the kitchen for coffee. There was a long knife on the counter. In fear and rage, he picked it up, and he held it pointed toward his abdomen, into his pubic hair. It trembled there in his hand, the point pressing the skin.

"Fuck it," he roared into the empty flat. The knife clattered on the counter where he threw it.

He brewed coffee and then sipped from the mug of hot, brown liquid, holding himself steady, girded with rage.

A cramp stabbed at his gut, and he walked painstakingly to the toilet. He sat naked and in agony on the seat. From him flowed a helpless shit of New Year's Eve caviar and quail, endive and frites, Queen of Sheba, and Chateaux de Nerval and Paradis, bourbon and vermouth and vodka, an excrement of associations. He wiped and flushed and turned the shower on.

Jack stood beneath the warm stream and welcomed the water beating against his skin, against the odor in his nose and mouth, against his head aching with hangover and rage. He lathered his limbs and groin and trunk, his face and hair, rubbing to cleanse himself of hurt. As he washed, the blade of rage and terror always hung over him, over his penis and belly, and over his neck as he stood with the shower needling into his back and the base of his brain.

Wet from his shower, he took a towel from the bathroom cabinet, dried himself, and walked into his bedroom. His damp, ocean-smelling clothes were on the rug by his bed, and the veiled images of drinking and talking, ocean and drizzle, drowned him now. What had Joseph done after pulling him from the water's edge and taking him home, after entering his bed? It was as if he were disentangling the riddle of a murder. His memory blacked out, Jack felt on the verge of erasure, assaulted, fucked. Urgently, he tried to retrieve the lost memory.

Mounted on the closet door was a mirror. He looked into it, and the curtain over his consciousness slightly lifted as he saw himself there, his staring, green eyes, the angry brow and wild hair and broad chin, the stony legs and clenched fists. Bitterness and fear gripped him. Perhaps Jack no longer existed, and only this mirror image remained, this naked fake whose penis hung, at once vulnerable and slightly erect, below brown hair and rosy white skin. Appalled and incensed, he stared at this shard of himself: his double, pale with European genes, bleached by Polish pogroms and Teutonic rape. He lifted his fists in the air, poised to attack his own image.

He began to strike out, thrusting his naked body up against the mirror and pummeling the glass, on the verge of cracking. "Fuck you," he kept shouting, "fuck you!"

Then he staggered back, falling to the rug, collapsed, wordless, blasted. Here, he knew, was the nadir of his plummet west, the going downward to a raw, gray is. He felt a mute horror in the present.

Yet words came to him, a slow, severed sound from his throat and mouth.

"Who is I?" he said, word by word. "Who is you, this fucking you?"

He wanted to be clothed then, to cover his lack of being. He lifted himself up, and from his dresser, he took clothes and put on a clean, blue tee-shirt, undershirts and jeans, socks and then an old pair of Keds. He walked to the living room couch and sat, stiff and vacant.

He had to confront Joseph. He must find out, must face and know what had happened. Even if Joseph had gone no further than what he remembered, even then there was some violation and betrayal of Jack—and of Sarah. The three of them were entangled together in an odd, incestuous web.

Rage and appalled pity welled together in him. Joseph had alighted on the stripped-down, blank part of Jack where he sought to be open to whatever life brought. Now, that part was turned into an object, betrayed, dead. Always he had risked being the fool who strove to affirm all he experienced and all he imagined as well. But a bridling rage and bitterness came between him and that fullness of being. Now he felt he was a discard of being, a shard of a person.

He rose to write his emptiness down, to begin the journal of the new year, already flattened by the blast of his exploded self.

The phone rang. He let its deadened A-flat clang repeat three times. Then he sat back down on the couch and picked up the receiver.

"Jack?"

"Mom." The room came sharply into focus, the gray light filtering through the windows, the clouded, rainy afternoon.

"Are you all right?" His mother's concern warred with her pleasant warmth. Her voice plucked at him, drawing feeling from him, inviting him to be a son.

"I'm okay," he said, a blank voice hiding his gratitude and terror.

"Happy New Year."

"Happy New Year," he said.

"Did you get my card?"

"Yes: 'Happy New Year.' Did you celebrate?"

"You know your father. We stayed home and had the Liebermans over. They played string trios, and we made merry. How about you?"

"I saw the Petrovs. The children."

"Did you have a good time?"

"I had a time. It was okay."

"Just okay," she paused, and he was silent.

"You know Dad is coming out there in February—their west coast tour. Well, we've decided I'll fly out too, to see you."

"If you don't mind a double-bed, you two can sleep in my bedroom. I'll use the couch."

"If it's okay with you. To be with you. Instead of the hotel. We'll rough it for a couple of days. Why not?"

"It's fine with me." An old part of him was engaged now, open to her, appreciating her placid sensitivity. "I'd love to see you."

"Maybe we'll see Sasha and Helen," Rosa said.

"That may be difficult. They're not feeling well lately," he said with forced calm and objectivity, his father's calm.

"Oh, that's sad. I hope it's not serious. What do their children think?"

"Sarah helps them. She lives there."

"If we can't see them, we can't. We'll see."

"How are you and Dad?"

"He says hello." She began to talk about them, his work, hers at the Cleveland Heights library. As she spoke, he felt each breath he took in the gray room. She asked him about his studio work and his composing. After twenty minutes, the time she allotted herself for long-distance expired. He hung the phone up, and his hand fell to the arm of the couch.

Then he walked to the table, sat on an armless, wooden chair, and reached for the new, wire-bound notebook he had bought. He inked on the cover, 1973, and opened to the first page with its blank staves. He began to write along the lines and in the empty spaces between:

Jan. l: Happy fucking new year. I'm fucked, and sealed inside, a high wind of fucking blasts and levels everything in me. Let me out. Let me out. The images of my face and body are trapped in glass, and the walls of my body turn to stone. How can I compose this self turned to stone? How can I break free from the impotent sealed airless halt of sound? All I would compose now is the music of paralysis. Of my hopelessness. My halting scream. I sit here dead-still. I've lost all balance and grace and life. I'm left only with the obscenities gaping on this page.

He sat before the music paper. He had no heart or mind to compose the Adagio he had planned. He would not let his music play a part in his self-betrayal and become an art of lying.

At the end of his 1972 journal, he had made a clean copy of the finished Scherzo, the second movement of his sonata, and he took the notebook to the piano, opening it to the movement. He began to play the upright Knabe, choosing anarchic, bitter variations of tempo, grotesquely emphasizing the explosive freedom of the work.

The three bald geniuses danced from the raw, gray daylight into the living room. Even the Viennese Jew, serious and aloof, smiled at what Jack played. The thin Russian said: "This is true drunkard's music, yes! Surpassing even the drinking songs of my Hungarian colleague there, sneering in the shadow. It's like the peasant dances I knew as a child; I will illustrate." He danced and shouted to Jack's wavering beat, stomping his feet, jutting his legs like a Cossack straight out in air, stumbling, and brushing against Beethoven who roared into the room. He glared at the wispy, dancing Russian as short as himself. Karl Beethoven flickered at the door, looking like his uncle's son, the eyes blinking and shifting, even more possessed, a criminal's eyes. His uncle had seen enough and walked toward the piano.

Jack rose from the bench and edged to the table, where he sat before his new notebook, transfixed with alarm and pain and wonder.

Sitting at the piano before the inked sonata pages, Beethoven had an aura of tangled, electric hair sticking out from his head. He hunched before the keys and began to play loud and unhesitating. Obscenities flowed from his lips, snatches of Italian, Russian, Hungarian, and German. His eyes were fixed on Jack's score, and his hands pounded everything, playing wrong notes, extending and further distorting allusions to his own sonatas. The pale Hungarian sat again at the end of the table, the Russian on the couch, the Viennese Jew on the stuffed chair.

At Scherzo's end, Beethoven began to play a wavering snatch of his last sonata, opus 111, the opening of the Arietta. Suddenly he stopped and swung on the piano bench to face them.

"Our whole disassembly present?" he said, bitterly eyeing his nephew who sat on a straight-backed chair he had taken from the table to a corner, between the front door and the entry to the kitchen. Karl frowned there, hang-dog and accusative, looking at them all with punishing resentment.

"See my nephew Karl. I love him like a son, and he hates me. But I know I demand and impose. I am an ass. Write that down," he said bitterly, and he pointed imperiously to the 1973 journal, its first page open on the table in front of Jack. "Write me down an ass! Write me down an ass-hole! It doesn't matter." His voice was hoarse and loud with words he could not hear. "What matters is that we seek eternity, that we are condemned to everlasting redemption."

Against the wind, Jack slowly shepherded himself across Speedway, across the beach, to the shifting sand at the edge of the Pacific. His jacket flew open, and the wind buffeted him. Alone, he faced the dancing wind-driven waves and the wide current eddying far out in the frenzied ocean.

❀   ❀   ❀

Jack pressed the doorbell by the front door of the Petrovs' home. He waited for half a minute and pressed again. Sarah did the household shopping on Saturday. The garage was closed, and he could not see whether her covered jeep was parked inside. He had called her at nine, telling her he needed to talk—though he did not know how to express what welled within him. He knew he must talk with Joseph, but first he had to find out what Sarah knew, to see if she needed his help. He began to knock on the weathered, dark brown wood. It was just after one in the afternoon, the sixth day of the new year.

"Hello," Mrs. Petrov said, dignified and remote, at the open door. The short woman was dressed in her flowered housecoat. The gray daylight illuminated the mask of her puffy face. In the three months he had known her, she had grown this exhausted mask, and Jack reached with gentle pity to shake her small, swollen hand.

"How are you?" he said, looking with a sort of probity into her dark eyes.

"Fine, thank you," she said irritably.

"Is Sarah in?"

She was not yet home, and Mrs. Petrov led him down the hall to wait in the music studio. She walked with a tired gait, slow and resolute.

"My husband is out also," she said as she opened the hall door to the studio. "He took the Chrysler. To do errands."

"I see."

"Do you remember our little talk in the garden, some months back?" she said standing before him in the study.

"Of course," Jack said, disturbed and peremptory.

"Yes, our little talk," she said, numb and distant. "I'm tired, Jack. Too many words. I have to rest."

He heard Mrs. Petrov's steps laboring up the stairs at the end of the hall, and he sat down on the worn couch facing the door to the garden. Cloudy, winter light deadened the colors of the room, of the oriental carpet, of the frayed fabric of the furniture. There was a dead stillness to the room, the house, the day. Jack got up and wandered about the empty studio, from one end to the other.

On the music rest of the piano there was a yellowed volume of music: Poèmes Juifs, the title read, by Alexander Petrov. At the bottom, there was the name of a publisher he did not recognize—and Los Angeles, California, 1943. Here was one of the virtuoso's own compositions. He glanced through the crumbling pages at the music, which read like dissonant Satie, demonic Poulenc. Jack felt appalled by Petrov's title, its flourishing embrace of his mother's desperately vanishing people, its arch refusal of the German, its bravado introducing music of miniature, derivative artifice. The dead light through the glass enveloped the room, and he returned to pacing, restlessly, aimlessly. Rage invaded him: toward the arrangements of the decaying room, of the decaying family—Joseph, Sasha, Helen, even Sarah. He wanted to demolish the cage of a room, to fuck the couches, the black piano, the grass walls, the oak floor, the oriental carpet: a great fucking of defiance and destruction. He paced and stretched, half to serve the anger of his arousal, half to quell it. Thrust back into a primal, violent narcissism, he would straddle the whole room and shove his penis into its corrupt crevices. He reached down to touch his crotch when the sliding door rattled.

Sarah knocked at it, smiling in the cloudy light and holding a bag of groceries in each arm. He walked to the door, taut with amazement at his own, pent rage—and at her image there, on the other side of the glass. Her rosy skin was bleached by the gray daylight which lightened the dark gold of her hair and exposed the demure calm of her Mediterranean eyes. Framed by the door, she seemed to Jack a blanched canvas by Botticelli, or Leonardo's Adoration.

"I knew you'd be here," she said with a flourish when he slid the door open for her.

"She said you'd be here," Joseph's voice said, and he walked toward them through the backyard, with groceries in his arms.

"Joseph is with you," Jack mumbled. He felt the flinch of tendons in his legs and stomach.

"Joey gives me a hand sometimes on Saturdays," she said. Holding the groceries, the two of them stood together now, smiling.

"Let me help you with those," Jack said, taking the bags from her arms, and they walked through the dark hall to the kitchen. He understood what he must do now.

Brother and sister ritualistically put away the groceries. Sarah talked about Joseph's concert trip to the northwest. He would fly to Seattle next Friday, perform there Saturday and the next week in Oregon. Joseph bent to put groceries under the counter, a box of detergent and a can of cleanser under the sink. He did not speak; finally he glanced up tensely.

"Joseph, do you have time to talk?" Jack said.

"I have time."

"We'll take a walk, Sarah," Jack said. "We'll be back soon."

"Sure," she said, placid, somehow pleased that the two men talked. "Take your time. I have things to do."

In their jackets, they walked on the unweeded path down the hill through dead brush to the foot of Petrov's property. They turned to the right on Benedict Canyon Drive, trudging past Jack's green VW, up the incline of the street. Neither man talked. Saturday afternoon traffic swerved sometimes by them, and Jack would step off the street onto the dirt shoulder.

"I want to talk about New Year's Eve," Jack said.

"Yes."

"For days, I felt angry and confused. Fuck it, I feel angry and confused. As if I've lost a part of myself. I can't remember, Joseph. Tell me what happened after you took me home."

"What happened?" Joseph stopped on the edge of the street. A barreling white car honked at him; for a moment it looked like Petrov's Chrysler, but it was a BMW that skidded around him.

"You came into my bed, I remember, before I passed out. What happened, Joseph?"

"What do you mean what happened?" he said, looking up surprised and distressed.

Jack stared at the pale, unkempt man. His dark eyes were intensely quizzical now. "I drank, I listened, amazed at all that bravado, I blacked out, and now, shit, I feel fucked! Even if you did no more than make a pass…"

"More than make a pass?" Jack was silent, and Joseph went on, "Yes, I thought you'd respond; I thought you seemed open. I was wrong. You passed out, Jack. I didn't do anything else; I wouldn't do anything else! It's terrible that you feel so bad. I feel terrible about it."

"But why would you try? Fuck it! Your sister and I love each other. How could you betray her?"

"I didn't mean to hurt you. Or her. Sarah and I are pretty open with…You seemed so completely to accept me, Jack. You seemed so open. I can't tell you how terrible I feel about it," he said, his voice rasping, on the verge of cracking.

A tanned couple in white sweats whisked past, jogging, smiling.

Jack found that tears formed in his eyes. Suddenly he felt released from six days of doubt and rage; compassion began to take the place of fear and anger. "Don't feel terrible," he said sadly. "Who am I? Being open, but not being open. Both. And I was so hurt and angry. But I'm to blame, too."

Joseph suddenly began striding up the incline of Benedict Canyon, and Jack followed, saying: "Do you see what it's been like since New Year's?"

"I can see," Joseph gave him a glance, strained now; almost in flight, he walked steadily up the road.

"I wonder, Joseph, am I ever truly open? Do I ever truly connect? When I love, am I really just fucking myself? With my fake openness, who am I really? I wonder about all my feelings, my choices in life." He reached to slow the other man, and Joseph wheeled away, his hands clenched at his chest to hold himself back, it seemed. Then he turned to face Jack.

"Your choices aren't the issue," Joseph said. "I feel terrible about the way you feel, Jack. But I thought—I thought you were open to it. I don't mean your choosing to be open, Jack; it's a matter of who you are." Joseph walked behind his friend now. "What you do is the result of the person you are. I'm gay; I didn't choose to be gay."

They walked silently past hills of dry brush sweeping down to the road. The teeming, clouded basin of Los Angeles loomed beyond the scattered homes below them to the south.

"But it's not a matter of who you are," Jack said. "Because sex isn't the issue. Trying to be human, not to hurt others, to be decent—that's what matters."

"Sex is the issue, Jack. It's what you are."

"What you are?"

"Yes, what and who you are."

"I don't think so. You come into the world, struggling to be whatever you become. But what actually happens is the striving itself from moment to moment, even if the selves you become are as unchangeable as the fundamental and dominant of the scale. It's the movement from one to the other, right through the scale, that's really life. What's hard is struggling to live at all." Jack kicked at the weedy brush, and earth caught in his shoe. "Gay or straight, both or neither, is any feeling possible now, here?" He sat on the dirt by the road, untied one of his black Keds, emptied it of pebbles, and squatting in the dirt he laced it back up. "What we need to do is discover and connect and grow beyond this fucking root between our legs. That's the struggle. All that root-bound force in you, Joseph. We should be like fountains, like flowers bursting toward the light. Whether man or woman, 'give me the light.'"

Jack scrambled up from the earth, hitting his hands against the back of his jeans to get rid of the dirt. Then he turned about, to continue talking, but Joseph suddenly began to speak in the driven, gravely voice he had on Christmas Day.

"I feel awful about it, Jack. I thought you understood. I wanted to enter your world, as intensely as I could. It's bullshit about your not being open. I love your openness, your unsure, constant striving to keep true and alive, *your force*. You, Jack," he said, looking directly at his friend's face.

Suddenly Jack was stunned to recognize Joseph's love. Absorbed by the trauma of feeling assaulted and betrayed, the composer had failed to listen, had been unable to hear and comprehend. Now the prospect of Joseph's love presented itself to Jack, unmediated, unmuddled by resentment or rationalization, full with the call of empathy and desire, if desire it be. "I understand, Joseph," he said shyly. "I was angry and upset, but you know I feel love for you too, even if…" He paused, and Joseph answered.

"I didn't want you to feel upset or hurt."

The two men began to walk, and together they rounded the bend of Benedict to the top. In the dreary, winter light filtering from the high clouds, two cities stretched out on both sides below them, the split, flattened plains, north and south, of L.A..

"When you and Sarah came to the studio door, you can't imagine what I was about to do, what I wanted to do."

"I think I can guess."

"No. I wanted to give that room such a giant fuck of fury and destruction. I mean, literally."

"I've felt that," Joseph laughed softly and looked now at the other man. "You don't know how often, and how often I did it."

Jack looked back with a steady glance of recognition. He knew—standing above the vast city—that a part of him had become the extension of a single family's will and want.

2

Jack inked notes of his Adagio on the staves in his journal. He had begun to sketch it out, each night this week after he returned home from work at the studio on Peckinpah's new project. After talking with Joseph last weekend, he found himself able to compose, not easily, not without a blank angst gripping him at moments, but he was able to jot fragments and effects which formed a frozen swirl of possibilities, like a blasted galaxy unfolding imperceptibly in time. It was Saturday morning now, and he attempted to consolidate his ideas for the opening of the sonata's third movement. After noon, he was going to the Petrovs' again, to talk with Sarah alone, for Joseph had flown to Seattle yesterday. Later, at three, Petrov expected to go through another sonata with Jack.

The threads of music before him seemed severed from one another, and he yearned to unite them. Yet he knew they would not coalesce until he allowed them to expand, even to the point of mutual destruction. Each thematic element signified a warring part to Jack, and the elements grouped themselves always in three—music of will and soul and passion, classical and romantic and barbarous, mind and heart and genitals, F-sharp minor and G major and F-sharp major. As the movement grew, he opposed theme to theme, key to key. The groupings clustered against each other, all sounded together. It was music of abandon, of concepts colliding and shattering all around. Each note became a dissonant cluster of three half-tones, and at wavering moments all twelve half-tones resonated together. The music slowly exploded; the frozen emptiness sang. He was composing the landscape of blasted self he had known in the first week of the year.

Jack ceased blacking in the notes. He wanted another music to envelop and accompany, another vantage from which to view the blast, as if truly its sound were heard across the singing, galactic emptiness. He sought a music of infinite acceptance, beyond rage, beyond resignation: a song of transcendent and eternal generation.

He could not continue, and he rose from his chair before the table. The gray, winter light flooded in from the window and the sea. At his shelves of books and records, he took out a blue volume, softened and darkened with use, the second half of Beethoven's sonatas. He opened it to the Adagio sostenuto of the Hammerklavier and set it before him at the Knabe. The chords of mourning—quiet, passionate, con molto sentimento—flowed slowly from the piano. It was the profundity of their understanding of grief that Jack sought. He played the transition from F-sharp minor, moving a half-tone up, released from the echo of grieving minor into G major. He held the gentle stillness of this beautiful acceptance in his hands, and the few, simple notes generated an openness even to the surrounding grief.

Loud, staccato notes and chords interrupted. He no longer pressed the muting una corda with his foot, and the con grand'espressione theme ambled out, a possessed parody of the opening octaves and chords of mourning. Beethoven understood the exploded world, how the identical configuration of consonance or dissonance can keen or blast, kiss or spit, solace or enrage. Jack emphasized the vicious, driven syncopation, the snarls of melody, the demonic transformation of grief.

The wispy Russian strolled in, solo and sullenly elegant. He strangely swayed as if invisible strings pulled him to Beethoven's staccato beat. Jack glanced for a second at the leering figure. His white shirt and black pants were oddly decked with decorative trim, a frill at collar and cuffs. Jack sensed eyes observing from the shelves and woodwork, the Hungarian's, the Jew's. The waltz the Russian danced was fey and grotesque. Jack saw black mascaraed circles around his eyes, and the circle of his sneering mouth was open in a silent scream. Pirouetting in a travesty of salon elegance, his was a dance of death.

As the Adagio's beat broke down and yielded the hovering serenity of D and A major triplets—making way for Beethoven's thirty-second note transfiguration of mourning—the thin Russian began to waver and evanesce. The overwrought decoration disappeared from his clothes. His face became glassy and transparent. Just as he expired into thin air, he said: "Beware of one deformed. He wears a key in his ear, and a lock hangs from it."

❀   ❀   ❀

Jack drove his Bug over the freeway toward Beverly Hills and then headed north on Robertson. It was a dead-winter, L.A. day. A congested, dreary light lit the boutiques and fast-food joints and hair-dressers he passed—stores selling lamps and artificial limbs and books, drug-stores and cafés and cleaners. Jack was held in empty thrall by the press of stores and the passing pedestrians in coats and hooded sweatshirts against the cool wind, just below fifty degrees. He wondered at his own vacancy, minute after minute, driving mile after mile, his own blankness as he approached the distressed, compelling, haunted home of Sarah, Helen, and Petrov.

Sarah let him in. They sat next to each other on the worn, brown velvet couch facing the glass. She had closed the studio's door to the hall. Again the winter light blanched her skin and hair. He wanted to touch a wavy strand falling over an eye and cheek, to smooth it to her ear. Yet the clench of sorrow and worry held him unmoving by her. He gazed at the demure assurance of her eyes and mouth as he spoke.

"I need to talk about Joseph. And it's difficult."

The curve of her brows rose slightly as her gaze held him.

"I know about him," Jack said. "He told me."

"You know he's gay," she said in her high, clear voice.

"Yes," he said. He felt as if he were blind when all could see, as if he stammered in a foreign tongue. He wanted to speak what he needed to say, yet he hardly knew what words to use. "After we dropped you here on New Year's Eve, Joseph brought out a flask of Stolichnaya, however you pronounce it. We drank. In the car." He stopped. He was a fool, faltering, not saying what he needed to say. "Joseph told me." He almost demonstrated it, Jack wanted to say, feeling out what truth was speakable for him, holding back what he thought would hurt irremediably.

"He made a pass at you," Sarah said. "That's what he told me, before he left for Portland."

Jack looked at her in dismay. She was holding her arms together archly, almost dramatically, and he recognized the edge of hysteria in her high voice and its detached, ironic tone. A war must rage in her, he thought, between her injured sensitivity and her insistence on facing and voicing what she knew. The strain showed on her face, and he wondered what conflict marked his own. Suspended on the verge of understanding, he stared at her. In music, he sought to listen for the unvoiced, the silenced, the layer below, and the layer below that. But not yet fully in life, he realized, not yet and not enough.

"He says you'll not be in each other's little black books."

"Must I burn my library?" he said, amazed to hear himself produce with her these fractured ironies.

"He says you love him but don't want to fuck him."

"Yes."

"He says he loves you, but he doesn't think of fucking you anymore."

She gave him a sudden, disarming smile.

"There was a time," she said, "Joey used to hang on men like a disease. In his early twenties. He was more easily caught than the flu, and whoever caught him would always go immediately mad. He'd walk around Hollywood, and his affections would change with every block, like the fashion of his shirts. But then that passed, and…"

"Then he tried to love me," Jack said, dismayed now by how detached she seemed, how blasé both of them had sounded. "My god, don't you feel hurt, Sarah? I was so upset—more than upset. And I thought you'd want to cage him up and throw the key away. Or cage me up."

She stared, fixed and dramatic, at Jack. Suddenly her voice took flight, the beautiful soprano filling the music room.

"Yes, I'm hurt, Jack. That he even tried! But he's so fucking self-absorbed, he doesn't even realize it," she said. "When he first moved back from New York, he brought home, you know, a friend. Father raged through the house, and Mother was upset. She asked me to talk with Joseph. True to form, Father exploded, mother protected, and all three of them expected me to negotiate, to do the practical thing. Joey said he was testing all of us, that it didn't matter. Then he moved to his apartment on Franklin. But, Jack, what really hurts now are his drugs. He drinks, he smokes dope, and now he's doing crack. I know on New Year's Eve he was betraying me and you. But what hurts me most of all—truly, Jack—are the drugs. I'd do anything to make him stop."

"Let me help. Tell me what I can do."

"Kill him," she said, throwing up her hands in the air between them, her laughter singing out suddenly, desperately. "Short of that, I don't know."

Her bitter words were spoken with such vulnerable, desperate laughter—they startled him. The gap between the cynicism in her and the love she felt, this splitness in Sarah was as deeply a part of her, he realized, as the soaring beauty of her voice. Yet the passionate tenderness and concern there—in her eyes, in her voice, her slender hands—drew him implacably toward her.

"Come live with me, Sarah." The words came unbidden, and both of them looked now in dismay at each other. "I know it would be hard, but there's nothing you can do for Joseph—except be his friend. And most of what you do for your parents a housekeeper can do. You could visit them—daily. I love you. Move in with…"

"I can't," she said, tense now and desperate. "I can't help it, Jack. My parents need me!" she cried out, and she reached her hands out dramatically to hold onto his, as if he alone could keep her from sinking into the earth where she stood. "I love you, Jack. But I can't. Not right now."

Together they were silent then, and he shifted himself over, close by her on the couch. He wondered that time and family conspired to delay, even to void the possibility of their being together.

Then Sarah suddenly changed the subject. Once again she was detached, her voice objective. She spoke of Watergate, of Liddy and McCord and the trial.

"Nixon is such a son of a bitch, manipulating the press with blatant lies," she said. "But his government is falling apart. The cover-up is so corrupt it can't last! So manipulative and hypocritical a state of evil."

Petrov pushed the door open without knocking.

"Hello, Father," she said, rising quickly from the couch. "How are you feeling?"

"Acceptably," he said and touched her arm benignly with his big hand. "How are you, Jack?" he said, walking up to the man, who stood now. The old pianist neither smiled at him nor shook his hand.

"I'm fine. Ready for opus 109, more or less."

"I have to go," Sarah said and turned to Jack: "I'll see you later."

"What have we here?" Petrov walked now to the liquor cabinet. He made two drinks, brought them to the couches, and handed him a glass of watered Scotch. Like father, like son, Jack thought and put the glass down on a coaster by a book on the coffee table.

Petrov reached for the slim volume and sat down on the beige sofa across from Jack.

"Sarah's Christmas present to me, a book of poems by a new Israeli poet." He laughed. "Yehuda Amichai. *Time*—a nice little title, no? There's a poem in it you'd like." He opened the book, paging through it, sometimes glancing at Jack. "Here it is. Number thirty. That's your age, if I'm not mistaken."

"Not quite. On March fifteenth."

Petrov began to read aloud. His rim of white hair was carefully trimmed, and his face had the blushing hue of age and a lifetime of shaves. His voice cracked occasionally with the full baritone he mustered for his performance. In the poem, an elder's voice was addressing—even dressing down—a man half his age. At one point Petrov glanced up with a penetrating leer: the elder spoke of his own penis as a bridgehead suspended now over the new wave of just grown-up girls, as if his were the last organ of hope and help against all the inevitable disappointments and disasters of love. But the young man he addressed was drowning in just such pollution and disasters: lovers and children and—now Petrov wore an amused expression as he intoned—music even and musical instruments: all of it, the elder said, was like the detritus of driftwood and dead grass for a bonfire on the beach "in which you'll burn." Petrov was finished, and he closed the volume of Amichai.

Looking at Jack, he said, "I don't read badly, do I? I'm not an actor, but I read well. What does Nietzsche say? 'Only actors arouse great enthusiasm nowadays.' You know, a musician can be as temperamental as Olivier, as egotistical as Brando, but an actor can never be like us! No matter what I perform, I can smile or cry, tease or fart or laugh, as often happens. But not Sir Lawrence—he can't do any of that."

Jack laughed in recognition, and Petrov smiled then, point-blank at him. "You know, Number 30 reminded me of you."

"Of me?"

"Yes, the whole poem. Except for the children. So far," he said and sipped his Scotch. "Be prepared for the dry grass and kindling wood, Jack."

"I suppose. It's quite a poem," he said, subdued and ironic. "As for the bonfire in which I'll burn, I've been expecting it for quite a while now."

"Yes, you must, Jack; there's been so much death, so much burning and ashes…in the forties…millions. Millions," Petrov said, vague and distracted now. "And Bruno, Jack, there was my friend Bruno…and to this day, more and more. My fellow émigrés! The acquaintances, the friends, the geniuses. Schoenberg, and a few years ago Stravinsky, Adorno, Walter, Casadesus. All mowed down! Of course, you're interested in Arnold and Igor, no? Of course."

"Sure. But not only them, Sasha," he said, calmly waiting for the story which loomed in the room. Once more Petrov was attempting, he thought, to plumb and even possess his inner world. Such was Jack's worry and suspicion, yet he simultaneously felt gratitude for Petrov's affection and for the generous energy of his memories, his stories, and even his fantasies of Stravinsky and Schoenberg in the forties.

"In 1942. I told you. They sat here together, your 'friends' Igor and Arnold, with Thomas Mann, Bruno Fried, et cetera, all gathered in my music room. 1942 was quite a year of death."

Petrov's voice was intense and morose, imposing an uncanny drama and distance on his words. "I told them about a letter from my cousin Eugene in Moscow. He wrote that the Nazis had overrun the Tchaikovsky museum in Klin. They destroyed the house, but at least Tchaikovsky's piano had been removed, and the manuscripts. Mann answered me from the couch where you sit now; as always, he kept his hand in his suit pocket like this." Petrov illustrated by lodging his flat hand next to his broad hip. "'Yes,' Thomas said, 'they can overrun Tchaikovsky's house. Tchaikovsky can even overrun himself with his agonizing about love and sex and his morbidity. Even so…'

"'Even so!' Arnold scoffed. He quietly seethed with outrage. 'Tommy, the Angel of Death is sweeping his wings over all Europe, as far as Moscow, and you say "even so." Is death so heimlich for you, so comfortable a feeling? Do you say: "Of course we gather round, but naturally we are all dead!" That's a species of schadenfreude more cold-blooded than I'd hoped to hear from you."

"Hearing this, Thomas was quite upset. 'Arnold, you misunderstand!' he said; 'I have fled from the Angel of Death too, no? And come all the way to the edge of this ruined world. But music, I believe…'

"'No "but music,"' Arnold said. 'No "even so." Music can only be the mouthpiece for scorn now.'

"'Yes, Arnold, but music also transcends scorn and destruction and self-destruction. It's that insubstantial and permanent. But the letter you read me—your letter recently from Bartok'—always Thomas was keeping tabs like that. 'It says the same thing:
 No longer does the body feel the Danube waters.
 No longer do the lips drink from the glass.'

"'Now only the crystal clear water,' Arnold continued, and this whole room, all of us here felt bound together by the sense of communion coming suddenly from Arnold's severe face. His voice! 'Certainly, I remember Bela's letter. I can't forget it.' Then he spoke from memory: '"There are times here in New York when I become aware again—as in the past—that I am absolutely alone. And I know that this loneliness is my destiny. I search through the music of the Hungarian folk, now vanishing, and I bind my isolation, my inner music, to the individual peculiarities of this folk music. I penetrate and expose its uniqueness. And I transform it into the music I hear deep within me. That music speaks a language not unlike your own. And I write now from the Bronx only to state my profound regard for your daring, imposing advance of music, only to say do not forget that in my way, I too hear and confront the frenzied soul dancing through our century."'"

Suddenly Petrov rose into the space between the couch and the coffee table, and unsteadily he walked to the piano.

"I could not resist then," he said. "I played for them the opening of the Bartok sonata. Just as I was about to start, Thomas said ironically, 'What time must it be now in the Bronx?' And Bruno answered: 'They're asleep in New York, just as they're asleep all over America!'"

Petrov's hands punched the Steinway's keyboard now, and Bartok's striding melody filled Jack's ears. It felt to him as if Petrov were attempting once again to reach Jack at the level of his deepest hearing, his deepest understanding of the three great progenitors of twentieth century music. The pianist's right hand played a high folk theme which searched out new regions of harmony, while his left hand took the thudding base punctuation to the edge of uncontrol. Roughened, punched chords questioned new regions of rhythm, and the opening trumpeted alarums kept returning, and all was drawn into the speeding circle of energy, a hammering round of alarming violence. Yet Jack knew that the hope of this Allegro moderato was that its energy expressed not only barbarism and violence but the energy of meaning and new life.

Petrov stopped and glanced at Jack, who said, "Oh my god, don't stop. Continue, please continue."

The Sostenuto e pesante plunged both listener and player into the prison and mire of single, slowly repeated tones and chords, bare and rising yet in repetition always the same. The same, never mind that other melodies entwined them, these same repeated tones remained bare and stray and scattered, barely retrieved and so repeated hypnotically, like rubbed stones or relics. The momentary richness of intervening chords thick with notes, seven, eight, nine, voiced a tragic yearning for release, sought for amid the simple, repeated, rising tones. The final repetitions—the do re mi, over and over—spoke out hope against hope that the origin of still living music had been discovered, some tragic cherishing of these few, bare, elemental tones.

Petrov did not pause: he raced into the Allegro molto, with its folkish theme springing out life and energy. The possibility of clemency sang out now and danced above the hammering, fragmenting, idly exploding chords. Finally, Petrov's hands hurtled the final, percussive cluster of chords out toward Jack, like a Hungarian baton to be tossed back in delight, or like a bomb to explode in his hands.

Jack applauded vigorously and alone, as Petrov—with a mocking and apologetic smile—returned to his seat on the tattered couch opposite him.

"Yes," he said, "Bartok was dying in those years, and yet he composed wonderful things then. And he kept trying to tour. After all he was broke; he had to scrape pennies! As Teddy would say: society hasn't any use for genuine art, and its responses to it are pathological. You know, in the cities Bartok visited, he used to go to ghetto jazz clubs. He wanted to hear the 'boogie-woogies.' He loved hearing the scales in all modes, like strings of pearls. The flatted notes and chords: the ninth, the eleventh, the thirteenth sounding together. Boogie-woogie, indeed! In the smoky haze, he would write down the essential bits in a little notebook. Always the musicologist. The jazz musicians said he would never get it! But of course, they were wrong; he got it, no?" Petrov laughter sounded pained, like a bitter pleasure.

"I remember," Jack said, "my father's favorite cellist died in the early forties. Feuermann. He told me he almost gave up the cello when he first heard him play. It didn't seem possible, he said, the expressive depth and precision. And Feuermann was only thirty-nine. Evidently one of the greatest: to hear him must have been incredible."

"Not Casals," Petrov said, "but very fine. Yes. Even brilliant! But he wasn't the only one. In 1942, Paderewski died, but of course he was an old man then, and still box-office! Schoenberg's teacher died that year in Saratoga, New York. Zemlinsky. I remember Arnold told us: 'He was my teacher in Vienna a half century ago. It's as if it were yesterday that he said: "Arnold, it's up to you. Decide whether you want to be on this side of the barricades or that one." He was a great citizen of the world. He fled from the Nazis, and it broke him down. The Anschluss in Vienna. It broke him profoundly.'

"Then Igor suddenly slammed his little hands on the red arms of that chair over there, and he hissed: 'The goddamn Nazis! I've been told that now Jews, Catholics, Gypsies, Communists, homosexuals are all being packed into Nazi stockcars. They are sent east. To die? How? Have you heard? They're being massacred in droves. The Germans are a very industrious people, with a questionable soul, no? The sons-of-bitches have found it possible to do a very lively business in death.'

"You could hear a pin drop. I looked at Thomas Mann, and he sat very still and rigid next to his wife Katia, who was Jewish. I broke the silence, Jack. I said, How, how could I not see at first? Unbelievable. Grotesque. How could it be, I kept thinking. I was able to stay, until 1938, and I tried to help people, but what could I do. I shouldn't have waited: I put Helen in danger and myself. But I thought, this too shall pass. What an ass I was. A blind fool, I said, and Bruno said, 'Fuck it, Sasha! You were human. Don't blame yourself. Blame the fucking Nazis, who are bringing death and more death into this world.' And Igor said, 'Nineteenfortytwo. Another year of death. In Europe and in Russia, Africa, the Pacific. And also here.'"

Suddenly Petrov's voice began to dwindle, on the point of vanishing: "Without words, our little group registered all the deaths, counted...and uncounted:

"But we don't have to be so silent, Jack. You play Opus 109 now."

The young composer protested, but Petrov insisted. "I'll tell you where you go right, and where you go left!"

Jack sat on the bench before the black concert grand, and he felt a detachment he had not known so intensely before at this piano. That he should attempt to play a late Beethoven sonata now, after such a story, seemed stunningly incongruous, yet Petrov would have his way. All they had exchanged in the last twenty minutes—including the poem which Petrov let hang in the air between them—was only another sign of the spiky, recalcitrant life which kicked and screamed, it seemed, in each of the Petrovs and in Jack too these last months. Whatever happened between them took on a momentum and inevitability of its own.

He began the Vivace ma non troppo of Beethoven's thirtieth sonata, and within ten bars, as he headed into the Adagio espressivo, Petrov was shouting censure and instruction from above.

"Yes, very fast at first, very fleet, and the line is clear. But the Adagio, I can't stand it! Stop, and play it again, Jack. This is not opera," he bellowed in his aging baritone, "this is not supposed to be pretty. Play it loud. It must be a gaping fissure, cracking open in the music. Very quiet, then sudden crescendos. Make them sforzandi. Who cares what's written! Editors! Make it quake fortissimo!"

❁ ❁ ❁

He drove up Highland and onto the highway entrance ramp, heading north on 101. When he left the UA office on Melrose, noontime clouds had gathered low and dense overhead, and the salty scent of rain blew in the wind. Now the dark clouds emptied themselves onto L.A.. The slapping wipers hardly cleared the windshield. It was getting dark, too dark to see, and he turned on his headlights, concentrating on the cars swimming, finned and bloated, past his VW. At the first Burbank exit, he turned off the freeway, with Mulholland looming in the black sky to the southwest. In the foothills and flat land east of the freeway were Universal's offices, its studios, its staging hangars for props. A few minutes before one o'clock, he parked and sat for a time in the car, beneath the stream and dark which blotted out the low studio buildings. The roof and glass were inundated by noisy driven rain falling from the long black clouds coming down from the low hills to the south. He ran through the blast to the door of the recording studio.

There was a crowd of production people and hangers-on in the wide hall. He opened the door to an insulated, recording complex. All week, they had been taping the soundtrack for Pat Garrett and Billy the Kid. This was the last day, and he had gone through these same motions each day, finding his seat near the sound engineer's bank of buttons and levers, putting on a pair of heavy, brown earphones, and staring through the glass in front of him. One seat over, Brian nodded his greeting. He was helping conduct a sound check.

In the sealed, recording area, Alias sat on a high stool, surrounded by instruments on or by or leaning against chairs: cellos, guitars, a base, a tambourine, flute, banjo, harmonium, drums. Alias was plucking at his guitar strings, picking out a hootenanny tune. He hummed along. A cellist sat a few yards away, his instrument loosely held between his legs and against his leaning shoulder.

"Jesus, this pipe is rusting," Alias said, tapping his throat and laughing quietly. "It's so fucking strange when you look out at a horde of hearers in a hall and you sing to them with a goddamn rusty pipe, or you with your cat guts, and it draws men's souls clean out of their bodies and you think you see them dancing and cart-wheeling right there in the emptiness above their heads." Other musicians and singers were filtering in, returning to their instruments, checking the tuning.

"If you want to talk more," the sound engineer said over the PA, "do it in notes."

Alias cocked his head, playing at a look of stoned vacancy, and he stared through the glass at the big engineer sitting on the other side of Brian.

"Ah, sir, note this before my notes," Alias said, nasal and mocking: "there's not a note I play that's worth noting."

"Shit," the fat engineer said with his intercom off, "the son-of-a-bitch speaks notes. Note his notes and fucking nothing!" Then he switched his microphone back on and said, "Final theme, take one, gentlemen and ladies."

The day wore on. At a break, Jack walked down the hall and pushed open the door to the storm outside. The hard rain still fell; a flood of run-off ran down the gutters near the open door. The blowing wind hit him bracingly in the face, refreshing him. He shut the door but hesitated to walk back to the recording rooms. Instead, he wanted to go back out into the rainy day, drive his car off the lot and return to Highway 101. He wanted to be released from the desolate contrivances of the recording session, the multiple repetitions of songs, the ego-games, the interminable waiting—for what? For the fourth and positively last take, the engineer would say, loud and lying, over the PA.

Jack walked back through the hall. All along it, he watched production assistants, sitting or standing; there were some of the bearded, boisterous characters who had surrounded Sam and Alias at Randy Schott's New Year's Eve party. Were they bodyguards? Musicians? Or just masters of hanging out and hanging on?

The sound booth was crowded now. Four actors from the movie had come to hear Alias record this last song. Billy and Maria were there, not thin phantoms but warm, rounded, humorous humans. They joked with Garrett and the Governor who had the tanned, gaunt freakishness of stars off-screen—the Governor's older face looking more haunted and disturbed. Jack sat back down by Brian who said, "Here goes nothing," and he put on his heavy earphones. Beyond the glass, Alias sat with three singers and three musicians, bass, guitar and drums. The cellist, the tambourine man, and the others had vanished.

"Knockin' on Heaven's Door, take one, ladies and gentlemen."

Jack heard an echo from the sound-feed for the visitors intruding on his earphones, and it sounded to him as if Alias sang in a vast hall, not just ten feet in front of him. The sound of his throaty voice quieted everyone in the booth. Its plaintive wail seemed to compel attention from the core of their hearing: Alias had freed his voice now of false irony or stoned affectation. Brian took notes on knobs to turn, balances to change: he was going to polish the gem, once he took a copy of the tape back to their Melrose studio. The song ended, and someone left the sound room suddenly, slamming a door behind him.

There were more takes, and before the fourth, the engineer boomed on the intercom, obsequious and presumptuous, "One more time, if that's all right. Let's not tax your voice; you don't want to slander your own music."

After the fourth take, Jack had heard the title phrase repeated thirty-two times. He got up from his chair, and the Governor sat down on it: "Do you mind?"

"No," Jack said. Not thinking twice, he headed out to the arching hallway: it was all over for him now. He only pitied this zero of a profession, bound in a closed circle of utterly predictable repetitions, of recycled sentiments, of packaged talent, and—in Alias's case—of his exploited, charismatic power.

He sat on one of the chairs lining the hall and watched Sam talking with Alias's cronies. The director glanced at Jack and turned away. The singer emerged through a door, thin and sad-eyed, looking like a Jewish cowboy in his black shirt and shades. He nodded gloomily at Jack as he passed and made his way into the circle of his friends. Punchy laughter erupted from them. Alias stomped off, saying, "Shit, it takes a lot to laugh at your fucking jokes." After a few minutes, Brian came down the hall and sat by Jack.

"Well, the shit has hit the fan," he said. "We have here what I call a deteriorating situation. Did you hear Jerry's exit after the first take of Knockin?"

"That was Jerry?"

"That was Jerry. I found him in one of the inner offices. Jerry says Knockin is a piece of shit, and he won't touch the project again."

"You're kidding." The studio composer had seemed always devoted to Peckinpah, committed and supportive.

"No," Brian said. Officious, with his Anglo-American sneer, he continued: "He says Bobby and his band are a bunch of scrambling, out-facing, fashion-mongering boys who flout and deprave and go anticly about, show outward hideousness, and have a half-dozen dangerous words as their whole vocabulary. So it seems we're left to clean up the mess and finish the job."

"Not me."

"What do you mean, 'not me'?"

"The job is pointless, repetitive, and second-hand, and anything you plan gets aborted by the fucking producers. Go do the job yourself. I can't stand it anymore!" Jack said, opposed and decisive. Then he smiled: he realized he had used Petrov's phrase and his son's. He said, lightened and released, "I feel I'm knock, knock, knockin' on heaven's door myself."

"Well, it's all much ado about nothing to me."

Jack walked steadily through the still sheeting rain, stepping around wide puddles which seemed to swell from a subterranean source, not pour from above. There was a blue cast to the clouds now. He revved the motor of the car, skidding out of his parking place. The VW sputtered and rolled through the inch-deep layer of run-off, like a skipping stone over water. The title of one of Alias's songs suddenly, oddly occurred to Jack; feeling both freed and homesick, for his parents would be flying into L.A. tomorrow, he began to hum It Ain't Me, Babe, as he drove up the freeway ramp and merged with the homeward-bound, rush-hour traffic inching south on 101.

3

The hibachi's coals were white with glowing red flecks and patches. Jack put nine loin lamb chops on, and he heard the singeing sizzle when they touched the hot grill. He had marinated the meat since noon, an hour before he drove to L.A. International Airport to pick up his parents. He smelled the barbecued lamb and the marinade smoking off it: chopped red onion and parsley, olive oil and vinegar, salt, ground pepper, and a few shakes of Lea and Perrins. That morning, the clouds had blown off, and now a mild sun shone above the clear horizon of the Pacific. Jack glimpsed Janice across the path, at her window to try to see what he did and who was there, he thought. He stood and glanced around at the chaise and chairs. The patio smelled fresh, washed clean by yesterday's late February storm.

His parents were indoors, Julius reading the Friday L.A. *Times*, Rosa making a salad in the kitchen. He remembered her great salad, how she finely sliced celery, green pepper, cucumber Israeli-style and chopped parsley, sprinkling them over cut tomatoes and lettuce, how she added a dressing of olive oil, vinegar, basil and crushed garlic. And he remembered how sloppily she worked, in her enthusiasm strewing discards of food on the counter, pieces and crumbs falling to the floor. His mother was a fine, slovenly cook, and both parents were disheveled, at least in the home, leaving dirty cups and plates and newspapers about, oblivious to the clothes they wore or left off. He remembered being raised as if he were hardly present. As a boy, he would walk down the hall, and one of his parents would come from a room, surprised that he was there, sometimes indifferent, sometimes delighted that this stranger absent from their consciousness for a minute or a day had returned. Of course, they had cared for him, clothed and fed him, loved and supported him. And perhaps their detachment had freed him to become the spry fool and criminal of perception he was at seven—and later to become whatever he was now.

He brought in the chops, medium rare and medium for his father. He walked over bits of celery and lettuce in the kitchen to make sure the pilaf was hot (coil vermicelli browned in butter, and rice, salt, pepper, chicken broth). They sat to eat at the living room table he had cleared of his notebooks and papers. His father sat at one end, his hair thinning but still brown at fifty-seven. His graying, red-headed mother sat by Jack, looking out to the ocean.

"So you quit?" his father said, sipping at a beer.

"It was hack work, Dad. And it interfered with what I really need to do," he said between mouthfuls of pilaf. "They treat you like shit; all decisions are made by committee, which in practice means they're made by the director and the producer. You don't know how much unreality there is in that world."

"You sure do know how to cook!" his mother said. "Molly or what was the other one's name taught you some fine moves, in the kitchen," she laughed, plump and brimming.

"It was Susan—she was Armenian. You remember, the violinist's daughter. How do you like L.A. now?" he asked her.

"God, it's changed. That airport is twenty times bigger than it was. And the freeways!" He had waited for his parents at the gate. The plane-load of musicians had walked through the ramp and filed by him, old émigrés among them, and occasionally a new, young, bushy-haired addition to the Orchestra, mostly men, with a few women sauntering by, some curious, some jaded, relaxed, professional. Finally, he had seen them, his father thin and wide-eyed, the same height as his plump, smiling mother who had said: "My god, it's warm," as she reached to hug him.

"So, how are you going to support yourself?" his father asked now, objective, calm, yet concerned. He forked salad from his plate.

"They did pay me a decent wage, so I saved a lot. I can survive for quite a while on it. Don't worry. And last night, I typed letters—inquiries, applications for support. You know what I mean. Commissions, too. I'll be fine." He had adopted the shot-gun approach, writing to: Erb, Dick who was just retiring, Babin at the Cleveland Institute of Music, the Gund, Chandler, Simon, and other Foundations, the Portfolio group, the Cleveland Orchestra, the Cleveland Area and the Ohio Arts Councils, the L.A. and California Arts Councils, the Ojai, Graf, and other Festivals, the new National Endowment for the Arts, Rockefeller, Ford, etc.

After dinner, they walked over the sand out to the ocean. "Do you know what it was in Cleveland when we left?" his mother said with glee, plopping down on the beach in the twilight. "Twenty-five and snowing." Later, he and his father had played music together. The Knabe was tuned for their visit and for the Petrovs who—responding to Jack's tentative invitation—agreed to come for dinner on Sunday evening. Jack and Julius played the Bach G-minor and the Brahms F-major cello piano sonatas: it was a form of communion father and son had experienced since Jack was in his mid-teens—a form of mutual pleasure and acceptance, no matter the intervening resentments and rebellions.

The next morning, his father rose at eight. Jack was going to drive him on the freeway to the downtown hotel where the other orchestra members were staying and from which they would be bused to the morning rehearsal. Rosa slept late. As his father showered, Jack put on his jeans and tee-shirt, took the blanket and sheet from the living room couch, and folded them into a pile on the stuffed chair. He went into the kitchen to make coffee.

"Jack," his father stood, stark naked, in the doorway, "can I have a cup of that?"

Jack brought the cups in and sat at the table as his father laid out his dark suit, shirt, tie, socks, and underwear on the couch.

He was seven when he realized it was strange that his father did not shut doors for privacy, let it all hang out as he shaved in the open bathroom, or just lounged around nude. That year, he heard odd, droning groans and hums from his parents, through their open, bedroom door. He thought it was a sort of music they made, and he walked in, curious and then amazed. There was Dad on top of Mom, naked, hugging, pushing himself against her, his thin body and her fat body swaying back and forth together. He had tiptoed out before they noticed him.

Now his father pulled on boxer shorts, over his aging, veined legs, his genitals, his graying pubic hair.

"We're both war babies, you know," he said. "I was born in 1915, you in '43. As I grew up, I thought life hung by a thread over some mysterious chasm—some cataclysm, no less. The Great War. Then the boom which never touched your grandpa and grandma. And the depression which bowled them over. Then, of all things, I became a musician. A cellist. That's always struck me as an unreal choice, under the circumstances. Catastrophe and music. Those were the two ingredients of my growing up. Destruction and some unreal sort of creativity. And all my life, the two have gotten mixed up in me. So Mom and I sometimes lived as if there were no tomorrow, we were so impractical and confused."

"You weren't bad. That's just being human."

"But I wonder, Jack. I worry whether all my confusion has somehow hurt you." Now he wore everything but his tie and suit coat. He sat on the couch and held the fingers of his veined hands together to form a grid like a cage of ribs. "Are you all right, son?"

"You were fine parents. So you were confused or into yourselves: that didn't hurt me. You raised me and then let me go. You could have done worse."

"But are you okay?" On the floor near Julius, his cello lay in the red interior of its case.

"What's okay? Just because I quit an insane job doesn't mean I'm not okay. It means I know what I want to do and what I don't. You always told me there were times when you almost gave up the cello. When you heard Feuermann for the first time. Or when Szell was driving everybody crazy. Do you remember what you used to say?"

"The orchestra plays brilliantly, and one's personal attitude becomes irrelevant," Julius smiled and leaned to tie his shoe laces.

"Right, but a little more resentfully than that," Jack said. The cellist sat up, his face serious now.

"You know, I've been thinking a lot about the fact that we play German music for the most part."

"You mean the basic repertoire?"

"And many of the players are Jews, no? Here we are haunting L.A. and Cleveland."

"You're not an accomplice, Dad."

"I don't know. At times, performing, I hear German music whisper: Use the Jews, use the Jews."

Jack was silent. He knew his father spoke from his generation's perspective: teetering above the abyss of another horror, as awful as they come. Jack thought of Adorno and Arendt.

"I don't mean, say, how Mozart used Da Ponte," Julius continued. "Or the way Austrian and German orchestras chewed up and spat out so many brilliant Jews. Over the generations. It's more than any one thing. It's that all my Jewish soul, my capacity to be generous, devoted, a mensch, is squeezed for all it's worth by those beloved masters! It must be their function, I think. God knows, I hear their barely audible whisper as I play. Use the Jews. You probably don't understand what I'm saying."

"I know what you mean, but I wouldn't say use and I wouldn't say Jews. Every human being is capable of feeling that call. To their souls. They don't even have to be musicians to feel it."

They were ready to leave. Julius made sure Rosa was all right. She said she knew where they went and would be fine, and she went back to sleep. So Jack drove father and cello downtown to rehearsal. The son kept thinking all the while of how many Jews had devoted their lives to music.

Among the hundreds of musical Jews and similarly inclined half-Jews who preoccupied Jack as he drove through the mild, smoggy, winter morning, the following is a sampling of names: Auer, Babin, Copland, Dylan, Eisler, Feuermann, Gershwin, Horowitz, Imber, Joachim, Korngold, Lhevinne, Mahler,

Newman, Oistrakh, Petrov, Rubinstein, Serkin, Toch, Ulanowsky, Volpe, Weill, Yard-heimi, Zoocoughski. Et cetera.

❈   ❈   ❈

The Petrovs sat on Jack's couch, talking with his parents—Rosa on the stuffed armchair and Julius on a straight chair he had taken from the laden table.

"Do you remember Los Angeles, thirty years ago?" Helen, erect and polite, asked Rosa.

"Of course, I do. I remember the evenings at your home, and how you were so kind when Julius was looking for work. How are your friends the Viertels?"

"Both have died," Helen said.

"Oh, I'm sorry to hear. The Franks?"

"Dead," said Petrov. "The Walters, the Werfels, the Dieterles, the Manns, Schoenberg, Stravinsky—all dead."

"Szigeti died last week," Julius said, treading this nether region with his usual calm and sympathy. "Such a great violinist, Sasha. Incredible insights, he had. I listen to…"

"Out of tune," Sasha said, "and wayward rhythms. Gifted, but uneven."

Jack watched his father engaging Petrov—Julius always objective and responsive, just as he was last night in the midst of Mahler's Sixth. The conductor Abbado fervently beat and pointed, drawing a pure unison and an operatic drama from the banks of cellos, violins, woodwinds, brass. All the while, his father watched from the fifth chair of his section, absorbing, participating, and always, it seemed to Jack, witnessing. Afterwards, the son had packed him and his cello into the VW's back seat and his mother into the passenger's seat which was pulled all the way forward; they had driven home on 110, 10, and 1. "So you're merely a technician, then?" Jack had teased his father. "We fiddle," Julius said matter-of-factly and then began to laugh, quoting himself: "'The orchestra plays brilliantly. One's personal attitude becomes irrelevant.'"

Now Jack rose from the table by Sarah. "How about some dinner?" he said, pulling his chair to one side and gesturing to the dishes there. "I hope you don't mind how informal it is."

Helen Petrov rose and came to scrutinize the bounty on the table. "Not at all," she said.

"It looks very good, Jack," Petrov said, standing and putting down his emptied glass of Scotch.

Jack had converted his wide work table into a buffet dining table. He and his mother had shopped on Saturday afternoon, and together they had bought up the following storm of provisions: dry Italian salami, kosher salami, sliced turkey and ham, rye bread and sourdough, potato salad, cole slaw, humus (Jack had made it: garbanzos blended with garlic, olive oil, lemon, tahini, sprinkled with cumin and cayenne), Greek olives, California olives (black and green), pickles, sliced tomatoes and cucumber, Coke, ginger ale, beer, wine, Scotch, and vodka. Devil's food cake and cheese cake waited in the kitchen for later.

A black Triumph squealed to a stop on Speedway, outside the windows by the table, and Jack went to the front door to let in Joseph, the last to arrive.

"We just started eating," Jack said quietly at the door.

"I'm sorry I'm late," he said, his face ashen, his black hair tousled.

Jack's parents greeted Joseph warmly. Julius reminded the young pianist that they had chatted one summer two years ago, when Joseph had played Mozart's 23rd concerto with the Orchestra at Blossom. Rosa told him what she had told Sarah, that she remembered them as babies.

"Hello, Joseph," Petrov said, and his son slightly nodded, then waved at his mother, short and gray, as she silently filled her plate with food from the table. They all sat to eat, the older generation at plastic TV tables before them on the couch and chairs. The younger generation crowded their plates and drinks—coke, wine, and vodka—next to the platters and containers laid out on the table. Jack sat next to Sarah in front of the food, facing the windows; Joseph sat at the end of the table, nearest the front door.

Jack had not seen him since his return from the northwest early in February. Work on the job he had just quit occupied him, and he had hoarded nights and weekends for work on his Adagio. Two weeks ago he had spent the evening with Sarah, seeing Last Tango in Paris; afterwards, they were sitting and holding each other in his car, and she had said, "We're like castaways, I mean our real selves. Not as a daughter or son, sister or brother. I mean you. Me. Here we are drifting along these fucking freeways and boulevards." Later, they had sipped coffee in a booth at Ships on Olympic, until one in the morning.

"How did the concerts go?" Jack asked Joseph now, as the food was being passed and eaten.

"They went okay," the pianist said with careful detachment; his face was bloodless, as if he had taken a drug—Jack thought—or was in need of one.

"Let me show you something," Sarah said quietly, reaching for her purse on the floor by her chair. "It's a review Joey got in The Oregonian." She handed

Jack the newspaper clipping, and he began reading it to himself, as their parents visited.

"In one stroke Tuesday, a brilliant piano recital by Joseph Petrov overturned two myths: that a predominantly twentieth century program cannot attract a significant audience, much less win its whole-hearted approval; and that great musical talent does not pass from one generation to the next, father to son. In the large recital hall, packed to capacity, at the University of Portland's new music building, there were justified enthusiasm and cheers for the performances of Berg, Webern, Ligeti, Mozart and Scriabin by Petrov, son of the great, retired virtuoso of yesteryear, Alexander Petrov."

"My god, this is a classic. Is yesteryear still a word people use?" Jack said. "Do you know this Carmichael, Joseph?"

"I never met him in my life," he smiled palely, raising his hands, pleading innocent, and then lighting a cigarette from a pack he placed by his now empty plate on the table.

"What are you reading, Jack?" his father said, listening from his chair between the table and the couch.

"A review of Joseph's Portland concert. A classic."

"Read it aloud, Jack," Julius said.

"Oh, please, no," the pianist groaned from the table.

"No, read it," Jack's father said, eager and insistent. "So we all can hear."

He read the opening, and at yesteryear Helen raised her eyebrows and Sasha stiffened on the couch. Jack continued through the paragraphs on Joseph's Berg and Webern, up to: "'Petrov shared the music's secrets in passionate declamations, whispered messages, and dramatic developments. The sparkling, crystal clear piano playing was propulsive and always gave an extra dose of drama.' Have you heard enough already?" Jack asked, in the maw of the prose.

"Why not read the rest?" his father said, looking around him, curious and patient.

Finally, Jack came to the last paragraph: "'Petrov's concert went a long way toward dispelling the unfair myth of modern music as strange and difficult, giving no real meaning or pleasure to the listener. The Berg, Webern and Ligeti he played gave the capacity audience an extremely generous serving. They responded with a standing ovation. His concert also dispelled any illusion that great musical gifts do not recur in the next generation. The great recording of Beethoven's Hammerklavier sonata by Joseph's father, Alexander Petrov, set the benchmark, as far as I am concerned, for all subsequent performances. It is my belief that Joseph Petrov is similarly endowed and promises to set a benchmark in the repertoire he plays. His Scriabin already comes very close.'"

"What a great review!" Rosa said.

"Joseph is as obsessed by the piano as I am," Petrov said, lighting a cigar. "It's the family disease."

Helen sat quietly on the couch, her eyes searching out her son's. Joseph looked nowhere, nursing a glass of vodka at the table.

"I don't think it's a disease," Julius said, finishing his beer. "It's a fate. Really, a contribution. It's a contribution especially Jews have been fortunate to make. That's a historical fact, Sasha. From generation to generation, it's been our task, all right our obsession to communicate to the gentiles. Through music, through words, through ideas. To explain, to express that there are other ways to be than business as usual. Of course, not all Jews. And not only Jews. But certain Jews. I'm not saying it right." He got up, went to the nearby shelves, and took out a thick book designed for coffee tables and public libraries in Jewish neighborhoods. "Jack, I found this when I looked through your shelves Friday night. We gave it to you some time ago, remember? Next Year in Jerusalem."

"I remember," he said, though he barely did and had barely read it. Julius sat back down and opened the book.

"There's a brilliant little essay by George Steiner in it. Here: 'Some "Meta-Rabbis."' Don't worry," he said jovially, "only a sample." He read a paragraph about three great tendencies characterizing Jewish intellectuals in modernity: a hyper-sensitivity to language, an acute consciousness of history, and a passion for encompassing conceptual insights. Driven by these three obsessions, Jews—orthodox but above all assimilated (which Jack understood to include partial and agnostic Jews)—shaped essential elements in each field of art or science to which they contributed.

As his father read aloud, Sarah leaned—quiet, tender, yet apparently aloof—to Jack by her at the table. "Do you want me?" she shaped her phrase almost silently.

"But it's a brave new world, Mr. Weinstein," Joseph said from the end of the table. His voice was at once remote, earnest, and ironic. He spoke only to Jack's father, as if no one else were present.

"Please, call me Julius."

"Modern culture hardly exists anymore, as you understand it," he said. "The ideas Steiner is talking about have been supplanted by media images. It's an electronic world out there now."

"Look at Watergate," Sarah spoke up, between Joseph and Jack. "The media is so manipulative—and we are so manipulated. You simply don't know what are lies and what is truth anymore."

"Under those circumstances," Julius patiently argued, "there's all the greater need for music and art. To make a thoughtful contribution."

Joseph had risen, vodka in one hand, a cigarette in the other, and he meandered to the other end of the table, closer to Julius, so that the older man turned his chair about, between Petrov smoking on the couch and Joseph standing against the table.

"What's the artist to do," Joseph said, "in light of the media? In that flickering, electronic light? In light of the disaster?" His face was masked by a pleasant, aloof grin. "The artist ought to say no, and spit in the eye of his so-called culture. With all his being, he should say: I will not serve your images."

"But the problem," Jack spoke up gently, looking at the black haired pianist standing unsteadily at the table's end, "the problem is deciding how and when to say no, and whether saying no will even help. And first, before anything else, he needs to decide how to be. The artist who spits in their eye may only end up at best getting shoved up against the wall and at worst getting his head bashed in. Or maybe even beating it in himself."

Jack's mother had stopped chatting with Helen, and she assumed a look of absorption, swimming now in Joseph's unsteady glance as he sipped from his glass. All of them were stunned into attention by his warm, obscure engagement of his friend's father. His eyes searched the room now, the books and records ranged on shelves, the ceiling. His grin tightened, and his breathing quietly heaved beneath a flourishing quotation and a rush of sentences.

"'Thou wast not born for death, immortal bird. No hungry generations tread thee down.' But the world today has given up on art. It's no longer"—Joseph's free hand flew out, his thighs leaning against the table, his pale face turning now directly to his father, who had risen from the stuffed couch—"the ordered and humane world which, of course, we all used to inhabit."

The old pianist stood by the Knabe now and struck a chord forte with both hands. He lifted all his big, dexterous fingers except the right thumb on A.

"Let's play," he said to Julius, with a bitter, snapping intensity. He pointed imperiously to the cello in the corner by the couch. "The dead boys over there are immune to flattery," he said, grinning across the room. "My son gets wonderful reviews, and he worries that modern culture is going to hell. He reminds me of Oskar Fisch, the king of cabaret in Berlin, before he came to Hollywood.

'Nothing,' Oskar would laugh in his beautiful, rasping baritone, 'nothing is harder than saying no to one's time! No?'"

The cello case bared its velvet lining next to Helen who moved to the corner of the couch. Joseph, his face frozen in a broken grin, returned to his chair; his hands lay like pale bones on the table before him.

"Here, I found this on these shelves of music," the cellist said.

Petrov took the volume of Beethoven, and he said, "Let youth keep their self-doubts. Their good reviews. Their bravura technique! The reason for calluses like burns on our hands. On our lives. It's not technique. It's not mere, wishy-washy angst! No, 'dem Manne muss Musik Feuer aus dem Geiste schlagen,' Beethoven said: to strike fire from the mind, that has been our task. Imagine the conditions under which he said this. Deaf, isolated—in both body and soul! And what a father *he* had. He would beat the boy and call his improvisations 'stupid trash!' But then he took credit for his success. Naturally! As for his mother, she used to send the boy to bars to retrieve his drunken father, sometimes to intercede with the police. 'No man knows who has begotten him,' he would say. But despite everything, yes, he struck fire from the mind!" Petrov tapped gingerly on the volume of music he had taken. Smoke trailed from the cigar in his mouth, and on the music rack before him, he opened the volume to the third cello piano sonata, Opus 69.

Joseph sat back in his chair, his long white fingers grasping the top of the table. From his eyes came tears, which eased down his smiling face. Sarah darted an alarmed, imploring glance at Jack, as if he could say something, could intervene. But it was not possible. He could not plumb, let alone enter, the obscure depth of anger and need between father and son.

Sasha and Julius began to play the opening movement, Allegro ma non tanto. Unaccompanied at first, the cellist played a naked, rising fifth, bowing it awkwardly as if his fine tone were dangerous to produce. The piano entered, insouciant and assured, and the ensuing conversation juxtaposed affirmation to affirmation, upwards fifths to downwards fifths, agitation answering agitation, warmth merging with warmth, bravura with bravura, and at the end delicacy with delicacy. When they began the Scherzo's off-beat theme, the upbeat was continually stressed with fleet, intensifying precision and power by Sasha, the cigar stub dead in his mouth, and by Julius, who smiled, without a sneer, smiling at the challenges his arms and veined hands met.

Helen quietly rose from the couch, walked to the kitchen, and closed the swinging door. After a minute, as the Scherzo's trio poured out its manic hymn, Jack followed her into the kitchen and softly swung the door shut behind him.

The short, gray woman was taking small paces back and forth across the linoleum, registering the stress of the music. She looked up at Jack and stopped. Her thick, agitated face reassembled itself into a polite mask. She touched the sleeve of her beige dress as if to straighten it.

"Can I get you anything?" Jack asked softly.

"Nothing at all," she said and then gave him a disarming smile. "I don't know why, but I couldn't stand sitting anymore."

"Well, all the noise, the music."

"Yes, the noise. How," she said in a harsh, slow whisper, as if her words disclosed a profound and secret truth, "how could he connect Joseph with Oskar Fisch...the lunatic! I remember seeing a Fisch film in the early forties. A private showing, I don't remember whose house. Always beautiful young men! In Nazi uniforms, the beautiful boys would shoot people right in their faces or herd them together like cattle. Horrible fantasies, I thought! Always the faces of the handsome Nazis were virile and virginal and unmoved. Blank they were, as they stomped on bodies or mowed them down with mechanical guns or hacked them up with axes. Horrible, horrible. At the end, there were hills of bodies piled up, naked, their heads shaved, and the virgin Nazis played with the dead, kicking and shooting to make them bounce and shudder. Atrocious premonitions! I fainted right there, yes, I remember it was on a couch at the Viertels. And then the women there did a little dance of kindness around me, trying to retrieve me from the place of horror Fisch had sadistically led us into. Salka, Vera, even Alma lay their hands on my arm, my forehead, to soothe me. It's curious how one's humanity becomes more precious to others, just when it threatens to disappear."

"My god, yes," Jack said, anxious that the distressed woman might collapse even now. But she had begun calmly to study Jack, his face, his hands, his clothes.

"You like Sarah quite a bit, don't you?" she said. "Naturally. But she can be erratic, you know. For example, she shows little restraint with me. She is not as wild as Alma Mahler was, but she does need to learn restraint—like her father." Jack lifted his hands as if to reassure her, but before he could speak, she said, "You have such fine hands. And you like subdued colors. Your sweater is a mauve, a beautiful, subtle mauve."

"I guess that's the word for it."

"You prefer subtle colors, don't you?" she laughed softly. "You've acquired the habit of protective coloration." Then she looked down at her beige dress. "I believe life has taught me that habit too. We have it in common, Jack."

As the evening was ending after the music, after the dessert, the Petrovs were saying good-bye near the doorway. Sarah would drive them back to Benedict Canyon in their old, white Chrysler. Joseph slowly approached the door and shook hands with Jack's parents. Then, suddenly, he wheeled to Petrov, and the son's words snapped out.

"Don't you ever listen to yourself? Your complacency? Your murderous egotism? Such a great man, of course! Such a great man, and you care for nothing except yourself. The Nazis should have caught you and finished you off. Then generation after generation of this hell would have come to an end once and for all."

Rosa and Julius took quick, quiet steps back into the living room and down the hall. Jack and the four Petrovs stood in a tight circle at the door.

"Joey," Sarah pleaded.

"Joseph," Petrov said icily, "this is killing. It is sick."

Joseph's hands fought helplessly out of their black sleeves. "There is killing, and there is killing." His stiffening arms reached forward, his fists held in the air before his father's face.

Petrov looked now with blank eyes at his son, his shut mouth rigid.

Joseph, frozen before him, spit out each word.

"You asshole. You fucking asshole. Who do you think you are?" Suddenly he swayed back, turning to Jack, and with one hand, he grabbed for his friend's arm. "I can't take it anymore," he rasped out. With the other hand, still a fist, he weakly reached toward his father.

❀ ❀ ❀

The phone rang. His hand was wrapped over his sleeping head. He reached up from the couch to the telephone table.

"Jack?"

"Yeah."

"It's Sarah."

"What time…?"

"Two." Her voice was thin and stricken. Jack sat up, naked on the couch, suddenly awake.

"What is it?"

"Joey is in the hospital. I'm here too. Father and Mother are. Joey crashed his car." She began softly to cry and immediately stopped herself. "Jack, please come. I need you."

He dressed in the dark, hearing the constant sweep and surge of the waves in the distance. He wrote a note to his parents and taped it to the open door of the bedroom where they slept. At noon, he would need to drive them to the airport.

The dark, moonless night hung over the VW as Jack traveled north on 1, then east on 10. On the phone, Sarah had given him directions to Cedars Sinai, and she told him what the police had said. Joseph must have driven up the coast when he left Jack's flat and then turned east on Mulholland, curving along the ridge of the Santa Monica Mountains. The police had been alerted by scattered residents high above L.A.. They had heard the midnight screech and the shattering, resounding thud of Joseph's Triumph plowing into the hill just below the turn down into Benedict Canyon. The police had found the black sports car smashed and wedged into the hillside where, two months before, Jack had kneeled to empty and retie his shoe. Shattered glass spread out over the dark canyon road. Joseph was unconscious, his legs broken. He bled internally, and his face was torn open by the glass.

Jack turned off the freeway and drove north on Robertson. A cool wind blew across L.A., through the dark and the circles of light from signs and street lamps. Dust and trash swirled about the empty streets. Now, after two, the boulevard was abandoned.

Poor Joseph, poor man, Jack thought. Was his crash unintentional, or was it in some way suicidal? Perhaps he was seeking to stop time, to end the brute motion of life with a final brutality. Or had Joseph wanted to punish himself, out of some misconceived sense of failure and self-censure, as if the skidding collisions of one's life meant that its motion deserved to stop? Or was it possible that Joseph had wanted to punish the survivors, to place everything always in the perspective of his crack-up and his death: their lives, their failure to hate his father as he did, their acceptance of Sasha and even the possibility of their love for him—for his vitality, his humanity, even his flaws. All of it would be mutilated by suicide if Joseph died.

At Robertson and Third, Jack parked his VW near Cedars Sinai. He rode the elevator to Intensive Care, and in the waiting room Sarah sat staring straight ahead at nothing. The ropes of her gold hair were unbrushed and pushed back. Her face was mottled, a pallid whiteness beating back patches of blushing rose. She turned to see him, and her dark eyes seemed unable to fix on his image.

She walked toward him and buried her head against his shoulder. They stood together, silently buffeted, holding each other.

"Where are your parents?"

She lifted her head from him and said, "They left after I called. Mother was getting ill. Father said he'd drive."

"Have you heard any more?"

"No. He's still in critical condition. They won't let me see him," she began to cry now and walked back to her seat. There was a glowering couple in their fifties across the circle of upholstered chairs, and they stared at Jack and Sarah, sitting together.

"Something was bound to happen," Sarah said in a soft high voice, wiping her face with kleenex from the low table by her. "The drugs. The drinking. And the insults. The resentments. The constant struggle between them. He drank so much last night. They both did."

"There's so much disdain and hate between them," Jack said. "Neither has a monopoly on valor, but…"

"I'm living in hell, Jack. I'm shackled there, like a slave. In the fire." Her piercing eyes fixed on him now as they sat together in the waiting room.

Later, a doctor—balding and looking harassed—entered the room. "Petrov," he said. Sarah stood and walked to him. "The sister?" he said with bleak indifference.

"How is he?"

"He's out of critical. Most likely, he'll live."

She held Jack's hand tightly and asked, "What does most likely mean?"

"The man is in serious condition. He's semi-conscious. His liver only just stopped bleeding. His legs are broken. His face is hanging on by my threads. But he'll live. Most likely."

"What's your name, doctor?" Jack asked.

"Latner. What's it to you?"

"He's with me," Sarah said, her arm clinging to Jack's waist now.

"Your brother's blood alcohol was point one four. There was some cocaine in the car. Quite a joy ride," he laughed suddenly, unexpectedly from a hidden well of bitterness. "He'll need reconstructive surgery, and he'll be in a cast for months. I told him, and I think he understands. He tried to lift his hand." The doctor ushered them into the darkened hospital room.

Joseph was a figure in gauze. His legs and head and face were swathed in white, tinged aquarium green by the monitor lights. There was a constant gurgle and whir from the life-support equipment.

"Joey," Sarah said, by him. There was no sound and no movement. She reached out to his swathed body.

"Don't touch. He's asleep now," the doctor said. "You'll have to leave."

It was four-thirty in the morning, and Jack drove Sarah through Benedict Canyon. She had phoned her mother from the hospital; Helen had wanted her to call if anything changed, for good or ill. They parked at the base of the Petrovs' driveway and walked up the path to the yard. On the step outside the sealed music studio door, they sat together, canted over the void of blackened, flickering L.A., below them in the moonless dark. A police cruiser slowly descended the canyon drive and disappeared. The air was raw and moist, devoid now of Benedict's indigenous odors of chlorinated pools, marijuana, and scented wealth.

"Fuck it," Sarah started softly and numbly to chant, barely containing her bitterness. "Fuck it. Fuck it. Fuck it. Why did he do this?"

They heard a thin wail from deep inside the darkened house, the sporadic sound of Helen keening. Suddenly it vanished, and everything was hushed in the house and yard.

"It's so still now," Jack said, not touching Sarah, who sat quietly next to him, "like heaven or some graced hell, moist and silvery; the dew's indifferent to where it falls."

"Come with me. Upstairs," Sarah said. Jack shook his head, mouthing the words: it's insane. Neither of them moved. "Please, hold me, Jack. They'll never notice."

Jack mouthed the words, "You're insane," as the two of them tiptoed up the stairs to the second story hall. Together, they had been assaulted, pared down to a terrible vulnerability by Joseph's accident, his self-destruction. Yet the vulnerability in her high voice and being seemed always to give rise to a compensating desperation. And he realized that both the fragility and the steely desperation in her needed him, his chaperoning and protection.

In the hall, the door to the Petrov's dark bedroom was slightly ajar, and Jack could hear snatches of distant talk.

"I'm in critical condition too," Petrov snarled. "Do you know what my disease is?" There was silence.

"What?" Helen mumbled sleepily.

"Paralysis." Again, there was silence. "Paralysis of mind, heart, and soul."

Sarah gently closed and locked the door to her room. The whole family was teetering on the abyss, and Jack felt he too was drawing close to the edge, joining the Petrovs suspended there. In the near darkness, Sarah wore only her slip, and she put a record on the player, its volume almost inaudible. Jack left on his shorts and tee-shirt, and he got under the covers she opened for him.

He held her softly against him, his face against her hair, his hands stroking her shoulders. She began to whimper without words, repeating the same single tone over and over, a bare, high, quiet, elemental moan. Jack held her gently as the hushed sound sang in her throat. Then she pulled him tightly to her and began to kiss his mouth, a gnawing, desperate kiss. They took off the rest of their clothes, and she seemed so bare and almost vanished to him: he pulled the sheet over them and covered her body with his own. Over and over, his lips kissed her face as if to hallow it, to protect her, to retrieve her from the place of vanishing.

He heard more clearly now the voice from the record. He registered it, detached, accepting it: Dylan's voice.

Their bodies joined together were like the fated song in Sarah's throat, yearning to be retrieved from the prison and mire of the room, the story, the house, the canyon. Always repeating over and over the same motion, the elemental thrusting of their bodies rose together toward climax, toward a desperate cherishing of their bare, essential joining.

PART IV

❀

Largo—Allegro risoluto: The Ides of March—Spring, Summer, and Fall 1973

1

The L.A. days floated out of time. Each day, with Sarah, he visited the hospital where Joseph was being fed through tubes hanging from bottles slung above his bed—intravenous medicine and nutrients, blood in reserve. He hardly moved. He did not speak. His black eyes gazed remotely through the rent in the swath of gauze. He stared—from some location in stopped time—at the white space of bandages and sheets which was his bed, never at Sarah or Jack, or the nurses and doctors, or his parents. And each night, Jack saw Sarah at her home, sometimes staying with her, and he would leave—listening to make sure the coast was clear, as he did the first night—at six or seven in the morning, before the Petrovs rose: they seemed not to sense his early morning presence, twenty yards away on the second story. In this way, Sarah and Jack kept barely intact the primitive, imperfect song of their bodies' joining.

On Saturday afternoon, March 3, the sixth day after Joseph's crash, Jack walked up the Petrov's front path. The dense, dead scrub on the bushes and trees had begun to mutate and sprout a cover of tender, pale leaves. There was a glaring, smoggy brightness to the air. The sun had poured in on him when he had awakened at home late in the morning. He had dressed and left the bed unmade. Dishes accumulated, unwashed, in the kitchen; clothes and papers were strewn about his bungalow. The 1973 notebook containing the completed Adagio of his sonata was unopened on the table. He could compose no more. There was no time, no heart.

The garage was shut again, and Jack could not see whether Sarah's Jeep was back from her shopping for the week's food. He rang and knocked. After a minute, the door opened on Petrov's bulky form. Gray stubble grew on his face, and the halo of white hair edging his pate was untrimmed. He wore his long-sleeved, brown plaid shirt with its empty pockets.

"Oh, Jack," he mumbled, vague and obstreperous. "Sarah couldn't reach you. She had errands to run...she told me to tell you. She won't be home until the afternoon." Petrov's tone was not angry; he must not know, Jack thought, about his sporadic early morning exits. "We could talk, if you'd like," he continued. His vestige of an accent was oddly noticeable, the British inflected echoes of German.

"Sure," Jack said.

"Why don't we walk? It's mild for winter," he said off-handedly; they stepped out onto the porch, shutting the door behind them, and Jack followed him down the stairs onto the unirrigated lawn.

"I once strolled in the garden here with your composer friends," he said, unsmiling in the smoggy glare. He did not look at Jack and took short tired steps over the ragged grass. "Arnold said, 'Let's see the grounds of your mansion,' so naturally I took them for a walk. Even cigars I offered; Igor took one, but Schoenberg never smoked—after all it was asthma that drove him to seek this 'perfect' air in the first place."

Petrov gestured at the unkempt bushes, the withered chrysanthemum beds: "I told them, 'See what my Helen grows, the beautiful flowers. The vegetables.' There were tomatoes, thick and red. And peppers, dangling from stalks. And nests of basil, mint, oregano. And big sunflowers. Huge, glaring." Whatever the content of his words, his voice remained quiet and mechanical, his tone sad. "The grass was green as can be, and the flower beds were fit as a fiddle: yellow roses and red ones, big chrysanthemum of all colors, paradise flowers all around. Of course, there were the exuberant singing birds, and we saw even a rabbit. 'Too bad,' Igor said, 'we've no weapon handy.'"

Jack and Petrov walked slowly past a bloomless bank of oleander. Beyond it—in a wedge shaped indentation in the hills—was what would have been L.A., veiled in a gray-green shroud.

In the backyard, Petrov pulled open the sliding wall of glass, the patio door to the music room. Inside, in the uncanny wintry light, Jack was struck once again by the tattered glory of the room, rising from the oak floor to a high ceiling with embedded redwood beams. On the floor at their feet, the big ragged oriental rug was hidden beneath the coffee table, the old couches and chairs. Petrov pulled the glass door's curtain closed—not speaking now, as if he were alone. He went to the low, liquor cabinet and bent to pour himself a glass of Scotch, neat. Sarah had said her father had begun this week to drink sometimes as early as noon, yet he seemed to her always the same, never drunk.

"Do you want something?" he mumbled to Jack.

"Thanks anyway. No."

"We missed our session last month," Petrov said from one couch. "The next sonata. Should we do it now?"

"The Hammerklavier. I can make an attempt…do you have time?" Jack said, sitting on the couch opposite.

"Time?" Petrov said vaguely, not rising. Having offered, he seemed not eager to act. "I've been thinking lately—about when Joseph was a child, when we were new here in Los Angeles. It was a grotesque time, Jack. I don't know how else to say it." He paused to sip from his glass of Scotch; hunching slightly, the heavy man seemed to be shrinking into the couch. "Here's a story for you," he said. "I told you my friend Bruno Fried worked for Max Steiner. In the Bureau of Studio Composers, he called it. Once at a party here, Bruno made his way to my piano, cautiously, bowing all the way. He told us: 'Right now we're finishing work on Casablanca, an anti-Nazi romance—it will be out soon. You have no idea what crap Max has thrown into that pot: Deutschland uber alles, Die Wacht am Rhein, La Marseillaise, Ippolitov's Caucasian Sketches. And the theme song!' Bruno suddenly was shouting. 'How Max hates it, As Time Goes By, indeed! "This is dreck!" Max says. But a few weeks ago, the producer Wallis calls down to say he wants it scored even more heavily, at open and close. As Time Goes By for full orchestra.' Then Bruno began to play and sing in his squeaking voice, and he makes the English sound like German:

You must remember thisss,
A kisss is just a kisss…

Et cetera.

Thomas and Katia Mann were there. He laughed so hard his wife, always upright and vigilant, glared at him."

Jack couldn't help grinning, there was so much irony and laughter in what he heard, and for a moment Petrov smiled at him. "Then, even Katia Mann joined with us, to applaud Bruno's impersonation of Ingrid Bergman imitating Dooley Wilson's swing and pace. 'Play it again, Bruno,' Thomas called out. 'If you can stand it, I can.' But Bruno had inched back to the end of the couch. 'I can't stand it!' he moaned. And the fact is he couldn't. Once Jack Warner, the producer, had cornered him at one of Max's parties: 'You people are like my writers, you're shit beneath my feet.' Of course, as a result, movies got the music they deserved, no? Then as now, I assume."

Jack nodded as Petrov's voice continued unabated.

"Do you know the old Dada joke: What is German culture? Answer: Shit. Hollywood was not unlike Berlin in that respect. Except for the Nazis, the killers. But the movie men and the newsmen and the academicians were all performing the same rape of culture, turning everything into shit, into propaganda. A grotesque time, yes. Think of how Bruno felt: he was like the gifted poet who works as a copy editor for your leading newspaper. The part of him that remains a poet struggles to keep alive even just the sound of genuine poetry, the holy sanctuary, yes? At least not the journalistic shit. Then at a minimum the sounds, say, of King Lear might survive…'nothing can come of nothing.' Of course, that would be a desperate alchemy in German, sound for sound: Noch hing'gen kaum Freund…noch ihn." Petrov looked up at Jack with a raised eyebrow and said, "Bruno was so bitter he quit life before he could quit the studios. It's good to see that you have quit the studio first."

Jack was startled by Petrov's sudden reference to him. He wondered whether the brilliant, droned story and now this pointed pause were all a sort of strategy. Petrov had said he was thinking of Joseph; maybe all he did now was an avoidance and defense against the impossibility of speaking directly of his son, who was still in serious condition at the hospital. Jack smiled warily as he said, "What did they call the artistic use of noise, like your German English? Noise as art, or the art of noise?"

"You know Bruno hated Los Angeles," Petrov said, focusing his eyes on Jack and ignoring his question. "But he was the first to admit we had all idealized America—Hollywood, New York, Chicago, the Wild West. In Berlin, he said, we had tried to imagine America: a liberal Eden, tolerant, eclectic, and infinitely expressive…open to all difference, to both the primitive and the sophisticated, both the avant-garde and the popular. In short, an America which never existed. And when we came here, fleeing for our lives, what did we do? We built Berlin here by the Pacific, and inside it we continued to imagine the America we wanted to exist, the America we know exists nowhere. That's what music in the Studios was all about: Bruno, Max, Eric Korngold, Franz Wachsman—all of them wrote the music of an America we had invented in Berlin, in our dreams."

Hunched down in the couch, Petrov sipped the last of his drink. "That reminds me of you, Jack," he said icily.

"What do you mean?"

"I've been thinking about what you want from music. And from me, also. I think I know. You want something impossible, like our dream of America, but in your case backwards." He paused, and Jack warily watched the old pianist as he leaned forward to place his empty glass on the coffee table. "You're an American, but you want to become a European. With a capital E. If possible, a

European of the last century. That would be ideal for you. To become something which no born European like me could become! Something impossible. Something you can't have."

"Sasha, can we talk about the Hammerklavier, instead of me?" Jack said irritably. Accurate or not, he thought, Petrov's psychoanalysis felt stigmatizing and irrelevant to what truly bound their lives together, music and friendship and—carefully unmentioned—Joseph and Sarah. He began talking associatively about trying to play Beethoven's opus 106 in his teens. "Of course I can't bring it up to speed," he said. "Certainly not the 138 a half-note Beethoven asks. Now *that's* impossible."

"The new generation! You're so naive!" Petrov exploded. "You define rhythm according to the machine. The jet plane, the jackhammer, the sports car. For anyone who grew up before the world wars, your rhythm means the obliteration of rhythm. Listen to Casals. His is the rhythm of the body. The beat of the body is not mechanical or precise. I'm not a piece of artillery; you're not a machine-gun! The body wavers, it rises, it breathes. Its imprecision gives life. The Hammerklavier is like that. It's not all 138. The ritardandos, the ritards! Then the allegros shoot out of the blue. It breathes."

"I understand it's ever-changing. It's…"

"As for me," Petrov plunged on, "my youth was cut in two by the Great War. I have both rhythms, the machine and the body. I can fuck the piano, and I can make love to it." He laughed, not getting up, not even looking any longer at Jack, just blankly staring before him.

"I think there's a third kind of rhythm," Jack said. "A rhythm that may seem arbitrary, that improvises, that responds spontaneously, with insight and originality, to the choices of the moment. To whatever the moment brings."

"Whatever the moment brings?" Petrov laughed. "That's not a third rhythm. That's fate. I am always inside the moment, and outside it. Both inside and outside time."

"Yes. You're always using the third rhythm! I mean really the creativity of your rhythms, the idiosyncratic cast you put on them."

"Leave the idiosyncrasies to Gould. My rhythm isn't perverse! And I don't sway and hum at the piano. Though I think I'll try it."

"Gould may seem arbitrary, but you know he really isn't. What seems random from the outside is imaginative and original when you truly listen. The third sort of rhythm is a gift, and I hear it every time you play. Neither fucking nor dancing. You're projecting your unique sense of…"

"You're telling me I have an imagination. That I don't deny." He got up and walked slowly now to retrieve a volume of Beethoven from his wall of scores and books.

"Sit. Let's see what your rhythm is like," he said, gesturing Jack to the piano bench.

"It won't be 138."

"Just play as fast as you can."

Jack began the Allegro's opening leaps, not springing but revolving like Andromeda or Orion, a vaulting form in six and a half beats. Again, the cluster of leaping chords revealed their pattern of power.

"Yes. Interesting. Now, start again, and slightly stress the third beat in the bar. Good. It must be propulsive. Yes, always build to the third beat. Now come those staccato chords answering the theme. Make them a knife. Slash with them. But always cleanly, like a surgeon." Jack played into the second page, and Petrov kept on with his obbligato, sometimes mumbled, sometimes shouted. "Arpeggios like waves flowing down, then ritard, then again the waves. Stress the third bar of the four. Yes, the third: give it purpose. Destiny. Make it a search, a struggle. Always explore! Now this theme too. A mysterious, restless search." Jack started the Allegro's development, playing the octave alarums beginning the fugato. Petrov, gesturing for him to move over, sat down on the bench.

"Let me show you," he said. He began the fugal development, and he played with a concentrated hush which joined utter quiet to a shocking relentlessness, the counterpoint ineffably soft and clear and ceaseless. "Do you hear? This house, this city, this earth, how they vanish. Only the phrases you create remain." The pianist increased the volume of his playing and the pace to 138 as his hands began to play the louder, denser counterpoint of chords, and his fingers betrayed no curve of effort. "Your hands. They must be quiet. All violence, all danger, all pain will be like joyful laughter." His rigid hands produced great, explosive masses of clustered chords, the few missed notes lost in the relentless modulations from key to key. Amazed, Jack felt the troubled bulk of the old man's body by him on the bench. Just before the diminuendo into cantabile, Petrov sustained the final roaring chords with the pedal, and the virtuoso grabbed the top of the piano with clenched hands and outstretched arms.

He rose from the piano without speaking, walked to the cabinet to pour more Scotch, and then sat on the couch. He had taken two cigars from the humidor, and he insisted Jack try one. "Cubans. Illegal," he said and lit up now.

"You have an extraordinary capacity to listen, Jack. I've wanted to tell you that." It was clear he would not continue with the Hammerklavier; Petrov was settled, smoking on the couch, distracted and intent. Jack wandered to the couch opposite. He sat there and rested his unlit cigar on the coffee table in front of him.

"It's like your gift as a composer," Petrov said. "Your playing shows it, too. You hear in a transformative way. It touches me. It's a deeply attractive part of you. I mean it." He swallowed a mouthful of drink and suddenly grinned. "But, I tell you, even if I were attracted to you. Even if my penis grew in my pants, it would mean nothing. Because I honor your genius, and I do not choose fucking."

Jack stared speechless and amazed at the pianist. Suddenly he realized that the family's need—Petrov's, Joseph's, even Sarah's—was to fuck the intruder, to possess him body and soul. He felt that he plummeted somewhere out of time through a recurrent nightmare of misprision and assault.

"Do you know Rilke's Duino Elegies?" Petrov asked, breathing in his own smoke and unperturbed by Jack's glare. "Let me translate for you: An Angel is like Chartres…Or it is like music itself—in flight and transcendent. Or like the lover with her passion and despair. And yet you, Angel, dwarf all of these. Don't imagine that I desire you, Angel, and even if I desire you, you wouldn't come. For my cry is full of departure, mine—and yours. With the wind of my cry blasting from me, nothing can stay upright. Like a reaching arm, I cry, reaching to seize you, my open hand signaling before you, reaching, stretching, opening. As if fending off or, it may be, warning: You, unseizable one, high above."

Petrov sat, quietly possessed, on the beige couch. "Anyway, it's not *you* I desire. Not even your youth, though here you are like that giant angel before me. It's your capacity to hear profoundly, to create powerfully. It's your genius I love, and I don't want to fuck that."

Jack was listening, he thought, to the mad, not the dull moan and clack of usual madness, but the high, cracking scream of the extraordinarily mad. His acceptance must be the cause—or some deep kinship in him to the family's madness, or the allowance he offered this brilliant and disturbed spirit, the free rein he gave. Whatever its cause, Jack was alarmed by the license Petrov was taking.

"Sasha, I think I'm truly a member of the family now," Jack said angrily, and Petrov glanced at him sharply. "I'm moved by you, by your intimacy, your intensity, your vision, really. But my god, what are you doing? What are you saying? You upset me, Sasha. Restraint, some basic, needed restraint is missing. In your children too, I think. Do you know, most of all, you remind me of your son, of Joseph?"

Petrov, pained and exposed, stared now at Jack, the composer and recipient of Petrov's secrets, the lover of his daughter, the friend of his son.

"I hurt Joseph," he said, halting and intense. "I lacked, yes, the necessary restraint with him. Maybe, now, with you, too. But, Jack, he has a driven will! Impossible, even as a child. A will out of control. Nietzsche said, Lieber will noch der Mensch das Nicht wollen, als nicht wollen: man would rather will nothingness than not will—that is my son. And now he has tried to hurt his mother and me. Why? Because he's homosexual and I was not a hundred percent sympathetic? No, impossible. I care if his life is empty or full; otherwise there's nothing I would do either way. We all have pain. But to try recklessly to destroy yourself! Now, that lacks restraint." The old man's voice had become assured, detached, as if all this were what he had planned inevitably to say to Jack. "You know, I perform no more because of Joseph. Only my anniversary concert."

"You had a heart attack," Jack corrected, somber and dubious.

"Yes, I did. But I'd already quit. Let me tell you, he cannot bear me because of what I did to him. He cannot bear me to play. Even to breathe. I remember his last lesson with me, almost twenty years ago. I corrected him. In my way. I was smoking and telling him he made sloppy errors, a mess. Joseph began to shout obscenities at me. I think he was twelve. 'Fuck you, you fucker,' and things of that sort. I stared at him. Cold. I would not speak. Finally, I said, 'Leave the room, Joseph!' He came up to me, and he slapped the cigar from my mouth. I remember the burning ember there," Petrov said. Suddenly, he hurled his lit cigar beyond the dark oriental rug to the oak floor below the Steinway, and he pointed to the spot. "'Forgive me, forgive me,' the boy begged on hands and knees! But I neither looked nor spoke to him. My son went to the hall door there, and slammed it onto his hand. He fell crying to the floor. When I knelt over him, he shrank from me. You see, Jack. Fathers are evil incarnate."

Jack watched Petrov's trembling, stubbled face as he stared at the studio door. The composer felt sure it would open on some vision or apparition, perhaps that Sarah would be there, even that Joseph would appear. There was no one, nothing. No truce, no cherishing and reconciliation, no love offered or returned. Jack smelled the smoke from the thrown cigar, still burning on the polished oak floor of the music studio.

2

Waves of sound inundated him, sound alone, not harmony, not melody, not rhythm, only a dismembered roaring. Bits and pieces of the Hammerklavier flew past, mocked and transfigured by the roar. The sound—in no time or space he knew—filled his ears on the bed. By him were his parents. Julius reclined, unconscious, on the side away from him. Rosa held him closely, his face against her bosom. Her eyes were closed, and he smelled her fleshy, sleeping body. To his mute horror and fascination, his parents were transformed into Mr. and Mrs. Petrov. Sasha was numb and rigid on the bed, Helen fully awake, but absolutely still against him. Helen changed shape, unfolding into a youthful, gray-eyed woman, into Sarah who gripped him and held her roused body to him. Sarah stretched out against him and became Joseph who, scarred and paper-white, held him down with one arm and with the other pointed some vague weapon at his abdomen. Suddenly Joseph's shape merged with Petrov, on the verge of attack, of plunging a knife into him. He began to scream, the scream merging with the waves of disintegrating sound.

Jack awoke calling out in his Paloma house. He could not retrieve the images of his dream, only the dread and a memory of sound. He pulled on his clothes and clammily, groggily made himself coffee in the kitchen, taking the cup to his work table. He opened his notebook and looked at the slowly unfolding fragments he had sketched for the introduction to his sonata's fourth movement. He had struggled to free them from any restraint of bar line or tonal center or rhythmic structure or serial order, to allow the material an absolute liberty, the freest rein. The sequences he had written in the last ten days disclosed contortions and agonies of sound he had not foreseen; incidental consonances simply disintegrated before his eyes as he read through the lines of the introduction, up to the opening of the final fugue he had not and could not begin.

He remembered the sound of his dream, and he wanted now to recast parts of the movement's introduction, so that the roar of pure sound would become a sole recurrent, centering motif: a centering of pure, dread sound eating like acid at each tentative, freed and fragmentary transformation. In these acid pauses, time would stop, and the roaring sonic space would seem simultaneously full and utterly barren. He interspersed these new pauses now to punctuate the fragments he had already composed.

He heard mail being shoved in the box at the patio entrance. He opened the door, and the late morning sky was a clear, bright, overarching blue. A slight, salty breeze flowed from the Pacific. He walked to the box, and he saw Janice at the top of the stairs across the cement path, getting her mail from the metal bank of Ellison Hotel mail boxes. He felt an odd compassion for the tanned, thin, ageless woman, and wondered at the tie he had severed with her. She glanced curiously across the path, gave him a detached smile, and then swung open the glass door of the building, returning to her first floor apartment.

At his table, he opened the four envelopes he had gotten. One was from the Cleveland Institute of Music. His former teacher had responded; Erb would recommend him for a commission from the Gund and from the Portfolio performing group he helped direct. Another envelope held a Pacific Gas and Electric Co. bill. The third was from an old friend in Cleveland; Jay wrote a long, inchoate letter, indicating crisis, travel, disgust with Philosophy graduate school, and fondness—almost elegiac, at this distance—for Jack: he was going on a pilgrimage, he wrote, in his honor! Driving to Indianapolis, for he found that one of the composers Jack used to talk about was premiering a work there March 22, Ginastera's Second Piano Concerto. Jay was impulsive, even disturbed, but then Jack understood that a part of him too was mad, and so it seemed was a part of everyone to whom he drew close. The fourth envelope contained a card from his mother and father. Today was Thursday, March 15, his thirtieth birthday. Rosa's timing in such matters was nearly always perfect. He would save the fifty dollars they sent him: to extend his time to compose.

That afternoon, he again visited his injured friend in the hospital. Joseph would only occasionally lift a hand; he would not speak. Reconstructive surgery on his face was scheduled for next week, and if all went well, he would be out of his casts and mask by late spring.

In the early evening, Sarah drove him in her gray Jeep east on Sunset, on their way to the Greek Theater. She was giving him three birthday presents; two were on the back seat, and she said he should open them in the park they headed for. The third was tonight's concert for which she had bought tickets.

She turned north on Los Feliz, and the car radio played new rock of all sorts. As they made their way to Vermont and up Vermont to Griffith Park, they heard Crocodile Rock, You're So Vain, Walk on the Wild Side, and Killing Me Softly with His Song. After Roberta's slick, throaty ballad, Jack suddenly heard Richard Strauss pour from the speaker. "My god, what's that?" he said as Also Sprach Zarathustra disintegrated into pop-Brazilian dance music, replete with synthesizer and bongos. They listened to a minute of news—American Indians still at Wounded Knee, Watergate now heading toward a Congressional investigation. He watched her listening, the brushed silk of her hair, the ivory skin, the clarity and warmth of her glance as she drove. She had the air of intelligent, instinctive sensitivity which certain finely formed animals have, deer or gazelle.

She drove up the winding park road and stopped in the lot near Griffith Observatory. They walked along the paths, carrying a picnic basket, his wrapped presents, her camera, their coat and jacket. It was still warm with the sun just set beyond the hills and the sky a rare smog-less, deepening blue. They walked down a grassy incline and spread jacket and coat out on the dry, leaf-covered ground behind a bank of oleanders. Sarah began to unpack the meal she had made them: chicken baked with herbs—basil and oregano—and french bread and a salad of potatoes tossed in olive oil, lemon, and parsley.

"What are these?" Jack asked, holding up two plastic, champagne glasses.

"Open that," she said, pointing to one of his presents. He ripped the paper from the box, and he found inside, a bottle of Moet et Chandon resting on a rectangle of cold plastic. "Pour. I'll even have some."

As he popped open the bottle, she lifted her camera and began quietly shooting: the streaming of champagne into plastic glasses, Jack pushing a glass at her and then toasting the camera, one moment his arm stretched toward it, an eyebrow raised and a teasing mask of doubt and arrogance on his face; the next moment he was downing a glassful, his eyes wide, happy, focused nowhere. He tried to grab the camera from her, to take her picture, but she wouldn't have it. "The light," she said, "it's getting too dark."

They drank the rest of the champagne with his birthday dinner and then with éclairs she knew he liked. After, she had him open his second present. A record: Houses of the Holy. "It's very powerful, I think," she said. "And very advanced." They lay back next to each other, her hand in his, and dozed in the mild air beneath the oleanders.

Jack remembered hearing the band that played on the record she gave him. Two years ago, Jay had taken him to the Agora in order to initiate him into metal, as Jack had initiated his friend into Penderecki, Boulez, Ginastera, and the others. It was an early, small-scale tour, yet Led Zeppelin had the crisp power and excess of ambitious professionals. The songs shook the cavernous warehouse of a hall and bulldozed into the smoky, standing, hyped-up crowd. Always the music adhered to primitive forms, continually repeating the same harmonies, holding to blues and folk structures, improvising always on only a few notes and scales. Yet those improvisations rang and sputtered with electrified distortion coming from huge amplifiers. The guitarist took pleasure in a pure volume and violence of sound, in croaking speech-like noises, in a machine-like clank and roar. He shared the intensities he achieved with the singer whose penis seemed outlined beneath tightly stretched trousers. Long-haired and leaping, guitarist and singer exchanged riffs and phrases, and their shared music joined the sexual and the electric, male and female, the primitive and the technological. Yet their intensities had little purpose other than compelling display and spectacle, so that at a song's climactic scream, in self-celebration the guitarist lifted into the air the phallic totem of his instrument, electrified and still sounding. Jay had brought weed for them to smoke; it was the last time Jack had smoked dope. He felt his mind and body compress into a single, sensing instrument. The space expanded between him and his friend in the pressing crowd. Cleft, separate, and infinitely alone, he had risen into the isolating air where the waves of sound vibrated with their purposeless pulse. He wondered now about his openness to sound, whether Petrov for all his folly had yet been right, that his role and strength was to be a listener, or whether his hearing was actually a vulnerability, his flaw and failure.

Now, the sky above him was black and speckled with an extraordinary shimmering of stars. On his back, he stared up and thought he recognized Cassiopeia mother of Andromeda, the Gemini, Orion slain and slung up to the heavens, Andromeda herself saved from the monster of the deep, Venus, Mars.

Sarah stirred by him. He looked at her, his head in his hand, his elbow crooked on the ground. She gazed straight up at the stars, and she held her face still in a troubled mask.

"I'm sorry. I feel dead tonight," she said without moving or looking at him, her voice neutral and contracted.

He reached his arm to hold her waist and moved his body closer to protect, to comfort.

"I can't stop thinking about Joey, and Father. How much contempt there is between them. And I'm in the middle of all their hate and anger. Why do men have to use me to communicate? Men, with their penises, always trying to confront each other."

"Your brother's penis? Your father's?"

"Fuck, yes," she said and then paused. "I mean their goddamn insecurities, their insecure little egos. Enough is enough."

Her words stabbed. She was leading him into her hell, back to the place into which she was vanishing.

"And Father has started to talk about you. He feels threatened by you and me. He knows, and you're becoming a target. I have to talk to him. To make him understand." She turned on her side toward him, holding herself close to his sheltering limbs. "Jack, I don't know what to say to him."

She seemed to shrink in his arms, and he began to kiss her forehead, trying to revive her. She raised her head, and her mouth began to kiss his, blindly, with a sort of hysteria. She undid her skirt, he unzipped his jeans, and they began to stroke one another, hidden in the glade of bushes. Once joined with her, he looked out toward a glint of green beyond where they lay fucking under shelter of the oleanders—half humans fending off fear and fate, half animals desperately joining their bodies at the quick. Her delirium gripped Jack as she kept lifting her thighs hard, and he soon came with a sigh. She kept thrusting herself against his dull organ until she moaned and turned away. Then he sat cross-legged by her in the dark.

"Love can be very complicated, as your father once told me. It's unpredictable, that's for sure," he said, wryly smiling and looking at her back, hoping to penetrate the circle of distress which possessed her, constraining her voice, her spirit. "But really he meant any sort of love. The main thing is to honor its power, or it can destroy, no? I think that's what's happened to Joseph. It may have happened to your father and mother. Your father feels it, and he's worried."

"He's worried?" she said, doubt and irritation in her voice. Still she did not turn toward Jack, and he saw obscurely the dry eucalyptus and oleander leaves which had caught in her flowing hair.

"You talked about his insecurities—the same thing I'm trying to talk about. There's nothing you can do about it. Except support him and be kind. And prepare him, gently, without hurting, for your coming to live with me. Soon."

She rolled over to look directly at him. "I'm coming to live with you? Soon? Says who?" she said, smiling now.

""We'll live at my place, or we'll rent another apartment in Santa Monica or Venice."

"Could you do your work?" she asked, her voice high and lyrical.

"If there's a nook or a cranny," he said, pleased and ironic, "I'd go there and be alone enough to compose. Anyway, we can move to a larger place."

"You're an impossible person, and I love you," she said, sitting now cross-legged in front of him. Then she said cool and aloof: "I was a fool to fall for a man like you."

A blast of static walloped and rumbled the ground around them, and then a massive heartbeat began to burst in the air every second or so, as if the pulse of Griffith's earth were being miked and broadcast out for miles over Los Angeles.

Waves of mad laughter crashed over the hills and gullies around them, and a helicopter neared, louder and louder. Jack thought it headed for Sarah and him; he looked blankly at her, scrambled up, then understood, and both of them began to laugh. They were late. The concert had begun. The massive wattage of Pink Floyd's amplifiers a half-mile away in the Greek Theater blasted a huge crescendo of drum and guitar, and then Jack heard a skillful blend of pop-Hawaiian guitar, melancholy British voices, and synthesizer riffs.

They gathered their things to go to the open-air theater. Jack badly needed to piss, and he walked deeper into the bushes. Opening his zipper, he took out his penis, still moist from the wet of their arousal and coming. Sarah, he knew, used the pill to prevent conception. He thought of the myriad sperm and thousands of promised children smearing his fingers as he urinated onto the dry leaves below the poisonous bush.

❀   ❀   ❀

He parked his Bug and walked up the path with its blooming weeds and bushes. Last night, Sarah and he had gone to Ship's after the concert and sat in a booth, drinking coffee, for over an hour. Then she had driven her Jeep across Beverly Hills to the base of her driveway at two in the morning, letting him off so he could take his VW home. Before she drove the rest of the way up the asphalt drive, he asked her if she would be safe. He could see the house ablaze with lights in every window; Petrov must have stayed awake, waiting to greet her with his wrath and worry. She said she would be okay and disappeared up the hillcrest. Jack had waited, leaning against his car in the dark, and he heard no sound, only saw the lights systematically extinguished in the first floor windows.

Now he rang the bell next to the weathered, front door. It was early Friday afternoon, and soon he would be driving Sarah to the hospital to visit Joseph. Almost immediately the door swung open. Petrov stood before him. The pianist had several days' growth of stubbly gray beard, his fringe of white hair grew unkempt, and his bald pate had a gray pallor. His white shirt hung loose, not tucked into his trousers.

"I have something to say to you, young man." His hand seized the younger man's arm in a steely grip and pulled to bring him indoors. Jack grabbed the doorposts and wrested himself free.

"Is Sarah in?" he said, shocked and the adrenaline beating in his low voice.

"Sarah is home," Petrov said, decisive and intensely frustrated. "I beg to speak with you. Please come in," he said formally, slowly enunciating each word as if it were dangerous to speak, and the words dangerous to cross.

He walked with Jack down the hall and took short, intent steps in his slippers. Jack smelled the unbathed man next to him and the Scotch on his breath. In the music studio, Petrov pulled the green curtain shut against the smoggy glare. He stood there, gesturing for Jack to sit, and he began to speak.

"I am never reconciled! That is my secret, the secret to all my life and my art. And I will never be reconciled to you. To your nihilism."

"My nihilism!" Jack said, disbelieving what he heard. He sat on the red velvet chair in the open mouth of the U of old couches.

"Yes, your nihilism! The wayward naiveté of your decadence! The cynical pleasure in destruction that is your music! Why, my Poèmes Juifs are greater than anything you'll ever compose."

Jack was dumbfounded by the ire and gall he heard from the virtuoso, yet a part of him silently waited for whatever would come next.

"And the nihilism of your behavior! Making love to my daughter in my own house! While I slept! Nihilistic, decadent! Pathetic!" Petrov seemed to gasp for air now.

"Your parents! I remember when they lived in Los Angeles and we helped them, in the forties. Oh yes, we did! Your father had a heart murmur, it kept him from the Army, and they lived in a hovel, in the Fairfax ghetto—they were so miserably poor, jobless, pathetic. I helped him get work. And now I helped you. *This* is how you repay me! I let you into my home, I revealed things to you, my secrets. I trusted you!" He was shouting now. "But you are hardly my friend! How dare you!"

"I am your friend, Sasha. And I love your daughter. Surely you realize...it's a wonderful thing, Sasha. You must understand. What are you really saying?" Jack had succeeded in interrupting the onslaught of the old man, who paced to and fro before him. He wanted to wake Petrov from the nightmare which trapped him, to lead him out of hell.

"What am I saying! You're taking my daughter away from me as if it were nothing, and you ask what am I saying. I told you, don't play the anarchist with her. Have you lost your hearing? Don't you listen anymore! Don't you understand how essential she is to me? This precious spirit, whose soul lives in her voice. I, I need her!" he screamed in a wrenched and frightened cry. "And she says she's moving out! With you!"

"Oh my god," Jack said. "Don't you see, Sasha? Sarah will always be here when you need her. I'm a lot like you, Sasha. I love and need her, too. Please, use restraint...you know what I mean. Please, remember. Don't hurt Sarah; don't hurt your daughter."

"Hurt her! I hurt her! Never!" Petrov jerked himself up to the seated man and shouted bitterly across the few feet between them. "How dare you! Who are you to come into my house and judge me? As if I were no one. Nothing. Where is your robe, Jack! Your bench!"

Jack's heart faltered. Always listening as deeply as he could, he felt incapable of the graced and necessary speech to salve Petrov's pain, to confirm the friendship which had developed in this room over these six months. His words had failed to divine any ground of mutual acceptance, to restore the sense of kinship between them. It would take a different larynx, a different mode from any he could now summon to lead him out of the inferno of fear and anger, which trapped the old man in front of him. Yet suddenly words again blurted from his mouth.

"I didn't mean to judge, Sasha. I love her, and I'm only worried that she's hurting now. I want to help."

"Hurting? I am the one who hurts," he cried out.

"I know, I know. We're each of us in pain, Sasha. We all need healing, and she will help you. Let me help you too. But Sasha, please, Sarah also needs..."

"Don't give me your comfort!" the old man shouted, violated and incensed. "I don't need this crap coming from your mouth. Bring me a father who's lost a daughter he loves as much as I. Him I'd listen to. Because his pain lasts the length and breadth of time. Because all his comfort turns to rage, which before could solace woe with words, and agony with music."

Petrov began to moan and weep the tears of the possessed, of maddened gall and self-absorption. He stood wringing his hands a few feet from the composer, who sat frozen with amazement before the wild, looming old man. Jack thought he heard Sarah pacing above them on the second floor.

Petrov looked up to the ceiling. "Sarah," he cried out in an agonized screamed chant, "Sarah, Sarah, Sarah, Sarah." He was stretching his arms out in a gesture of crucifixion or importuned embrace. Then his voice contracted to an inner whimper, "Take pity on your drunken father. Forgive me my trespasses."

The virtuoso lowered his arms, and now he stared, seething and contemptuous, at Jack. "I will forgive you all. You spoiled dead boys, you anarchists of sex, you plunderers of music, you sons of bitches. You are all made in the image of the beast. And carry his mark!" Breathless with rage, Petrov was holding his groin, the shiny black fabric bunched in his hand, and then he lifted his hands up, wringing them violently a few inches in front of Jack's face which was wide-eyed with panic and dismay. "And you will fall down on your knees before me, and weep. Or I'll take your hearing hostage, and keep the key forever." He reached his big, veined hands out. They trembled on either side of Jack's head.

Petrov smashed his hands together onto the composer's ears just as Jack unfroze, on guard and in motion. He grabbed at the old man's thick wrists and held them in both hands. He struggled up from the chair. His ears were ringing, his eyes blurred. Possessed, heavier than Jack, and inches taller, Petrov fought back, and they reeled together across the music room. Suddenly Jack let go of the wild man's wrists. Petrov plunged backwards, smashing his back against the curtain. The glass door shattered with a cracking roar behind the cloth. The sun and smoggy air streamed in over Petrov who sat on the floor, his shoulders draped in green.

"Out, get out of here," he screamed as his breathing heaved, "out of this house."

Jack stepped forward to see if the crazed old man needed his help.

"Get out," Petrov shouted. "You'll never step foot in my house again."

Jack opened the door to the hall. Holding the wooden edge in his hand, he felt again the panicked terror which held him in the red armchair. He shut the door. His ears still rang, and he stood in the dark hall, amazed at Petrov's extremity and his own paralysis before it.

Sarah stood halfway down the stairs at the end of the hall. "Go, Jack," she said in a cracking, broken voice. "I'm so sorry." She scurried the rest of the way down the stairs, opened the music studio door, and hurried across the studio. Jack stood frozen, watching from the hall. She leaned down, kneeling by him on the fallen drape, and she reached to hold Petrov's bald head in her hands.

"Father," she said gently, "should I get you a doctor? Poor Father."

"No, my Sarah," his voice was hoarse and piteous.

Tears filled her eyes, and she said, "So much anger, so much violence, so unnecessary. Poor father, poor lost father. So desperate. And for what? Jack and I would always…"

"Still Jack!" Petrov said. He moaned deeply, yet their hands remained entwined. "I need you, Sarah. Your being here."

"But I would come, and you have Mother."

"No, you must stay here!" he cried with urgency and despair. "Don't you see what your mother has done to me! I love her. I love her deeply. But is it love in her, that she patronizes me! That behind my back she insults me. I hear! Is this love, that she never returns my love? Never! Sarah, I'm afraid, afraid. I'm utterly alone. In this house. In my mind. Help me, Sarah. Help. Oh help," he cried, and his face wept as she held it against her. "A little patience. A little gentleness. Please, please. I'm a frightened old man. Don't leave me, Sarah."

Jack pulled himself away, hurrying down the hall.

A hissed whisper came from the dining room he passed. "Jack!"

He looked in and saw Helen Petrov sitting at her end of the dining table, near the credenza with the vegetation gods her father had carved on its doors. She hunched in her flowered housecoat, her face livid with knowledge and impatience.

"Jack, come here. Sit," she said, gesturing to the chair by her. He walked over and stood between her and the ornate chest.

"I heard him," she hissed out, cold and intense. "The madman. Raving at you. He has done worse to me, Jack. Poèmes Juifs, indeed. One would think he were a Zionist. I remember him, booming like a Nazi, he could not even decide to leave. It was I who convinced him. And it wasn't for me, I wasn't the Jew, but I made him leave his precious Berlin in thirty-eight, almost too late. I went up to him and screamed and shook him so he'd take me and his Swiss bank-books out of hell. Horrid. Horrible! And now he raves about his Poèmes Juifs. One would think he invented the tone-row! The big, pathetic man. And yet, Jack, my husband is a great man."

She looked closely now at the pale young man in shock before her. "Too bad, Jack. We'll never see you again." She stretched out her swollen hand to him. "Good-bye," she said, and they shook hands formally, like two, pleasantly parting, haut-bourgeois acquaintances.

As he fled the house, Jack's mind burst from the surfeit of grotesqueness he never thought possible. Blindly, desperately, he raced down the path through the smog to Benedict Canyon Road and his car. He saw father, mother, and daughter as nightmare phantoms, ever looming and pursing him. He forgot now that these same Petrovs—enraged, betraying, bitter—led parallel lives of struggling tenderness, generous intelligence, difficult hallowing love, even prophetic grace.

3

A dozen men and women were selected and assembled outside a large Quonset hut like those found on army bases or near nuclear installations. Each test subject was a Festival participant, either a musician or composer. They milled around in the sunny little garden cultivated at the entrance, exchanging their speculations about what the experiment involved. A woman said it concerned the measurement of sensitivity to subtle gradations of sound. A man believed the researchers tested the responses of humans to those pitches which certain animals use to communicate but which exceeded human hearing. Another subject thought that the twelve had been selected to measure their capacity to detect paranormal phenomena. One person at a time was admitted to the oversized hut by a bearded doctor with glasses. He smiled benignly and wore a white, laboratory coat. Egress after the experiment was through a separate door so that the untested had no contact with the tested. He was the last subject.

After an interminable wait, his turn came. The doctor, ushering him through a fluorescent-lit hall, explained that he would be provided with a score of music particularly suited to his being. He would hear this music from hidden speakers in the testing chamber. Afterwards, he would be subject to an extensive debriefing interview and questionnaire. The doctor opened a door like a space-lock, at the end of the hall, and he brought him into a circular room, completely gray from floor to ceiling. In the middle of the chamber, he sat on a chair, and a nurse attached sensors to his skin, his chest, his arms, his head. Before the doctor left, he explained the experiment's objective. It was to test his ability to sense if God were present at Graf.

The lights were diminished, and he was alone. Flickering shadows were now detectable on the curving walls of the chamber. In the low light, he saw the score on a table placed by him. He carefully reached for the slim volume so as not to disrupt the sensors bound and sticking to him. He wondered what other test subjects had been assigned, Bach or rock, Brahms or Berio. The score he held in his hands was a posthumous work by Schoenberg. Suddenly he was acutely aware of the silence in the flickering chamber. Its acoustic surface absorbed even the sound of his breathing. It was a depth of silence he had never before experienced. He opened the page of the score. There were no notes inked on the staves.

Jack awoke on his bed, fully clothed, with shoes and jacket still on. His limbs felt pummeled. Breathing was painful. Exhaustion held him as he made his way into the bathroom to urinate and the kitchen to make coffee. Every sound he heard seemed now a gift, the slip and clap of his shoes, the gurgle of piss in the bowl, the singing of water from the faucet, the toot of his fart, the hiss of the burner. Schoenberg had written no absolute farewell, no such declaration of an end to music. Yet he had come close, closer yet in the dream Jack began to forget.

He took his coffee cup to the table, sat, and reached for his 1972 notebook. On a middle page, he had noted some of the compositions from a program mailed to him that summer. He read some of the titles of works performed then at the Graf Festival: Constellazini, Dies Irae, Musica polymetrica, Polytrope, Strata, Unisons, Variationen, What's Next. He closed the notebook. His breathing was still oddly labored, and he went to the couch, stretching out and taking slow, conscious breaths.

Again he fought with the demonic old pianist. He twisted on the couch in repulsion and defense against his memory. He wanted to cry, to cry out. His eyes welled without tears. Poor father, she had wept. Help, Petrov had cried, help, oh help.

Collapsed in his car, he had driven down Sunset, autos honking at his slow pace, his erratic steering. At the base of Sunset, he must have stopped the car along the Pacific Coast Highway, for he remembered walking on the coast there. Waves dashed against outcroppings of rock and flooded the narrow band of sand. He lay curled in a foetal posture on a widening beach, and he fell into a dead, beaten sleep. Then he drove home at sunset and wandered to his bed. He slept immediately, fully clothed, until his dream of silence woke him.

Sorrow engulfed him, for himself, for Sarah, and for Petrov, who had tried to deafen him as he sat in shock, stock still on the chair before the assault. Only once before in his life had he felt so frozen in the face of menace and dismay. The summer between college and graduate school, he had backpacked through Europe. He stepped through the swinging glass doors of the State Classical Archeology Museum in Berlin, and an abject terror seized and paralyzed him. He could neither advance nor retreat. Hundreds of naked men and women stared at him from stone and plaster faces. The gods were ranked in rows, each poised in the gesture of his myth, about to step out of eternity, to confront Jack and enact his deepest dreaming. There were Apollo and Athena, Eros, Medusa, Dionysus. Finally he found himself able to move, and he fled from the concentration camp of stone.

Lucky Jack possessed the unwitting charm of one who walks where angels fear, yet this had costs he began only gropingly to see: Blood and paradox mark the entry to the heart of life, mark any opening to the gods' descent in water, earth, sun, and sound itself. He struggled with a vague, troubled sense of his openness to such descent, his vulnerability to the fateful incursions and ambiguities. All depended, he thought, on his readiness, his willingness to struggle, his refusal of passivity even as he would not, and could not, refuse his openness.

He reached for the phone by his head, put it on the floor, and dialed the Petrovs' number. There was a connection after four rings.

"Hello," Petrov said. Jack paused and decided.

"Sasha, let me talk." The line went dead. He tried again, but there was no answer. He hardly knew what he would have said to him or to her if he reached her: that he was desperately hurt by Sasha's violent breakdown, and yet he knew that they all—Joseph, Sarah, Helen, and Jack—had driven him to this break point, and he felt such sorrow. Yet they must all keep trying. His choice, he knew, would be to persevere.

That summer, six years ago in Berlin, Jack had steeled himself, returned to the museum, and seen the frozen denizens of Olympus. He walked from row to row of statues, exploring the hall of gods and humans, containing the entire pantheon—from Zeus and Leda, through Achilles and Athena, to Orpheus, Clytemnestra, and Joscasta.

It was noon now, and he fixed himself a sandwich of Monterey Jack, sliced tomato and lettuce in Arabic bread, with shriveled black Greek olives. As he sat to munch and sip a Coke, he realized he had eaten nothing for twenty-four hours. After lunch, he opened his notebook. He would struggle to begin the fugue to end his sonata. The essential theme must wind its way out of the tentative, searching liberties and the obliterating noise and silence of the introduction. He wanted this new, winding, cascading, struggling theme to echo the main fugal subject of the Hammerklavier. What Beethoven in his late works had done to Bach—joyously plundering, adapting, absorbing and transforming the play with line and gesture, counterpoint and cadence: that was what Jack wanted to do with Beethoven. To celebrate and transform, to swipe his music and play joyously with it in this murderous time as the eighth decade of the century wound its third year tighter and his own third decade came to an end. He inked in a dissonant, streaming theme, and he made the counter theme a melody of absences, always oblique, always suggesting the chromatic notes missing at any moment in the main theme. In this way through streaming and obliquity, through theft and struggle, the field of tones and of his deepest creative impulses would be exposed, sing, and cry out.

In the weeks which followed, Jack worked on his triple fugue. He sketched episodes which travestied and transformed the music of Schoenberg, Bartok, and Stravinsky, absorbing their onus and impetus into the grateful motion of his work. On April 1, he made still another call to the Petrovs. For two weeks he had tried without success to reach Sasha or Sarah. To his dismay, even she would hang up when he called. And at the hospital, when he visited Joseph, unspeaking still and swathed anew after the operation on his face, Sarah was never there. She must have decided to avoid any possibility of meeting, to visit her brother only when Jack would not be there.

Yet he tried calling every few days. On the first of April—the day after Joseph left the hospital—Sarah answered the phone at their house, and she stayed on the line when he said hello.

"How have you been?" she asked politely, as if all were as usual and these weeks had not passed—as if the two of them were thrown back six months to October.

"Oh my god, Sarah," he said, "you'll speak to me."

"How have you been?" she said again, her extraordinary voice diminished, constrained.

"Not good at all. How else could I be?"

"I understand," she said with implacable detachment.

Almost in compensation for the straight-jacket of her voice, compassion and sorrow rose in him. "Sarah, tell me how you are."

"Joseph came home yesterday," she said, still muted but with greater purpose now. "We fixed his room with a hospital bed. He has begun to speak." She sounded as if she reported weather changes or plane departures. "He calls Father maestro. When the ambulance brought him, he said, 'I hope the Maestro doesn't mind my staying in his house.' Father said, 'I'm glad you're here.'" Suddenly she was hurried. "Things are back to normal. I have to go."

"But, Sarah, tell me how you are. Can we see each other?"

"That's not possible. Good-bye."

In the mornings and evenings, then, Jack began to take hour-long walks along the coast, near the clapping surf, and he would return to work, clear and determined. After two weeks of his regimen, he felt exhausted, as if he had fallen into a pit of ink and the ocean had too few drops to wash him clean, too little salt to purge the sweat and taint of his labor. In need of rest, he stopped composing, his fugue almost a quarter completed.

On Monday, April 16, he drove down Santa Monica Boulevard, dropped his income tax forms in the mail just in time. He stopped by one of the single-story buildings a score of blocks from the Pacific. Browsing among the art books and novels, the paperbacks of philosophy and poetry in Papa Bach, he lighted on a used volume of Rilke. He had read the Sonnets to Orpheus as an undergraduate, but not the Elegies. In defiance of the lion's mouth, he thought, he bought the book. He took it home to his Paloma bungalow and sat with it open at his table.

The high, clear wind of the poems blew through and around him. He read first the Sonnets to Orpheus, how they strove to build a temple inside his hearing, to hallow and revive, to affirm that song was reality, like nothing for a god, but when could humans be real? He found the poem To Music, its declaration of a language beyond language, the breathing of gods. Then he steeled himself to explore the Duino Elegies, first searching for the passage Petrov had recited. It was in the Seventh, and he found that Petrov had mistranslated it intentionally, it must be, subtly deflating its wooing of eternity into blank desire. Yes, that was how Petrov read and listened; the power of his will grasped and reshaped all he heard. There was a kinship between them, Jack realized then: how much they shared in the willful, transformative ways each listened and felt. Despite the sad collision between them, there was—he thought—a not unlike effort of visionary hearing in his struggle to compose and in Petrov's playing. It was reading Rilke that helped him to see this. As he read further he found passages on hearing the call of the archaic torso of Apollo, the message which formed itself out of silence, the wave upon wave of anguish transformed into praise and jubilation.

❦   ❦   ❦

Late every morning and afternoon through April and into May, he lolled about the patio, sunbathing in his cut-offs on the recliner. The chair's strips of plastic stretched under his body's weight, marking his tanned skin. The flat and lazy banana leaves, the bushy bamboo, and the short palms lined the edges of his patio, giving him privacy. Oblivious to the noise of passers-by, he opened himself to the sun, taking in its healing heat and light. He felt that some knowledge like compassion flowed through him, a tempered acceptance, harmed by fate yet still open. His body seemed to drink in the infinity of light the sun shed on him, as if he were himself a constellated body stretched out in the vast heavens. His arms and legs relaxed over the frame of chrome and plastic. He felt as if his face and limbs were the receptacle through which flowed neither ego nor sex nor power, but an openness to the void.

"Jack," a voice said at his gate. His eyes, blinded in the sun, saw only a flood of white. He sat up, his legs swinging from the chaise to the cement patio. Finally his eyes adjusted to the afternoon light. Janice was peeking over the wooden slats.

"How are you, Jack?"

"All right."

"Do you have a minute?"

"Sure."

She opened the gate and sat on one of the dilapidated director's chairs near him. She wore a black bikini. The thin bones of her shoulders and face showed beneath her tan.

"How are you?" he said.

"Okay, I guess." She stared at his tanned indifference, sitting on the chaise. "You know you used me, Jack."

"What?" He looked nonplussed at the woman with her blackish-purple hair cut short now, her fine-boned, weathered face, her tanned body.

"You cut me. Last November. Fucked me and threw me away."

Jack had not the words or will to voice his thoughts. He saw that the indifference and even the fleeting compassion he felt for her now were equally self-deceiving.

"I'm sorry," he finally said. "I should have been honest."

"Yeah. Another should've. I've heard it before."

"I got involved with another woman, Janice. With her family, really. Obsessed. But it's over now."

"Were you as honest with them as you were with me?"

Her face was bitter, and again he could not reply. There were so many levels of obsession to answer on, no, to answer for. He could not separate one from another.

"I quit my job in February," he said.

"I can see you're not working."

He did not tell her he had been working on his sonata, morning, noon and night. The final fugue was almost half finished, and he felt drained, emptied, in need of the hours he spent in the sun: the suspension and renewal which the light and stillness yielded. When she left, he went indoors to his table and his work.

She began visiting him when he sunbathed, sometimes catching him on her way home from work baking and cooking at the café. She had cut her hair short, and she said she was beginning to feel hopeless about life. Everyone she knew felt it too, as if head and heart and hands were disconnected from each other. Maybe it was her age, or the times, or the Nixon thing: the government falling apart. The Watergate Hearings began to be broadcast on TV, and they both were watching when they could. Finally, Jack invited her in. When he closed the door, she reached her hand to his. The sun streamed through the lace at the windows. He kicked off his cut-offs, she slipped out of her bathing suit, and in the bedroom, they fell to the mattress in a blind swoon of fucking.

Jack stopped composing. Janice began to stay the night at his unkempt house across from the Ellison. She brought over an airline bag with changes of clothes, toiletries, cosmetics. One morning, he found an empty bottle of hair dye on the bathroom sink and stains of purple on the porcelain and floor. He cleaned, and he cooked for them.

Occasionally he looked at the three movements he had completed of his sonata. Janice came up to him at the table.

"What's that?"

"A sonata. I'm working on it," he lied. He looked at the curve of her tan breast at eye level to him.

"I remember your playing part of it."

"It's in praise of your beauty."

"You're kidding."

"No. It's in such an elevated style that no man will ever have come over it."

"No man will ever come over me?" She laughed and poked his ribs.

Together they would lounge on the couch and watch the Watergate Hearings on a black and white portable Jack had purchased. White House aides testified in front of the Senators—Ervin fat and unflappable, his southern accent giving a down-home imprimatur to his sharp barbs and love of law, Inouye the undaunted, righteous alien, Baker debonair, punctilious and efficient.

Janice was out shopping one afternoon in early June. Jack sunbathed on the patio. When he went inside, he sat at his table and re-opened the notebook he had stopped working in. He saw the fragment of flowing fugue cut off in mid-flight. Just after the last notes he had inked on the page weeks ago, he began now to write a journal entry.

June 4: Is this fucking trash I've written? My disorientation is complete. I'm stumbling ahead. My fulcrum has shifted finally away from Benedict Canyon, away from the Petrovs' possessed and troubled souls. I live on the western rim now, the ocean's edge. I've drifted into the arms of a woman whose waves of short hair form a purple aureole on the pillow next to me when we wake. She holds me in the morning sun and asks, "Are you comfortable, honey?" Yes, and more. So why do I distrust this comfort? Am I so ruled by my generation's insatiability? My comfort and self-acceptance with her seem unacceptable. And anyway, how can I be entitled?

The sunny room suddenly soaked up all noise from man or car, sealing Jack's ears with silence. The Viennese Jew, sallow now beneath his tan, groped to the stuffed armchair. Beethoven's nephew followed, sitting on a straight chair at the end of the table by Jack. Karl's thin voice penetrated the silence.

"I couldn't stand it anymore. I climbed that hilly mountain near Baden, and I put a bullet in my scalp. But I had already vanished. I, Karl, did not exist. I was merely an extension of his punishing resentments and confusions, an actor in his drama, serving his needs. Yet never could I please him. And I didn't succeed in suicide either. Only later could I feel reconciled; he was dying, and part of me was dead already. Death is liberation!"

Jack wanted to solace this bitter boy, to reach out to the shade, to the pith and pain buried deep inside nephew and uncle both. He wanted to say that not only death, but life too could liberate and soothe. Yet it was not possible. Karl withdrew toward the door, and now the bald genius sitting in the armchair spoke. His remote, insistent voice became the sole sound Jack heard.

"The composer uses a language he does not comprehend and reveals a wisdom he cannot bear to follow," the bald Jew said, his eyes fixing Jack in their imperious gaze. "When you find your own vision unbearable and leave it unfinished, it is a disaster. If you let your work collapse, it will become reduced to the merely human: they will say, this hate is there, or that painful love. Yet your deepest music should expose the true morphology of feeling where sadness and happiness, love and hate, are one: the identical form can subsume each."

Beethoven, disheveled and impatient, barged through the swinging kitchen door. He stood between Jack and the old man in the armchair, to whom he said: "Silence, you're the best heir of my inventions. Do right by me, and be merry! I've surveyed this kitchen and find it lacking. Where are the beans to grind for coffee? There are only cans of grounds. And no Hungarian wine. Only brandy: do you want my liver to shrivel into a green sponge? Good cousin, enough hectoring and lecturing. For an eternal watchman like you to talk and babble is most tolerable, and not to be endured. We are all ancient and most quiet watchmen, and our waking sleep would not offend, but inspirit and transcend."

He glanced at his nephew who glowered from a straight chair he had pulled away from the table. Then, the composer sat in a chair next to Jack who stared through wide open eyes at his visitor with an electric haze of hair on his head.

Cantankerous and curious, he stared back. "If I were tedious as a king," he said, pointing to the bald composer on the armchair, "I'd be tempted to bestow all the tedium in the world on him." He put the open notebook in front of him and took Jack's pen in hand. "The body of your discourse is sometimes guarded with fragments," he bellowed, marking, rearranging, inking in new notes. "We before you are also desperate. Yet we composed, and we endure. You must create imposed shapes fierce enough to survive the death of your ears, your brother, your child." He lifted the pen from the staves, stood, and gestured for the Viennese Jew to follow. He glanced about the living room, at the papers and dirty plates on the floor, at Janice's panties on the rug in front of the couch.

"When my listeners sobbed before me," he said as he disappeared, "I laughed. I called them fools and asses. I told them: Do not receive without giving. Use your mind and gut, not only tear ducts and dick. And when I was alone, as I must be to compose, I looked above my desk to read again the motto of Isis framed there: I am all, what is, what was, what will be."

One Friday in mid-June, Jack sat riveted on the couch, watching and listening as the Senators and their Counsel moved moment by moment closer to some clenching revelation about Nixon and the White House.

"I've not heard this one," Janice said, sitting on the floor next to Jack's shelves of records, fingering through the rock and jazz. She held up Houses of the Holy. "Let's listen."

"Not now. Let's listen to the Hearings. They're..."

"I'll play it soft," she said and put the record on the player.

"I am sorry to interrupt you," Baker said, "but tell me again, exactly at this point, and as you understand it. What did the President know, and when did he know it?"

Led Zeppelin's patented sunshine lyrics fought their way into the room, and after a few minutes, Jack turned off the television.

"You know, I've started to work," he said, but his voice was blotted out by a breathlessly driven song with violently associative lyrics about the woman next door.

"I don't think this is working out, Janice."

The side ended, and she did not turn over the record. She sat by him and softly stroked his arm.

"What's wrong?"

"It's not working, Janice. I clean and cook, and sometimes I feel like I'm turning into your smiling slave. And I've started to compose again. I'm trying to be honest. With you, with myself."

"You know you like it with me, Jack."

"I like it. I like you."

"Is there someone else?"

"No. No one. It's my fault. I just don't think I can live with anyone. I need to be alone. It's my own obsession. I need to compose, and I need to be alone to do it."

She got up and walked through the hall to the bedroom, then noisily to the bathroom. She returned with her airline bag clutched in her arms.

"I guess that's it, Jack. You're like my main man in the sixties, my folkie love, and I should have known better than to get involved with another musician. You're no virgin hippie, but you come close. You're a god-damn pleasant son-of-a-bitch, Jack."

She slammed the door on the way out, leaving him in the empty room. The amplification of electric silence trembled from his speakers.

4

Jack drove north onto the Pacific Coast Highway, past the cliffs at the end of Wilshire and Ocean. On the way to Malibu, a sign finally said Sunset. There was a restaurant on his left, overhanging the clump of rocks jutting into the Pacific. Swerving right, he drove east on Sunset Boulevard.

He climbed past a meditation center and some sprawling Pacific Palisades homes; dipped down a hill by Will Rogers' ranch; sped by Rockingham (where Schoenberg had lived), and crossed the San Diego Freeway at Sepulveda. His VW slightly skidded down the hill past Veteran, and he put on his brakes to see the towering steel and glass city which was UCLA nestling below Bel-Air and above Westwood. He passed mansions obliterating any sight of golf-courses, of the city itself; raced through Beverly Hills but slowed as he passed Benedict and the hotel; then sped past the gated mansions of gangsters and corporate owners, stars and thieves. He ascended toward Hollywood, and near the French and Scandinavian (among other) restaurants between La Cienega and Fairfax, he turned north on Wetherly Drive (where Stravinsky had lived) and climbed into the Hollywood Hills.

He stopped his VW in front of a ragged lawn, yellowing in the smoggy afternoon. Rosebuds and camellia blossoms clustered on irrigated bushes ringing the one-story house. Brian had called and invited him to Sunday dinner. As soon as he stepped foot across the threshold, Jack's ears were filled with studio gossip and gripes. It did not cease as Brian's family swirled around him, his harassed American wife preparing food in the kitchen, the son and daughter, nine and eleven, playing a game of Monopoly in the middle of the living room rug. Jack watched the children, their engagement of each other and the game, their seeming obliviousness to the adults around them. The son was a loud, towheaded miniature of his father. The daughter was a blossoming redhead, spontaneous and curious, who looked up at the adults from time to time, registering their cautions and absurdities. The children lacked any trace of their father's British inflection.

Brian and Jack, beers in hand, took rib steaks outside to the grill.

"Shit, Jack," Brian said as he prodded the barbecue with a long fork, "I could have used your help. Jerry left, you left, and then Peckinpah—actually it was Carroll, the producer—took the music editing away from me. You left me in the lurch."

"Jesus, Brian. I'm sorry. You don't know: things only got worse for me."

"*You* don't know. I was without a project for three months. If it weren't for the union, we wouldn't have made the mortgage payments. We'd be in the streets."

The two men sipped beer, each the survivor of a different war. Jack watched Brian's children sneaking up in back of him, and with wild, hugging abandon, they leapt on their father, the son on his back, the daughter on his side.

"Oh dear. Shit!" he laughed. Putting his beer down, he collapsed on the grass.

The next day was Monday, June 25. Jack watched John Dean sit in blazing TV lights before the senators. He was blond and clean-cut; hesitant at first, he began to read a statement. The earnest, soul-less good soldier reported with phenomenal compulsiveness on the conversations he had with his leader and on each Presidential directive he followed. Here was the moment of implication and complicity: the smoking gun, they called it—a murder and suicide, both.

That afternoon, Jack returned to work on the sonata's last movement. He would mark it Risoluto, in travesty and homage to the Hammerklavier's final fugue. Day and night, he sat composing at his table, and as he worked, he would mark the days with incidental annotations in his journal. On July 6, Klemperer died, and Jack realized he had not noted Picasso's death April 8 or Kertesz's drowning April 16. On July 16, Alexander Butterfield testified that Nixon had taped every conversation in the Oval Office of the White House. On July 28, Skylab 3 Astronauts began a try at living for two months on the outpost revolving slowly in deep space. On August 1, he received a phone call from Joseph. He wanted to see Jack.

It was nearly sunset that evening, when the pianist drove down the narrow lane of Speedway and parked a used MG, its top down, by his friend's bungalow. Outside his living room window, Jack glimpsed Joseph's head of black hair, inches longer than before and tinted brownish orange by the lowering sun.

The two men shook hands at the door. Joseph walked slowly with a limp and made his way to sit on the couch. A light red network of lines exfoliated over the edges of his face, branching beneath his shock of hair, in front of his ears, trailing down his jaw.

"I'm glad you're better," Jack said, sitting on the stuffed armchair.

"I'm lucky to be alive," Joseph said hoarsely. His hand trembled slightly as he lifted a glass of Coke toward his face. Before he drank, he looked at Jack and said: "They say the scars will fade."

"Have you been able to play, to practice?"

"Yes. The Maestro and I share the piano now. But he's deteriorating, Jack. I guess it started earlier. I'm sorry he put you through such shit, that we all did."

Jack held himself back; it was impossible for him to express the complexity of his feelings about Sasha, his hurt and his love, let alone his questions about Sarah.

"Now," Joseph said, "he pores over works he composed decades ago. In the forties. His Symphony. His Poèmes Juifs, which he wants to perform in October, at his anniversary concert. Along with the Hammerklavier!"

"Your father went through part of the Hammerklavier with me in March. He played like a demon. It was amazing. But his Poèmes Juifs. I saw them on the piano once. They're not so great. They're…"

"They're shit. And I made the mistake of telling him so. I'm still making mistakes he can't forgive me for. What I should be doing is accepting him. His life. And my own. What does Nietzsche say? Always affirm. Lead me into life and towards the death which life eternally witnesses."

Jack laughed softly.

"Why are you laughing?" Joseph said. He stared pointedly from his lined, distressed face, and he shifted now on the couch to ease his legs.

"Your father was fond of quoting Nietzsche, too. Not that I mind." Jack could not help himself: he felt an upwelling compassion for these tortured spirits. But he remained wary of their incestuous involutions—in father, son, mother, and daughter. He wanted to ask Joseph questions, invasions of his melancholy, his troubled wistfulness, his convoluted privacy, yet he asked only one.

"How is Sarah?"

"That's one reason I came. I'm worried about her, Jack. She's hitting bottom, under the pressure of our fucking family."

A responsive force filled Jack, as if through Joseph's words Sarah's need reached toward him, to the buried cords and muscle deep within. His arms and hands stretched over the arms of his chair. "If only I could talk with her," Jack said with a full voice. "I can help her, I can give her what…"

"Sure, just leave it to you—tanned and healthy Jack, right!" Joseph's voice was volatile and sarcastic; the injured man leaned forward on the couch. "No. No, all you can do for her is listen…if she'll talk with you. Your caring, your protection, and all the love and fucking in the world can't save her. No one can save her but herself."

Jack sat startled, vulnerable, listening, with his leaden arms on the stuffed chair.

Joseph stayed an hour, rasping out his concern and his bitterness about the Petrovs' paralysis. Muted and pained, he spoke of the damage the Maestro did them all—Sarah, himself, and his mother, not to mention Jack. There was a terrible need in Petrov to dominate and control: his father was evil, Joseph said.

Jack watched him drive away down Speedway, and then he walked out onto the beach. The sun was descending through clouds to the horizon, and in the mottled light he thought over Joseph's visit. Enraged, knotted together, the Petrov family always seemed to risk the greatest damage, to court disaster, to play always for keeps. Yet none of them seemed evil or malicious to Jack, for each of them had his or her grief to bear. Finally, their pain drew compassion from him, and not only compassion. Seeing the son, Jack realized how much he missed them all. His bonds to them had been severed, and he felt acutely the missing connection—to Sarah and Petrov too, even after what he'd done and now Joseph's assassination of his character. The tie to Sarah might be healed and restored, but he knew his friendship with Petrov was irremediably damaged; the old man had—with fury and despair—said it himself: he would never be reconciled.

Yet Jack felt the void all the more, and his mind began to fill with images and thoughts of their aborted friendship, never to be developed, never to be celebrated and affirmed again. Sorrow welled within him as he stood in the dusk near the roaring waves. Suddenly he understood that their six-month long friendship led a life of its own now within him. The unfinished exchanges between them would continue to mark his life, and Petrov's uncompleted stories still unfolded within him. He began to remember the tales of Bruno Fried, of Stravinsky and Schoenberg—Jack's friends, he had called them—or of Alma Mahler and her novelist.

Heading home across the sand, he began to imagine extensions and continuations of Petrov's stories. Perhaps, late in the afternoon, Alma sat on Petrov's couch with Jack's mother nearby, and Alma said to her: "Rosa, someday please take me to your neighborhood. To Fairfax, no? I would like to eat at one of your delicatessens. On dit, vraiment, ils sont les mieux."

Or perhaps Bruno Fried turned to Thomas Mann. "You know," he said, "Eisler and I are composing music for Oskar Fisch's new movie." Bruno might have looked around him slowly, noting that Schoenberg had gone down the hall to the kitchen or bathroom. "Tell me," he said, "what is the difference between what Eisler and I compose for Fisch, and what composers do outside the films? There's Copland now. I can hardly listen. The flatness and deadness of the American idiom in music. Just leave out a third and voila the lifeless, open fifths. The stillborn, derivative melodies. At best, Indian wardance rhythms."

"Schlamperei!" Alma Mahler Werfel must have spit out her late husband's word for all that is done complacently.

"Fisch understands," Bruno forged on, "in the avant-garde, we hope to transform the medium itself, to transform perception and so to transform society. That's why we work on his project for little or no salary."

"Yes, Bruno," Mann's voice was patrician and ironic. "As Adorno would say, expose the stereotyped, prefabricated sentiments for what they are. Undermine them by revealing their essential mechanisms. Like Hanns and Bertolt."

"And Arnold," Bruno softly added. "When society is transformed, Eisler says, a wonderful palace will be built for him. Made of glass, naturally, with fountains and singing birds like in A Thousand and One Nights. The old man will sit in that house of glass and design his twelve note series with note symbols on big cards, and he will be undisturbed by what's happening in the world at large. Meanwhile, some of us will build socialism around the edge of his glass castle." Bruno was glaring at Mann's arch and jovial face.

"I don't think Arnold would consent," Mann replied, raising his eyebrows. "You know what he is composing? Ode to Napoleon is not undisturbed by events in the world at large. Despair is what Arnold feels, and rightly so. When societies become oppressive, everyone is crushed and vulnerable, the sensitive as much as the numb, the elite as well as the ordinary, both of them thrust together in opposition. And yet their mutual opposition yields no unity, no relief. The man of the street recedes back into apathy or paranoia, and the intellectual—who wants to reach out to the populace—still creates in the self-obsessed manner of the bourgeois."

"Whatever you say, the fact remains we must oppose the oppressor. There is no choice. But, Thomas," Bruno's tongue darted from his mouth now, "at least let us build Arnold his glass castle, so he can create there in privileged isolation to the end of his life."

"And when I'm age hundred twenty five," Schoenberg would have said in a loud, abrasive voice, entering now from the hall, "I'll be universally acclaimed."

❀   ❀   ❀

It was nine in the morning. Jack walked up Rose to the bakery and, breathing its sweet, yeasty air, he bought croissants and muffins for Sarah's visit in half an hour. She had called yesterday, just as he was deciding to confront the lion at the gate and call the Petrovs' number. She said Joseph had insisted that she call him, that he wanted to talk. She would come for a visit, and now he walked back down Rose towards the beach, with the mid-August morning sun on his back. He saw her gray Jeep pass and caught a fleeting glimpse of her pale, tightened face, with her hair pulled into a knot in back. She was early. When he entered his patio, she was reclining, with her eyes closed, on the plastic and chrome chaise. In the slanting, early sun, her face seemed a mask of porcelain, smooth but tense, even in repose.

"Sarah."

"Oh, Jack," she said in her high voice, brittle now and tense. "I actually fell asleep for a second. I don't know why. How are you?" She stood by him as he unlocked the front door.

"I was out buying some breakfast for us."

"You didn't have to."

He brought her pastry and a cup of coffee he had brewed, and she put them on the low telephone table by her on the couch. He sat in the armchair near her, and suddenly an erratic flow of words came from her mouth, and her face seemed like a cracking mask. As she spoke, she kept glancing curiously around the room as if it were new to her.

"Father is deteriorating terribly. He's forgetting everything except his music. He keeps asking me to get my camera and shoot Joseph and him and Mother, as if that way he could keep track."

She paused, and Jack said, "How's your mother holding up?"

"Mother is remembering more and more! Morning and night, she tells me stories—about him. You don't want to hear what she says."

"She already told me one story, last March."

Sarah's face fell, unmasked and frightened.

"I'm sorry, truly, Jack. Father was desperate. Desperate. I hope you can forgive him, and me. We roped you into our hell. With Joseph and me, I think you became another of his victims and inheritors. He and mother are like the giants who crushed and consumed their young."

"You and Joseph and Sasha and Helen. It's an incestuous web, isn't it?" He looked at her troubled, turbulent face. His voice became quiet, filled with sorrow and distress. "You know, don't you? What your father tried to do, to deafen me…he was at the breaking point, and he slammed his hands over my ears. He must have thought, this is his Achilles' heel, his hearing."

"I know, Jack," she cried. "Now he won't even mention your name, I don't know if it's from anger or shame."

"But you know we drove him to it, Sarah. All of us."

She sat without replying, her face pained and tense. He wanted to reach over and soothe the tension from her, but he held himself back, his hands gripping the stuffed arms of his chair. "All of us," he said, "need to forgive, instead of hate. And be forgiven, no?"

"It's hopeless!" she blurted out. "He's terribly ill. And he intends to perform in six weeks! I can't stand to think of it. He keeps practicing those pieces—they're so deep in his memory."

"Is it painful to hear him play?" he asked tentatively, feeling his way.

"What do you think, Jack!" Her fine high voice burst from her, and her face was at once bitter and pleading. "I fucking hated his music a few years ago, but now? He's so ill and old—it's like a sacred chalice he tries to hold up to us now. Before, I used to feel how evil it all was, how poisonous was anything he held up for us to admire. I can't tell you how much I hated it. And how much I wanted to revenge myself. In 1969, when I was living in Laurel Canyon, my radical friends were going to disrupt one of Father's concerts, to expose its bourgeois complacency and seduction and corruption. It was my idea; I'd read about something like it happening in Germany: during the applause at the end, I was going to walk on stage with a dozen roses for him in my arms. Only, my dress was going to be unbuttoned and my breasts bared. I was going to caress his face. To humiliate him. To show him how sick it was…what he'd done to me and Joseph."

Jack stared at her. He realized whether or not Petrov had molested his children, it was as if he had. They felt he fed on their spirits, and revenge was still misshaping them.

"But I didn't do it," she pleaded with ringing intensity. "I couldn't. And I broke down. A few months later, he visited Rick and me, and you know what happened: he collapsed, and I moved home. I started taking care of *them*. They needed me so. And I didn't hate them any more."

"They still need you."

"But I can't stand it anymore." Tears sprang from her eyes, and quiet despair sounded in her voice. "If I stay there much longer, I'm going to fall apart.

Joseph is home now. He can help them. I've done all I can. I'm losing track of who I am, Jack, who I might be. I have to move out."

"Where to?" he asked softly now, watching her wipe tears away. It seemed to him that she had become more real, that she was playing at life no more, but witnessing and suffering from its entrapping complexities. He knew she was reaching out for him now, and a reciprocal yearning grew again in him for the erratic muse sitting before him. He heard once more the beautiful lyricism of her voice. He saw the sad, intense alertness of her moistened eyes, her eyebrows, her forehead, her slender neck, yet he remained rooted in his chair. Time was needed to regain trust, to grow, to choose, to touch.

"Whatever happens," he said, "you must know what's important for you, for Joseph, for your parents too: it's the opposite of all the humiliation and anger and hatred." His voice echoed in the room now, warm, welcome, yet still abstract. "Love. Wherever you find love. Isn't that what's important?"

Sarah was mute; her saddened eyes were flush from crying. She stared at the curtained vista of Pacific sky by Jack's table.

"Can I tell you a story?" she said in her high voice.

"Is it a tragedy or a comedy?"

"A woman met a man."

"Jesus, do they always begin that way?"

"She loved him, Jack. He opened up a new world for her full of compassion and awareness and sensitivity."

"Neither of our stories is very funny, is it? What about now?"

"I don't know what's right anymore. You changed me, Jack. I cut myself off from you once. I won't do it again."

"It's still a story without an ending."

❀ ❀ ❀

In the last week of September, he completed his revision and wrote out the final notes of the sonata. He had been thinking lately of ideas for a concerto, for piano and orchestra. He would begin sketching it on Tuesday, the day after Petrov's recital. During late August and September, Sarah and her brother had visited him almost every Saturday. When he finished his sonata, they met to celebrate on the last Saturday of September. It was an anniversary of sorts, too. For one year now, he had lived on Paloma in L.A..

Hot Italian sausages and Greek lamb-burgers sizzled on the hibachi. Joseph stretched on the chaise, a glass of red wine in his hand. Jack kept track of cooking the spicy, pungent meats, and Sarah efficiently, neatly prepared the salad and pilaf in his kitchen.

"So she's moving in with you soon," Joseph said quietly, sounding calm and reconciled. Jack had asked her to live with him in his Venice flat.

"Yes, soon. Will you be okay in Benedict Canyon, alone with them?"

"I think so. What they really need is a nurse and housekeeper."

"Yes. But your love too. And Sarah's."

"Someday I'll move out," he said, wry and detached. He glanced away from Jack, toward the expansive blue above the cement yard.

After they ate, the setting sun hung low in the hot Indian summer air, and the three of them walked in their swim clothes along the beach. Sarah talked about Judge Sirica, the continuing collapse of Nixon's government, and then the news report last week about the CIA's role in Allende's assassination.

Jack had given Joseph a copy of his completed sonata, and now the pianist said he wanted to perform it. Each movement had an uncanny power, Joseph said, a hallucinatory force as if Bartok or Schoenberg had found a new answering voice in these latter days. Jack said that he sometimes thought he was a post-everythingist: he would hear their voices, and then composing became for him a sort of listening.

The three of them walked, thoughtful and somber, over reddish gray sand in the sunset. Sarah drifted into the surf and kicked water up at the other two, who followed her into the ocean. Joseph walked waist high toward an oncoming wave, and he scooped water at his sister and at Jack, who reached for Sarah, his arms and legs circling her now in his familiar embrace, carrying her down with him into the dark and churning wave. The couple surfaced where Joseph was, and feet, limbs, hands and heads tumbled together in the bath of turbulent Pacific water. Then Jack scrambled onto Joseph in the rush of water. Grabbing him between his legs, laughing face to face, he dunked his friend's head, letting him slip from the grip of his legs, down into the shadowy green water. The memory of New Year's Eve flashed into Jack's mind, then the walk they took in Benedict Canyon. The images hovered for a moment, distant, accepted, a sort of testimony to the struggle of their friendship. Then memory gave way, and the baptism of ocean waves hallowed each of them—Joseph, Sarah, and Jack—with the release of their laughter and play. Such was their fleeting victory over the terrors and emptiness of their time and of themselves.

They walked back in twilight to the Paloma house. For weeks, they had been planning for her to move in with him, for the struggling fullness of their bond had returned now. He understood the potential for destructiveness in Sarah, storming out at moments, so like her father in that but also in her capacity for lyric tenderness, for the deepening sensitivity and restraint he heard growing in her voice. What always compelled him was her voice. With more force than any photograph she had given him, her beautiful, high voice was the means by which he faced and saw himself, by which he heard the possibility of love, of meaning, within the death and silence of spirit which he felt descending everywhere, disfiguring their time and their lives.

5

It was almost 8 p.m. on Monday evening, October 1, and Jack sat in the last row of Royce Hall, near the wood-paneled back exit, on the keyboard side. He intended only to listen and not to be seen. Sarah and Joseph knew he would attend. The sister and brother sat with their mother in a front row, near the left stage exit. Helen came under duress, only because Sasha had put his foot down, in his fashion.

The Royce Hall lights dimmed, and Alexander Petrov—seventy-one years old, yet looking older than his years—walked with small, deliberate steps across the stage to his black Steinway grand. His rim of white hair was carefully barbered, and his ruddy face glistened. He sat down after offering a short bow, a minimal acknowledgment that the thousand men and women had assembled to hear him play.

Immediately, as was his way, Petrov threw his big hands at the keys, and Bach's Toccata in C sounded out, with a shockingly wrong note embedded in the flourish of the opening. Bach was a new choice for his concerts, and even with the missed notes, Petrov's power and Faustian brilliance transmuted the Toccata, as if his hands recreated now the essential elements of music itself from its primary materials, from the Prelude's basic scales and chords. Then, in the Intermezzo, with painful, revelatory slowness, Petrov relished each minor-key ornament and modulation of the Adagio: he seemed to use it as a sort of time-machine to swoop himself back to the poignant angst of youth, the fluid melancholy of traumatized adolescence. Finally, he played the fugue: strutting, showing off, playing suddenly muddied, or suddenly soft, or suddenly crystal-line and pedal-less, just to show the mass of listeners that he was in charge, that he would always have tricks up his sleeve, that his will was foremost at every instant. After the unfurling, fortissimo climax, the audience roared, and Petrov stood, grinning a broad arrogant smile, and finally bowing without compunction.

During the second work, Schoenberg's Suite Opus 25, Jack watched the remote reflection of Petrov's hands in the polished lid open over the keyboard of the Steinway. Two pairs of hands played, one belonging to the man who had smashed them together over Jack's ears, and one pair existing in another, obscurely shining world inside the ebony of the upright lid. And it seemed to be those other hands which disclosed the tragic power of Schoenberg's Suite, its bitter gaiety, travesty, and power, its searching beauty verging close to silence.

Finally, just before intermission, Petrov played the three pieces which comprised his Poèmes Juifs, all based on the same melismatic, Hebraic tone row—only each with a different tempo and style of ornament. All were faster, fleeter, clearer than Jack had imagined, when in January he had read through them, repulsed and enraged. He heard now their abjuring of tragedy, their consciously childish simplicity, their concerted imagining of a naive, womb-like rootedness. The three, derivative poems yet resonated with Petrov's troubled, willful brilliance. The applause which greeted the final wispy chord grew to full intensity, an embarrassed fervor of appropriation, as if these pieces too would become an accoutrement for the audience, a supplement to the evening's sheen and gloss.

During intermission, Sarah and her brother and mother disappeared backstage, and Jack wandered among the concertgoers, out across the plaza in front of Royce Hall. He sat on the library steps, looking back at the Hall, the clay-red hue of its tower illumined by spotlights and isolated against the autumn darkness. Against the blackened blue of the sky, it seemed to tremble like a red station in deep space. Coming towards him out of the buzzing, trembling circle of light, Joseph walked across the plaza, smoking a cigarette.

"Sarah and Mother are still back there talking with him. He's not well, Jack; he's terribly pale, his breathing is labored. We insisted he cancel the rest of the recital, but he's refusing, true to form. I've given up trying."

The lights of the lobby and facade of Royce Hall began to blink, on and off, on and off, as if the building were giving fair warning that it was about to take off into the sky above UCLA.

"We'd better go back in."

Petrov walked slowly across the stage, oblivious to the intense ovation, only nodding slightly, palely at the hall. His thick fingers stiffened to sound the opening leap of the Hammerklavier sonata, stiffening and hitting the keys just short of those he had to reach. Wrong notes sounded, and with his hands leaping, his fingers racing, he played each Allegro theme not as assertion and search but as a disastrous falling, sheared from any support, a plummeting, a collapsing. At the end of Beethoven's Allegro, his fingers took a handkerchief from the vest pocket of his shiny tux to wipe his glistening head. After, he stumbled through the Scherzo and began the Adagio, his heavy body contracting, his hands playing close to the keyboard, the work's fragments of sound vanishing into the black where the audience reared up to listen. Then Petrov's hands began to slip over the keys, the fugue racing out from the Largo introduction. The leaps, explosive and out of tune, placed their mangled, dissonant pattern in the darkness.

❀ ❀ ❀

Strained and worried, Sarah stood in the fluorescent white hallway.

"It's a waiting game the doctors say," she told Jack, who had walked with her from the visitors lounge. "Joey's driving mother home. She's decided to wait there."

Sarah's voice registered a brief lyric blip of pain and irony, but then again evened out: "Father says he wants to see you alone, Jack. Don't be shocked. He's very weak."

As she walked back to the space for waiting, he reached to open the door. Green monitors glowed in the shadows of the room, and a nurse stood by the instruments, jotting notes on her clip board. A night light was on by the bed. The bulk of Petrov's body was swathed in a white gown and sheets. This was not the looming enraged Petrov, who had attacked Jack's hearing. This was a frail contracted old man, transformed and luminous, his pale head floating above the pillow.

"Feel," he said to the woman in white. His breathing was erratic, and a weak laugh gurgled in his throat as he pulled at his gown. "Feel me. Feel. I can still give you a good time, dear. Feel. I'm not dead yet."

"No thanks, honey. Not tonight," she said. "Anyway, look. Here's your visitor."

"Where? Who's there?" Petrov stared from his circle of light. Jack stepped toward the bed. "Oh, Jack. I thought I saw half a person, but now I see. You came," he said, his voice frail and welling.

"I'm here. You didn't know, but I was in the audience at Royce, during the fugue, when you collapsed."

A shout had suddenly burst from Petrov's dry throat. His hands had grabbed the piano stool beneath him, his arms stiff and vertical. "This is not enough, ladies and gentlemen. Not…" Petrov's children rose from their seats. Joseph had leapt onto the platform, his hands struggling to lift Petrov from the stage where he had fallen.

"Only a few minutes, son," the nurse said and walked out the door, closing it behind her.

"What a fool I was," the old man said. His head, with its fringe of white, seemed evanescent in the light. Jack restrained an impulse to touch him, to soothe his pained face with its white stubble, once more to try comforting him.

"That's what I want to tell you," Petrov said weakly. "What a goddamn fool I was. It was wrong, what I did to you. Please forgive me."

"We were wrong, Sasha. You know how much pressure your children put on you, and how much pressure I was putting on you." The old man listened, calm and detached. "Whatever strengths I had, I felt somehow I was always a witness, outside of life, but you were helping me to feel inside life, Sasha. Instead of just struggling along, just…"

"But we're all just struggling along, Jack," Sasha interrupted quietly, whispering weakly. "You're like your father, you know. He has a rare quality. He's a generous hearted man, a mensch. You take after him. Generous, and brilliant too. He must be proud of you." Petrov was silent then; it was the old pianist who had the generous heart, Jack thought.

"Jack, have I told you about my father?" Petrov said in a hollow whisper; his face was paper white. "Do you know, I used to hate him. He was so domineering, always at attention. Always. Willful, rigid, he would march into any abyss. Always, impeccably dressed in his merchant's suit, his cravat, his top hat—like armor, he wore it. Now, I realize too late, I take after him. I too march into any abyss. I can't help it, this hunger, this love of life. When I am consuming and possessed, it's really that I love the intensity, the being possessed! But what damage I've done, my family cannot forgive me for it, Jack. When the children were small, I remember, once during a party I went to the kitchen. 'We need more ice,' I said, loud from all the noise and drink. My Sarah was a little girl, and she was there. And Joseph was just an infant in a cradle; she was tending to him there. Helen always disliked any raised voice: 'Bossiness,' she called it. As I went up to the ice box, she walked away from the counter where she was arranging pastries on a platter, and she stood next to the children near the kitchen table."

Jack—worried and absorbed—heard only Petrov's labored breathing now and the rhythmic beep of the heart monitor.

"Like a fool," the old man said, "I began to criticize her: 'I heard you pacing in the hall before. Why didn't you sit with us? What sort of game are you playing, that I must go search for you? Must I force you to entertain your guests?' Then Helen rasped out at me: 'All of them are false—all of these arrogant Russians and Germans and Jews slobbering after fame!' I said, 'You don't know anything about it.' 'Don't I?' she said, 'you little God almighty, out of my kitchen, out of my house. I've had enough,' she kept hissing at me; 'enough. You fool!' So what did I do? Possessed by wildness and resentment, I rushed at her, and we began silently to scuffle right there in front of the children. I remember tiny echoes and fragments of piano music filtered to the kitchen from the music studio. She beat my chest, and I held my hands up against her. Suddenly I spit out: 'You bitch,' and as I brought my hands down on her, I saw from the corner of my eye little Sarah staring at us. Oh my god, I thought, what am I doing! I was permanently injuring her. Just then the baby sensed something was wrong and began to cry. What shame I felt! Helen took the baby from Sarah and nursed Joseph at her breast. I remember walking back down the hall, clutching the ice bucket to me like some surgical apparatus. 'No, no, no, God, no,' I whispered in fury and despair. When I lit a cigar with our guests, there were tremors in my hands. After ten minutes, my Helen entered. Amazing…in a turquoise dress, she was radiant in the afternoon sun. She carried the silver platter covered with pastries, apricot and berry, Napoleons and rugela and little Greek almond cookies. I felt split open, Jack, by shame and pride—equally. I was possessed!" Petrov's hoarse whisper filled the darkened room.

"I understand, Sasha. I understand," Jack said, amazed and fearful for the old man. "You have to rest now, Sasha, to get better."

"No, I'll not get better…Feel here, my heart," Petrov said and reached weakly to bring Jack's hand to his chest. "Do you feel? My heart flutters. It wants to fly away, Jack. It wants to soar in some other place, some other time, some other body. It doesn't want to be here. Do you feel? How it flutters. Feel here. Here it is."

❁   ❁   ❁

"Mother wants to see you," Sarah said from the door of the music studio. "Could you go up? She says she can't leave her bed." Jack looked at Sarah, still in the black crepe dress she wore at the funeral, still with the look of stricken dismay and bearing-up which had marked her since Monday evening in the hospital. Now it was late Wednesday night. That morning, a salty breeze had swept the cemetery, and the Pacific flooded the horizon a mile away. Jack had felt weak and chilled in his dark brown coat and an earthen sweater. He held his arm over Sarah's shoulder and felt the warmth of her body through her black jacket. Before them were the rabbi, the casket, the open grave. Joseph stood on the other side of his sister and mother. The pained and pale features of his face were etched round with reddened lines. Petrov had died in his sleep Tuesday, and burial had been set within the prescribed twenty-four hours. Hundreds of mourners crowded before the grave, and beyond were grassy plots and stones with carvings in Hebrew and English.

Yisgadal V'yiskadash Shmey Rabbo: the prayer for the dead sounded from the rabbi's mouth. He was an old acquaintance, a music-lover, a noted Conservative rabbi. He had offered a warm and burnished tribute to the pianist, frozen and big as life in the open casket at the funeral home. Then, dazed by grief, Jack watched as Petrov was lowered into the California hillside. The gray wind off the Pacific promised rain. It blew at the black plumed hat and veil covering the face of the maestro's wife, rigid and mute at graveside. Afterwards, as the family walked to the waiting limousine, Helen Petrov had held Jack's arm and asked him to come to the house. He stood next to his VW as they drove by him, and he saw Joseph's face at the car window. Sarah had reached to rest her hand on Joseph's shoulder. His lips kept moving silently, and his palms and long fingers were stretched tight against the glass.

Jack stood now in the music room. A new, curtainless, sliding door looked out over the clouded darkness of Los Angeles. Dazed and disoriented, he followed Sarah into the hall. Stepping slowly up the stairs, he saw the frayed and thinning carpet of the runner; it was as if he walked on the moon, over some alien landscape where time was in suspense and movement was incommensurate with intention.

"Here he is, Mother," she said and left him at the bedroom door.

Helen sat up with pillows at her back, in the canopied bed. A shawl-like bedcoat covered her, and the blankets were pulled to her waist. Strewn over the bed were telegrams and letters and a book of signatures and messages which the funeral home had given her this afternoon.

"Would you shut the door, and please, sit down," she said as she looked up at Jack and gestured him to the red-stained leather armchair next to her side of the bed. The bedside lamp was on next to her, and in the light her plump face was placid and somber.

"So many condolences," she said. "I had thought most of our friends were dead. He had so many more than we thought. It's touching. But it's a bother, as well. I want to simplify my life, Jack. I've had enough sturm und drang…for more than a lifetime, and I want it quiet now." She looked carefully and thoughtfully at the thirty-year-old composer sitting near her.

"Sarah says that you and she plan to live together."

"Yes, she mentioned she'd told you."

"Good. I'm pleased. I think even Sasha, the poor man, would have accepted it. Do you know, these last weeks, he began to speak of you. 'Where is my prodigal son?' he would ask me." She stretched out her swollen hand to touch the bed next to her, as if he were under the covers there. "Poor, poor man. So brilliant, and so confused."

He had no heart to test whether she believed her husband were poor or not, whether she knew Petrov had seen him before he died, whether she were honest or merely beginning the process of rewriting the Petrovs' history. And he was too exhausted to take up the role the family had him play, his role as therapeutic listener and absorber of the Petrovs' rages and confessions.

"To think, he collapsed right in the middle of playing Poèmes Juifs! Those childish pieces! He came full circle. How ironic, and how sad. Such a sad man, at the end."

"It was during the Hammerklavier, the fugue, but it doesn't really matter," Jack said gently and lifted his hands in an apologetic, self-dismissive gesture.

"Oh yes. Do you know, you have beautiful hands? Such beautiful hands," Helen said. It seemed of equal note to her now, his hands or her husband's death. She looked down at the booklet and envelopes and papers covering the bed before her.

"He was losing his mind at the end, you know," she said. "Saliva used to hang from his lip! I had to remind him to wipe his mouth. When he practiced, how he stroked the keys! Like a naughty child. He was always so naive. A willful child of a man. I was twenty when I met him in Berlin. I was studying with Edwin Fischer, and I lived in a proper boarding school for girls. Every day, notes began to arrive for me, flowers, invitations. Should I tell you, Jack? Alexander Petrov, the brilliant pianist, advanced composer, intellectual. He was a vain, impossible young man. He even wrote to my parents in Athens: I must by all means stay in Berlin to marry him! He compromised me—fatally, let the expression be."

Helen riveted her bitter, abject glance on Jack. She watched him to see if she were disclosing too much of her martyred self to him. After a moment she continued: "A few years later, he made us stay in Berlin until death was certain, and we had to send desperate messages to Moscow, London, and New York. I remember the ship across the Atlantic, the *Illium*. I listened to him playing Chopin on the shiny white lounge piano. And he played with such vulnerability, such bared heart, that a rush welled in my own heart like upwelling blood, and tears came from my eyes. But then my husband decided to become drunk, to mark the escape from hell…naturlich! Unbearable…" Helen suddenly closed her eyes and shifted her face away.

Jack sat dumbfounded by what he heard. There was such suffering in her, such pain and anger. Her life was a nightmare of martyrdom, and he felt instinctively that he must turn away; he must save Sarah from her mother's bitterness, must save Petrov's memory from both his wife's rage and the dead man's own destructive wildness.

"Of course, I was passive by nature," Helen said with open eyes now, from her bed. "I had a temperament like my dear father. You won't believe it, but I had a good nature once. I paid for finding a mate like my mother, domineering, not to be satisfied. And how he drank. I think it wasn't his heart that killed him, but drink. I used to try to keep the bottles from him. Once when I hid the Scotch and wine, he pushed the water goblets right off the dining table, and they smashed on the floor. He grabbed me by the hair and dragged my face down into the broken glass. He was a big animal, and he pushed my face down in the glass, as he looked for bottles in the credenza. You have no idea. He held me down, I was kneeling in the glass, and he banged open those carved doors, hunting inside for bottles."

Suddenly she seemed on the verge of tears. She sat upright in her bed, and her head twisted from side to side. Her voice was hurried, filled with urgent desperation and self-exposure. "No, no," she chanted, "no, God, no. I don't want to be this bitter hag! But I can't help it, Jack. What could I do? He was a genius—a genius and a great man. I admired him. I loved him, in my way! But I tell you, I became frightened—to be alone with him, to be close to him. Would he attack or caress me? I never knew. He was out of control, from the start. We should have divorced, I know. But I admired him so. And he needed me! Then the children came. We had to raise them, and what would he have done to Sarah and Joseph without me always there! The years piled up heavier and heavier, and at the end, he wasn't even lucid more than a few minutes at a time. Nothing, I could do nothing. And neither could he. Nothing."

There was a knock at the door, and her flushed, bitter, grieving face awoke to the present moment.

"Come in," she said politely, contracting into herself automatically.

Sarah was at the door. She looked with curiosity and concern at Jack, and then her mother. "Are you talking about anything I should be in on?"

"Yes," Jack said tensely. Sarah sat on the edge of her mother's bed.

"We've had a chat about your father," Helen said. "Have you told Jack how Sasha was this summer? Tell him. Tell him about Maazel's visit."

"Why, mother?" Sarah said, defensive, her voice contracted.

"Tell him," she demanded.

Sarah sat stiffly on the edge of her mother's bed and said, "Maazel came from Cleveland to conduct at the Bowl."

"Yes," Helen said, "at Hollywood Bowl."

"Well, like so many," Sarah said, "he made a pilgrimage here to…"

"To honor the great man," Helen said. "But the great man was no longer himself. The great man hardly knew Maestro Maazel from Adam. But Sasha said, 'Yes, you should perform my works, why not! The first symphony of the great Alexander Petrov.' All the while, he smiled his childish smile, as the Maestro cringed and fawned. They all did that, no matter what Sasha said. 'Ho, ho,' he would laugh and shout: 'Schoenberg stole my idea of the tone-row, the son-of-a-bitch. My idea. The creation of Alexander Petrov.' At a certain point, he reached to pat my hand, across the couch; his teasing fingers stroked me, and he boomed out, 'We should have espresso,' meaning I or Sarah must get up to make it. And pick up the cups after. And empty the dirty grounds and lemon rinds into the shit hole of the sink disposal."

"How dare you, Mother!" Sarah cried into the shadowy room, and she rose abruptly from the bed. "How can you speak like that? As if you lived in hell."

"Do I speak—as you say—any differently from you?"

"A shit hole!" Sarah cried out, grief and anger churning in her voice. "Maybe you're right. Our shit hole in hell. Our Auschwitz. Yes, maybe you're dead. And Joey and I are dead too." She raised her fists in the air, shaking them at her mother who sat impenetrable on the bed. Jack stood now and walked a pace toward Sarah, to soothe and restrain her. "Maybe the Germans gassed us when we were two or three. We're all ghosts, haunting your shit hole of a house. Fuck, even Jack here is one of us," she shouted into Jack's face next to her. Suddenly she raised her fists up at him, and she held them up, unable to hit him. Her hands held no knife, yet as they gestured, it felt like hot iron piercing his chest. It's our perverse lot that we bear such assaults as signs not of sundering but of the deepest bonding.

She broke into tears, leaning against him, her arms slack. And then blindly she reached for her mother. Helen held her daughter's sobbing head against her bosom but did not speak at first. She only stared into the room. Then she said, "I must sleep, Sarah; I'm going to take one of the little pills the doctor gave me and go to sleep."

"Will you be all right?" Sarah said in the urgent, high voice of grief. She lifted herself up and stood now by Jack.

"Don't worry about me," Helen said automatically, as if no words had passed between them. "I want to be alone now."

"Joseph is home."

"Goodnight."

"Jack and I are going to his place."

"Goodbye, I'll see you tomorrow. Goodbye, Jack." She pushed the thick scattering of torn envelopes, letters, and telegrams off of the blanket covering her and onto Petrov's side of the bed.

As they walked down the hall, Jack saw Joseph in his room. The black haired man was stretched out on his bed, asleep in pants, shirt and socks. Sarah started to enter.

"Let him be," Jack said, edgy and exhausted. Petrov's son had met each commiserating friend of Helen and Sasha, visiting with them, offering a continual attentiveness and kindness over the past two days. Sarah reached for the wall switch and turned off his bedroom light. Next to her, Jack walked carefully down the stairs and tried to fix his mind on the myriad names of the old friends and musicians who had visited the house on Benedict Canyon Drive—the Weisbergs, the Kramers, the Filermans, the Luskins, et cetera. Then there were all those who had sent sympathy notes and telegrams, who had telephoned, who had signed the book at the funeral. As Jack left the house with Sarah, he thought of the friends, the acquaintances, the luminaries who wrote or visited, and the countless listeners who expressed their collective sense of loss—the music world of 1973:

6

They sat in the darkened living room several hundred yards from the ebb and flow of the Pacific. On the couch, almost touching, they quietly talked, struggling—as we do—to fill the impossible gap left by death, whether it be with words or other means to numb or heal. She loved her mother, yet she was right to resist her, Jack said. The only way they could help the grieving woman was by themselves not giving in to bitterness and despair. Only then, he told her, could they all move beyond cruelty and loss, only then might they stand unashamed before themselves and before each other.

A short lyric cry burst from Sarah. "I'm sorry, Jack" she said. "I tried to hit you. I'm so sorry."

He kissed her forehead and eyes. "Don't cry," he kept saying, and they began to touch and hold one another. They walked through the shadowed hall to the bedroom, past their fleet reflection in the mirror. On Jack's bed, they made fragile, tender love, gently, sadly. Afterwards, they curled together. Sarah lay warm and soft against him, and she descended with a shudder into unconsciousness.

Jack could not sleep. He lifted himself from the bed and walked out of his bedroom into the living room. The windows of the warm room faced west to the black ocean. He stood there stripped bare by fucking, and by his grief. Tears welled in his eyes. He sat on the armless wooden chair at his table, turned on a small lamp there, and began to write in his notebook.

Oct. 4: Helen, Joseph, Sarah, and I. We're all harmed, and all of us are capable of harming. All that keeps us from destroying those we love is this knowledge, this weak restraint, this placing ourselves in the position of another, so we know what it is to suffer our own destroying. Did Sasha and Helen practice restraint when it was most needed? And do we, their hybrid flowers, their double and triple spider mums, Joseph, Sarah—and Jack? It's nineteenseventythree, and here we are, like children, only at the start of learning the most basic lessons—how to live, how to love. Maybe it was the same in nineteenfortythree. From generation to generation, in this city, god help us. Is it L.A. which is mutilating our souls? No, it's we ourselves who injure and destroy, and it's we who must not harm the living or betray the dead, who must try to struggle beyond ourselves, to be more than the sum of our deformities.

As Jack put his pen down on the table, he saw at the top of the page the previous entry in his notebook.

Sept. 30: I met Janice unexpectedly Sunday. Over these months, we'd waved hello before. She must have seen Sarah and Joseph visit. This morning she walked right up to the front door, knocked, and came in to say good-bye. She's met someone, and they're moving north, back to the Bay Area; she said she forgives me: "Shit happens. It's just a passing pain in the ass. But, Jack, you have soul; I ought to know. I've been listening to what comes out of your windows, Christ, for a year now!" She wished me good luck, told me to take care of myself, whatever happens, and then she gave me a hug—of what? Affection, help, forgiveness. And I did something absurd: like an idiot, I started to cry. Just helpless tears. As if I were departing, not she.

He felt tired now, yet he stayed seated, naked on the chair in the circle of light by his table. No, we must not betray the living or the dead, he thought. That was it. Suddenly shuddering, he felt the full weight of Petrov's presence and his loss. How he missed the old man's voice, his startling intensities, his revelations, his stories. Yes, they were still stories without endings, and it was somehow his responsibility, Jack saw, to remember that amazing world of émigrés Petrov had brought to life for him. The ending of those stories depended on him. He began to imagine how Sasha's party finished in 1942, the guests departing. Jack's parents—Rosa and Julius—would have volunteered to drive the Stravinskys home, for it was east on Sunset near Fairfax where they lived for the time being. Schoenberg departed in the Manns' car. The Werfels and Bruno Fried, the last to leave, walked down the garden path to their cars at the base of the hill, and the Petrovs emerged onto their porch lit orange by the setting California sun. Helen waved to the three final guests down the hill as she reached with one hand for her husband's clenched fingers.

That was the way the wartime afternoon drew to a close, and all departed now into the future Jack occupied. Adorno spent the next twenty-seven years, in West Germany after 1949, writing Dialectic of the Enlightenment, Philosophy of Modern Music, etc., and he died in Frankfurt in 1969, both celebrated and attacked by the New Left. Bartok—whose music Petrov loved so—continued to compose in New York until his death in 1945, the Concerto for Orchestra, the Third Piano Concerto, etc. Also in 1945, Bruno Fried committed suicide by speeding his car west down Sunset Boulevard and at the Pacific Coast Highway plummeting off the rocks into the ocean; in the spring, he had learned that his mother, two brothers, and sister had been gassed and burned in Auschwitz ovens. Thomas Mann (with Katia) became an American citizen in 1944 and then published Doctor Faustus, Confessions of Felix Krull: Confi-

Daniel C. Melnick 177

dence Man, etc.; in 1955 he died in Switzerland, having exiled himself once again, this time from McCarthyite America. Schoenberg spent the next nine years teaching at UCLA, was denied a Guggenheim in 1947, and composed A Survivor from Warsaw, parts of Moses and Aaron, etc., all prayers for doubtful recovery; he died in West L.A. in 1951. Stravinsky continued to compose for more than two decades—The Rake's Progress, then Agon and other personalized adaptations of Schoenbergian technique, etc.; in 1971 he died in New York and was buried in Venice near Wagner's grave. Of the Werfels: Franz's success from the film of his Song of Bernadette was matched by that of his Jacobowsky and the Colonel on Broadway, and in 1945 he died in Santa Barbara, where Alma performed a Christian 'baptism by desire' on the lapsed Jew's corpse; Alma died, isolated and transplanted to New York, in 1964, having restored Mahler as her surname. Of the Weinsteins: Rosa gave birth to John (called Jack) on the ides of March 1943, and Julius played under Wallenstein at the L.A. Philharmonic until 1952 when Szell hired the cellist at Cleveland where the couple moved. Three decades later—Jack could not yet know—Julius, in his last concert before retirement under Dohnanyi, played Oceanlights by John Weinstein, Alfred Schnittke's Fourth Violin Concerto (Gidon Kremer, violinist), and Dvorak's New World Symphony.

❈   ❈   ❈

Joseph leaned forward on the couch in the living room. The windows were shut against the Pacific wind. In the light of the lamp, the lines about his face were pale and obscure, and on his lap was a photocopy of the first movement Jack had completed of his piano concerto. The composer had spent the weeks following the funeral working to create the movement, in face of death and disillusion. He kept working on his travesty and transfiguration of the warhorse form, in the wake of Petrov's death and, then, October 6, the Yom Kippur War; and October 20, Nixon's Saturday Night Massacre; and October 22, the death of Pablo Casals at ninety-six—he felt he was an unwitting ambassador of death as he made a second call to his parents that month and heard his father's saddened, thoughtful voice register the unheard news of death Jack bore.

"The cadenza takes off into the void," Joseph said. A grin spread across his face, enthusiastic and ironic at once. "Then the orchestra joins with the piano, playing the same mad arpeggios, up and down, over two octaves, then three, then four, then five! And as the piano's volume increases along with the full orchestra's, the daemon of bravura takes over: the pianist's hands will rise up over the keys, moving right and left, back and forth. They'll be transformed into demonic batons or wands drawing the blast and thunder from piano and orchestra alike, and you won't believe the piano isn't sounding because the orchestra is blasting at full tilt, and the pianist's hands have become merely commanding presences in air. They'll lift off together into outer space."

"That's how you'd perform it?" Jack said from the armchair.

"That's how I'd do it. Because that's how you wrote it," Joseph laughed. They had spent the evening discussing plans for Jack's music. It was the second Tuesday in November, and later in the month, his Movements would be performed at USC. In March, Joseph was going to premiere Jack's sonata—when the pianist was scheduling his first, return recital a year after his crash.

Sarah was spending the evening with Helen, and she would return by ten. Daughter and son traded times to spend with their mother, sharing the responsibility of taking care of her. Yet over the last six weeks, Helen had made it clear that she wanted her independence, even her isolation. She did not mind Joseph helping and living at the Benedict Canyon house, but she implied that she also would not mind his moving to an apartment of his own again. The mother wanted to be alone, and she welcomed her daughter's living at Jack's Paloma house. Sarah had found a larger place for them, and on January 1 the couple planned to move into two stories of a store-front building on Pico and Tenth.

"One thing I guess I absorbed—did I steal it?—from Father is a sort of sleight of hand, a sense of how to pull from music what's unique, what unique identity it has. Shit, did he have that in spades," Joseph said. His words, verging between irony and loss, unwittingly echoed his father's tone.

"I'll never forget once he sight-read my Variations," Jack said. "He'd never seen them before, yet he found the unique shape and life in each part. Sarah once told me we're inheritors. We should be so lucky. But it's an obligation, I think: we bear his chalice."

"Just give me a chance. Next March I'll show you what I can do with your sonata. Though your tempos, Jack, they give me a lot of fucking leeway. Maybe we should discuss the choices I make. They may not be right for you."

"But that's what I want. I want you to be free to choose. You should discover what's unique in you, not in me or my intentions. I'm not so much the composer as the composition. What I do is listen as best I can, and what I hear becomes the work. What you play finally will become what I hear."

"But you created it. You created these beautiful, shocking classical statues; you brought them to life. They're like the Commendatore sculpted by Praxiteles. Each movement of your sonata is a presence you hewed out of silence, each breathing fragment, each mangled arm and stony thigh."

Jack stared, wondering and grateful, at his friend, who could be as relentless and intense as his father.

"My task," Joseph said, "is to confront the audience with each breathing, stony fragment. Confrontation and assault are what we have for meaning now."

"I guess it's good we have that at least. But another time, another place, there were other ways of finding meaning, no?"

The three bald geniuses had returned to occupy the shadowed darkness by the entrance and the kitchen door. Standing impatiently, with Karl in tow, they talked together, and their voices whispered in a jangled accompaniment to what Beethoven produced at the piano, the final Fugue of the young composer's sonata. The three voices echoed the timbres of drum, guitar, and bass. At Joseph's side, the pallid Russian stood, a leer widening on his face, and he held a cup of brandy in the air. Reaching high, he threw the cup across the room, splattering brandy over Jack's face and hair, the cup careening and disappearing into his shelves of books and scores and records. The bald Russian spoke to Jack, his words an antiphony to Joseph's voice: "To hell with diminuendo and restraint. It's time for me to speak and you to hear. Are you asleep, or something worse? You know all that sturm und drang is shit: a momentary cramp! You know better, so come along. Enough. Beethoven, who occupies your piano bench, is a messenger from the future, from the only future I care about anyway." The short, thin man laughed his edgy laugh. "He more than any of us doth refine and exalt man to the height he would beare. Hear what arises from the piano, the phoenix from your ruins."

The front door opened. "Hi," Sarah said and walked with steady steps across the living room. She placed her purse on the end table and sat on one end of the piano bench. Jack watched her as she leaned forward and put her elbow on her knee, her chin in her hand, and she smiled at him.

"How is your mother?" he asked.

"She is herself; she's okay. What are you two up to?"

Jack lifted a half full glass of brandy at her: "Let me get you some." She shook her head no, and he said: "We were just talking about Joseph's concert next March."

"You should perform on October first," she said matter-of-factly to Joseph, and Jack's face opened into a broad smile.

"You kid me," Joseph said in his detached voice; "of all the times."

"I'm serious," she said. "In Royce Hall. Father would approve."

"He would not approve. He'd be spinning in his grave."

"You could play Jack's sonata or his variations, etcetera. Don't decide now. Just give me the word, and I'll try to arrange it."

"Sasha would love it, Joseph," Jack said, more loudly than he intended.

The Russian glanced at him and turned to face the pale Hungarian, the Viennese Jew with his California flush, and Nephew Karl. Beethoven—looking up occasionally—still played Jack's final Fugue, and the short Russian began in earnest to stomp out the dance he had attempted ten months before.

"Join me friends. Join me, my old Jew and you too my frail Magyar." Laughter possessed his aged face as he stomped and danced. Together—each with his distinct tone and timbre—the three bald shades chanted:

Weinstein knows
How to be
Weinstein knows
What death is
Weinstein knows
How to…

Out of doors now, Joseph stood by Jack in the patio of his Paloma place. The November evening was bright and cool. Sarah had gone to bed, and Joseph was talking again about Jack's sonata. The moonlight lit the pianist's shock of black hair and his thin, pale, lined face. The palm and bamboo leaves shimmered in the breeze.

"The audience will sit fucking bolt upright and face the music," Joseph gave Jack a warm, ironic smile, and then he said quietly, "I hope you'll feel I do right by it. By you."

"Right now I'm feeling as raw as when I finally got it all down," Jack said, "but you make me feel better." At this, Joseph couldn't help himself and laughed. Their eyes met, and they shook hands. Then, with a sudden affectionate flourish, they bowed to each other. It was late; Joseph turned to leave. There was the distant roar of planes ascending and descending at L.A. International. Chill from the ocean breeze, Jack returned to the living room.

Down the hall, Sarah slept, warm, waiting for him to come, to sleep huddled next to her. *Beethoven no longer glanced at his nephew or the others, as he played through the last page of Jack's sonata. When he finished, he rose, the three bald geniuses grabbed Karl, and all five exited through the walls, the shelves, the windows, the door.* Jack put the record of a late Beethoven quartet on the player, and his ears were filled with the soaring riffs and streaming shapes of music. It seemed to him he heard Sasha's voice echo in the fullness of sound which poured from his speakers. He sat listening on the stuffed chair. He did not see where his future led, or where his tie to Sarah would take him. He only knew what it was to feel broken and yet to struggle on, to try to stay alive, and there was no end he could see.

0-595-30803-1